The
Irish Nurse
at the
Lodging House

BOOKS BY NATALIE MEG EVANS

The Dress Thief
The Milliner's Secret
A Gown of Thorns
The Wardrobe Mistress
The Secret Vow
The Paris Girl
Into the Burning Dawn
The Italian Girl's Secret
The Girl with the Yellow Star
The Locket
The Paris Inheritance

The
Irish Nurse
at the
Lodging House

NATALIE MEG EVANS

bookouture

Published by Bookouture in 2025

An imprint of Storyfire Ltd.
Carmelite House
50 Victoria Embankment
London EC4Y 0DZ

www.bookouture.com

The authorised representative in the EEA is Hachette Ireland
8 Castlecourt Centre
Dublin 15 D15 XTP3
Ireland
(email: info@hbgi.ie)

ISBN: 978-1-83618-942-8
eBook ISBN: 978-1-83618-941-1

For Lynne.

Friendship can be a short story or a three-volume novel and ours is still being written.

1

GRACE

'Miss? Miss? Wake up.'

Grace opened her eyes, dazzled by the lights shining down on her. The voice had come from above her head. It took a few hard breaths for her to realise she was on the tube, jolting with the motion, and that a woman in a navy suit and pillbox hat was trying to rouse her.

The lady asked Grace if she was all right.

'No. I mean, yes. I fell asleep,' Grace muttered. Her heart was still hammering. 'I have to get out.'

'Of the train? We're still moving,' the smart woman informed her.

'Out of home, I mean. I have to get my own place, away from—' Grace realised she was saying too much. She sat up straighter. One eye, the left, felt painful and swollen. Tentatively, she touched it. *Ouch.* Why was it, every time she tried to make a go of something and improve her life, he was there, fists clenched, ready to knock her down?

It didn't help that she was so tired. The air raid siren had gone off at half three that morning, while she'd been on night shift. That unearthly, echoing wail, searchlights swinging, had affected her patients badly. It had been another false alarm, but by the time Grace had finally got to her bed, she'd been too weary to sleep. No wonder she'd dozed off here.

The woman offered a last piece of advice: 'Get that contusion around your eye seen to. Did someone do it? By "contusion", I mean—'

'I know what it means. Thank you,' Grace muttered.

'Walk into a lamp post, did you?' came an insinuating voice by Grace's ear. She realised she was sitting next to a soldier in uniform. He didn't smell too good. Cigarettes and yesterday's beer. He grinned. 'Everyone's doing it these days, aren't they, dearie?'

That uniform hadn't seen service since the last war, if Grace was any judge. Mind you, it was possible the gentleman was a volunteer, so instead of the brush-off that popped to her lips, she agreed, 'You're right. A lamp post it was.'

To discourage further conversation, she studied the map of the Central line on the opposite side of the carriage. She was on the right train at any rate. She needed to get off at Marble Arch. Pulling a hanky from her pocket, she dabbed her mouth. Pray to God she hadn't drooled.

'You were gabbling in your sleep, dearie. "Get away, I won't let you!"' To the impersonation of her accent, the man added a nudge. 'You'll be Irish, then, sweetheart?'

She angled herself away. Clearly, her accent slipped when she was sparko. Her family had settled in the East End from the West of Ireland, fifteen years ago. She'd called Dock Street, Whitechapel, home since then and had done her best to iron the Irish out of her voice, and to avoid a cockney twang. Sounding like you'd been to a nice girls' school was the only way out of poverty. She was on her way to an interview which would open a door to better things. Except this fat plum of an eye wouldn't help.

After her shift, she'd trudged home in the blackout and, just as the soldier guessed, she'd collided with something solid. Her brother Cormac's fist. He'd claimed it was unintentional, but the rage distorting his face had been real. All she'd done was tell him she was going for a job outside London. 'I can't take night shifts much longer, and this one's live-in. Two weekends off a month and better pay.' And her own little apartment.

Whump. Think again.

The soldier was peering at her black stockings. Grace shifted her legs and glared, so he stared instead at the white collar above the neck of her grey cape. He winked suggestively. 'Let me guess, a choirgirl. Innocent on top, fire beneath. I like a redhead.' His leer swept over her hair, rolled in a bun, the curls tamed with kirby grips. 'Redheads have a bit of spirit.'

That did it. 'Will you let me alone before I clock you one!'

'Only being friendly... to be sure, to be sure.'

A man seated opposite, reading a broadsheet that concealed everything but his knuckles and a half-inch of RAF blue cuff, lowered the paper and said, 'Cut the young lady some slack. Some of us don't like to talk in the morning.'

The accent wasn't as clipped as the pillbox hat lady's, but it was what Grace's mother would call 'nicely bred'. His cap was pulled low, giving Grace the idea that he'd been dozing more than reading. He pushed up the peak to reveal a lean face and eyes hollow with exhaustion. He was only a few years older than her, she realised. What those Air Force boys had gone through these last months...

The grubby soldier leaned forward and asked him, 'Where are you bound for, then?'

'RAF Hornchurch.'

'Essex? You're on the wrong train, mate.'

'I'm on the right one, but thanks for the advice.'

Feeling the deceleration of wheels, Grace got up and went to wait by the door. The window glass lightened to a blur of white tiles on a curved wall. Brakes squealed as the station's name flashed past. What, Shepherd's Bush? She'd slept past her stop and now she'd be late. She so needed this job. Three pounds a week. *Three.* Enough to help the family with the bills, to have a bit to spend and some for her future.

The doors rumbled open. Stepping onto the platform, Grace felt momentarily light-headed. Every muscle from her neck down was stiff and her gas mask in its box, compulsory wear, bumped her side. Cormac's fist had slammed her against the kitchen wall, a reminder that you should never take on a man in a small room with only one door.

'Miss, Miss!'

She turned, ready to give that khaki-wearing pest a piece of her mind, and saw the RAF pilot in the train doorway, holding a canvas bag aloft. 'Yours?'

'Yes – *yes.*' Panic fluttered. Lose that bag, she'd have to replace everything out of her salary. And as she didn't currently have a salary...

The doors were shutting.

'Throw it,' she begged.

The pilot thrust the doors open by brute force. 'Sure?'

'Yes!'

The bag thwacked onto the platform and she grabbed it. It held clean aprons, spare stockings, a wad of starched linen triangles and the precious final issue of *Peg's Paper*, dog-eared from repeat reading.

She gasped, 'Thank you. What's your name?' Startled by her own nerve, she added, 'I'm Grace.'

'Enjoy your day, Grace. The lady was right. Get that eye seen to and don't collide with any more lamp posts.'

So, he'd been listening from behind his copy of *The Times*.

The train doors rumbled shut and Grace wondered if he'd

meant to snub her, not sharing his name. Probably. If he was a fighter pilot, he'd be shooing women off like flies. There was a story in *Peg's Paper* about a girl who joined the WAAF as a cook, only for a chisel-jawed squadron leader to fall for her, though the base was full of shiny-haired debutantes in tailored uniforms.

Her pilot would have forgotten about her by the next station. He *was* on the wrong train for Hornchurch, as it happened. But that was his concern. Hers was to get to her interview and persuade the tyrant who ran the Root Agency that she, Grace Whelan, deserved the best job ever to land on its books.

2

____

The train back to Marble Arch had Grace biting her nails, which at least stopped her probing her sore eye. She stood all the way, as if it might make the wheels turn faster.

Already twenty minutes late by the time she stood at the junction of Park Lane and Cumberland Gate, Grace rocked impatiently from foot to foot. A policeman in shirtsleeves was directing traffic and had blown his whistle at her: *stay where you are!* The sandbags piled in front of Marble Arch looked threadbare in the bright August morning. The blast tape on the shop windows was getting shabby too. Well, it had been in place for a year. Everyone had gone into a frenzy at the outbreak of war, defending their properties against the enemy, but so far, the defences hadn't been needed.

They had come, the German bombers, but without releasing their firepower on the capital. Mostly, the skies buzzed with friendly aircraft.

A Rolls-Royce swept by, its flanks gleaming. Expecting the policeman to stop it, Grace stepped off the kerb. To her annoyance, he directed the car on, saluting it as it passed.

'To hell with that,' Grace muttered and darted after the

Rolls, ignoring the policeman's shout. From Park Lane, she turned into Upper Brook Street, where she paused to haul off her cape. It was that or expire.

The action revealed a short-sleeved dress the same blue as the sky, and a spotless white apron tied at the back. Gas mask bumping, she ran along Upper Brook Street, stopping at the scrubbed white steps of No. 88A, the Root Agency. Wiping her brow, she pressed the bell.

The door opened and Grace saw that, today, the tyrant was wearing a brown skirt and a blouse so starched, it creaked. Miss Root informed Grace what she already knew.

'Nurse Whelan, you are half an hour late. Where is your cap?'

In her bag, in its unfolded state. In her rush, she'd forgotten to put it on.

Grace lowered her head, to imply repentance and hide her injured eye. 'I'm sorry, Miss Root.'

'Your appointment was nine a.m. sharp. What delayed you?'

'I'm blaming the Luftwaffe on this occasion.'

'The all-clear went at four-fifty-eight this morning.'

Trust Miss Root to have noted the time.

Grace couldn't admit to dozing off on the train. Those of her lowly standing were not permitted human failings. She improvised. 'There was another false alarm at Liverpool Street and we weren't allowed into the tube station for almost an hour.'

Weak excuse, Miss Root's expression declared.

'Then, at Marble Arch,' Grace persisted, 'a policeman stopped me so the King and Queen could go past.'

'The King and Queen?'

Grace hadn't looked too hard at the Rolls-Royce, but there'd been a man and woman in the back. 'Unmistakeably,' she said.

Miss Root lifted a powdery grey eyebrow. 'How extraordinary as, yesterday, Their Majesties were touring the north-west, culminating in a visit to Crewe Alexandra Football Ground.'

Just her luck that Miss Root also studied the Court Circular.

'I'm sorry, but it really isn't my fault,' Grace said. 'Can we talk about my next position? I've finished at the nursing home now, and I can start right away. You said I was in with a chance as the family need someone urgently.' The job she wanted was at Potters Bar, an hour by train from central London. Grace had never heard of the place until a week ago, but her imagination had got to work. In her mind, it was a charming, olde-worlde town teeming with friendly locals. Not to forget three pounds a week wages. 'So, do I have the job, Miss Root?'

'You are the least experienced nurse on my books, and thanks to your conduct today, the least reliable.' Hard fingers took hold of Grace's chin, forcing her to look up. 'I knew you were hiding something. What have you done to your face?'

Grace offered up the story of the lamp post, only to be told that it sounded highly dubious. 'Your shift at Fenchurch House finished at five a.m., yes?'

'Yes.' Though these private nursing homes always found you one last job as you went to fetch your cape. 'It was more like five-thirty.'

'As it is summer, by five-thirty you would not be walking home in the dark.'

The woman was a meteorologist now?

'Ah, but it was foggy and the lamp post I collided with was painted grey.'

Miss Root was immovable. Grace could not represent the Root Agency while so disfigured. 'And this' – Miss Root, a former ward sister and zealous in her quest for perfection, wagged a finger at Grace's apron. 'There, right-hand side.'

Grace looked down. Oh, for Pete's sake! Five minutes without her cape on, and she'd caught her apron against some railings. Hating the world for turning against her, hating Cormac for pushing the first of a line of falling dominoes, she said desperately, 'You promised me this job, Miss Root.'

'Too late, Nurse. At precisely nine o'clock this morning, it was given to somebody else.'

3

____

Miss Root took Grace's silence for acceptance. 'Go home and don't come back until your eye is a normal colour.'

Grace was out of options, but it didn't stop her trying. 'Thing is, Miss Root, our rent is due at the start of next month, and Mam... I mean, my mother... forgot to put up the blackout a few nights ago and a lousy copper... a policeman, I should say... saw and now we've got a fine to pay. I need a position now, not in a week or two.'

Arriving home in the early hours, she'd found Mam crying in the kitchen and Cormac looming over her, having turned up unannounced. He had discovered that someone had spent the money in the rent tin.

Grace had walked in on the scene, Cormac laying into their mam because he knew, as Grace knew, that Mary Whelan was the culprit.

Spent on gin. Or, if not gin, Mam would have put it on the collection plate at Mass, as a desperate form of penance.

In a bid to calm the situation, Grace had mentioned her hopes of a better job.

'With that and what you contribute,' she'd explained to her

brother, 'we could find somewhere better to live. Somewhere with a bit of green, where the air doesn't smell of the fish market and the docks. Who knows, Mam might recover.'

Grace had no idea what part of that speech had done the damage, but fury had spurted from her brother like water from a burst main. Cormac had grown incoherent, ragged breaths interrupting profanities. Course, she'd lost her temper too and that was when he'd smacked her in the eye, though, afterwards, he'd accused her of moving at the wrong time. Hadn't he only meant to thump the air next to her face?

Mam had begged them to stop. Ricky, Cormac's twin, had stumbled in from his bedroom and done his best to get between them. Cormac had shoved him and, for a terrifying moment, Ricky had struggled for breath and looked as though he might collapse. Mam had screamed, 'You've murdered him!' and Cormac had stormed out.

Wanting the last word was an enduring Whelan trait. Grace had followed her brother outside and shouted, 'You should watch yourself. I heard the government's calling up all able-bodied men under the age of fifty. And you know what? When they march you away, I'll be giving the loudest cheer.'

He'd come back at her. 'I'm not joining up. Our dad did his bit for this family in the last fiasco.'

'You can't dodge a uniform for ever,' she'd warned him.

He'd stepped right up to her, his voice in her face. 'If I hear you've gone anywhere near a copper, Grace, I'll kill you.'

'You know I wouldn't do that.' The menace in his voice was like iced water tipped straight into her veins. 'Whelans don't rat.' For all that, a treacherous hope had come over her, that somebody *would*. A word in the right ear might get Cormac to a recruiting office and sent far, far away.

Until that blessed day came, she had a fight on her hands and with that in mind, she tried again to appeal to Miss Root. 'I need something permanent that pays every Friday on the nail. But more than that, I need to get out of Whitechapel. Sometimes I look at my life and I think it hasn't even started yet.'

Miss Root stared back at her. 'How old are you, Nurse Whelan? Twenty-one, twenty-two?'

'I'm only twenty.'

'Even so, it's not improbable that your life is already half over.'

'Half?'

'Accept that for a working-class girl like yourself, Irish to boot, a basic career in nursing is the best you can hope for. Be thankful.'

A ring at the door took Miss Root from the room, leaving Grace feeling she'd been thumped a second time. Was the woman saying she had a life expectancy of forty? She'd have stormed out, having first kicked over a chair, except that an altercation seemed to be taking place. Peering into the front lobby, she saw Miss Root framed in the open doorway. On the step was a nurse wearing a tunic in the agency's blue trading high-pitched opinions with the proprietress. They reached Grace loud and clear: 'You knew what you were sending me into, Miss Root. It's more than flesh and blood can take. Look at this. Look!' The nurse rolled up her sleeve to show her arm. 'I didn't qualify as a State Registered Nurse to have a malign child lob hairbrushes at me. Sod that. I quit.'

She spoke well, despite the profanity.

Imagine, being that lathered up but not letting the elocution slip, thought Grace. *If I could do that, people would treat me better.*

Miss Root was pleading. 'Come inside, Nurse Manning-Smythe. Let's talk this over.'

'I have already said, I quit.'

'But you can't.' For the first time in Grace's hearing, Miss Root sounded shaken. 'It was all going so well with the Ventnors. *And* I found you that lovely accommodation on Hill Street. Mayfair lodgings are gold dust. We can sort this out.'

Lovely accommodation? Grace echoed silently. *How come Nurse Manning-Whatever gets that, and where is Hill Street?*

'Too bloody late,' the well-bred voice shot back. 'Pay me for the days I've worked and take me off the books. I'm joining the Queen Alexandras.'

Grace leaped back into the office as Miss Root returned, followed by the pink-cheeked nurse, who threw Grace a comradely look, implying, *You know what I'm talking about.* She invited Grace to look at her arm.

'You tell me if you think it's all in a reasonable day's work.'

Grace sucked in a breath. A bruise reached from below the nurse's short cuff to her elbow, where the flesh was broken. 'That must hurt.'

'I'll say. The old cow waited till I was leaning across her bed and smashed her breakfast dish down on my arm.'

'*Language,* Nurse Manning-Smythe,' Miss Root begged.

Nurse Manning-Smythe rolled her eyes. She had not finished. 'She let me clean up, then lobbed her hairbrush at me. Look—' She pushed back her fringe, displaying another lesion. 'She could have killed me, the rotten bitch.'

'I thought you said "malign child"?' Grace had imagined an infant hurling toys.

'Lady Ventnor,' snarled Nurse Manning-Smythe. 'She doesn't need a nurse, she needs a wardress. Or a lion tamer.' Turning to Miss Root, she said, 'I'm signing up as a military nurse so I can be paid to have lethal weapons launched at me.'

Miss Root shook her head desperately. 'If you won't think of Lady Ventnor's family, think of this agency.' Belatedly realising that Grace was soaking it all up, she snapped, 'Nurse Manning-Smythe and I would like a moment's private conversation.'

Grace volunteered to make tea. An idea was taking hold and she wondered if she had the nerve to carry it through.

She was placing cups and saucers on a tray in the kitchen, when she heard the front door clash. 'Just tea for two, then,' she muttered. Better stir in extra sugar.

'This is a disaster,' Miss Root said as Grace shouldered into the office with her tray. 'The Ventnors live five doors down from here, and Sir Gideon Ventnor is a very influential man. I cannot have a nurse of mine walk out on him and his wife.'

Grace had known what she wanted from the moment she'd heard the front door slam, but not how to say it. Both feet in, the usual way? 'This is a daytime position, no night shifts?'

Miss Root nodded. 'Yes, just days. Another private nurse watches over Lady Ventnor at night. I understand where your mind is going, Nurse Whelan, but I couldn't possibly send you to the Ventnor residence looking as if you've been in a pub brawl.'

Grace handed Miss Root her tea. A job in Mayfair would answer her needs, and as it would keep her in London, Cormac couldn't object. Could he? 'How many people have injured themselves since the blackout started?' she said, pointing to her eye. 'A shiner shows you're doing your bit. Is Lady Ventnor really so bad?'

'I'm afraid so,' sighed Miss Root. 'She fancies she's had a stroke and she suffers from gout.'

Gout. The temper-twister.

'How much are they paying?' Grace had long ago dropped any pretension of nursing for the love of humanity. Well, at the start of her training maybe, but a few weeks being a probationer at the Royal London had snuffed out the rosy glow. Her wage was essential. Mam could no longer hold down a job and Ricky never kept one more than a week. Cormac made plenty with his after-dark activities, but he rationed his contribution to a fiver a month. When he dropped by home, he'd lay an extra pound note on the table, then pull up a chair and scoff everyone's rations, leaving the cupboard bare.

The Ventnors were paying one pound fifteen shillings per week, Miss Root informed her. 'Alternate Sundays off and one weekday afternoon per month.'

'One afternoon a month? What are they, licensed slavedrivers?'

'That's what they pay.'

Seven pounds a month in Upper Brook Street, minus agency commission, compared to twelve in Potters Bar. Only, that job had gone. A bird in the hand is worth two in the bush. An eel in your pie is worth twenty of the buggers in the Sargasso Sea. 'Will I get hot drinks and meals?'

'Ye-es.'

'Ye-es' meant stale sandwiches, bring your own milk ration.

Grace thought about it for a whole ten seconds. 'I'll start today.'

'Impossible.' Miss Root took a mouthful of tea and made a face. Too sweet. 'Lady Ventnor won't have a Nurse Whelan.'

'Because I never finished my training? I did, I just didn't take the final exam. I'm good, you know I am.'

'I'm not talking about your training.' The telephone rang and from the face Miss Root pulled, it was the call she dreaded. When she put the receiver down, she looked ragged. 'Sir Gideon Ventnor needs a replacement within the hour or they'll use another agency. I cannot lose this client. They're—'

'Highly influential, you said. And I've said I'll do the job.'

Miss Root shook her head. 'Lady Ventnor is fastidious. Nurse Manning-Smythe was a perfect choice. She went to school not a quarter of a mile from here.'

'You mean,' Grace said, translating, 'I sound too much County Mayo and not enough Mayfair?'

'Yes, since you say it. You are too Irish.'

'Then I'll change.' Grace crooked her little finger, holding her cup the way ladies did in Fortnum & Mason's tea salon, and gave her impersonation of Nurse Manning-Smythe. 'One could do very well in this position. However, one expects two pounds per week for the effort.'

'Then one will be disappointed,' Miss Root said curtly, but she made no more objection and set about the paperwork.

'You've spelled my name wrong,' Grace said as she took the typed letter of introduction from Miss Root. 'You've put "Wheeler" not "Whelan".'

'"Wheeler" will spare us unnecessary explanation. Temper your voice a little. Remember, the character you take over the Ventnors' threshold will be yours as long as you work there. Cap and clean apron, please. And one incidence of insubordination or cheek—'

'One will be out on one's ear.'

Grace retired to tidy herself up. Her left eye was beyond the help of face powder and it would look a sight uglier before it improved. But she had a job at one pound fifteen a week. Seven pounds a month... well, six pounds and twelve shillings after the Root Agency took its cut. Had she made another reckless decision? Being Nurse Wheeler made her feel she was stepping onto a stage without being given the lines. Pulling a comb through her hair, she told herself that she'd make it work. It wasn't what she'd hoped for, but with luck, it was the gateway into a different life.

4

Before she left, Miss Root re-pinned Grace's cap, tut-tutting because she couldn't get it to stay straight.

'A little glycerine on your hairbrush every morning would help, Nurse Whelan.'

'I thought I was Nurse Wheeler.' If Miss Root was forgetting, how was she meant to remember?

Leaving 88A Upper Brook Street, Grace felt Miss Root's judgement following her. What if Lady Ventnor didn't take to her, or worse, launched teacups or a bedpan at her?

At Ventnor House, she mentally prepared herself for a uniformed maid who would doubtless point a snooty nose at her. She wasn't expecting a butler in full morning coat, with a stand-up collar and cheerless demeanour.

'The Ventnor residence,' he informed her. 'May I help you?' His hair was greased to one side, some kind of blackener hiding the grey. Grace reckoned he was about her father's age – the age her dad would have been had he not died ten years ago at the docks.

She gave her name, stopping herself at the last moment from saying 'Whelan'. 'Nurse Wheeler, here to attend Lady

Ventnor.' Because she was trying to polish up her voice, she forgot to put the 'h' on 'here' and attached it to 'attend' instead.

'Oh, the replacement,' the butler grunted. 'You'd better come in. What happened to your eye?'

Grace was about to trot out her story of the blackout and a lamp post when she realised he was looking at her apron, which, even though it was fresh on five minutes ago, had managed to get a smut on it. 'Before coming here, I assisted at the scene of an accident,' she improvised. 'A rag-and-bone man's cart collided with a removals lorry on the Commercial Road.' And that was God's honest truth. The butler wasn't to know it happened last spring. 'Will you take me to my patient?'

Lady Ventnor was currently asleep, having passed a vexatious morning, she was informed. 'I will present you to Sir Gideon.' The butler told Grace to stay there.

She assumed he was going upstairs, or to a different wing, but all he did was cross a moderately sized marble lobby and tap on a panelled door. Grace had a moment in which to assess the Ventnor house. It was plum Mayfair territory and sizeable, but was there a faintly shabby air? Though who was she to judge. Flat 3, Victory Buildings, Whitechapel, the town residence of the Whelan family, was poky, dark and always messy.

The butler beckoned Grace over, saying, 'Go in.' He opened the door he'd tapped at and announced, 'Nurse Whitlow, Sir Gideon.'

'Wheeler, it's Wheeler,' Grace muttered. Heaven help her if everyone called her something different.

She walked into a room lined with rows of gilded, leatherbound spines. A man in khaki overalls stood at a circular table, staring down at an expanse of paper. She cleared her throat nervously. 'Are you Sir Gideon Ventnor?'

The man glanced up from his chart and said, 'I am' and put out his hand for Grace to shake. 'Goodness, Nurse, that's an impressive black eye. Don't tell me, fell over in the blackout?'

'Got it in one, Sir. Me and a lamp post had a tussle.'

Sir Gideon tutted. 'This wretched lights-out regime has caused more casualties so far than the enemy. Not that we have a choice, please don't take me for a revolutionary.'

Given that Sir Gideon sported a Lord Kitchener moustache, a fiercely military posture and officer's pips on his uniform, Grace could assure him that she would not. The armlet on his sleeve proclaimed 'LDV' – Local Defence Volunteers, recently renamed the Home Guard. Ten to one, he'd served in the last war and was back in uniform, doing his bit. Her anxieties diminished. It wouldn't be so bad if she had an ally in the master of the house.

'Good of you to come at such short notice,' he said and Grace couldn't miss the glance he exchanged with the butler, who had lingered in the doorway. 'We've had quite a morning.'

Unsure how much she was supposed to know of the rumpus between Lady Ventnor and Nurse Manning-Smythe, Grace smiled blandly. 'Every day offers a new start, Sir, is my motto.'

'That's encouraging, Miss, er, Wheeler. Have you come a long way?'

'Not far at all,' she answered with absolute truth. She wasn't about to mention Dock Street, not with the butler standing there like a pillar of doom. If she could change her name, she could change her address too – fake it, anyway. 'My abode is indeed very close by.'

'Your...? Ah, I see. Splendid. Keep it local,' agreed Sir Gideon. 'As my butler has informed us that Lady Ventnor is snoozing, how about you and I have a cup of tea, break the ice. Any chance of one, Buckland?'

'Tea, Sir?'

Grace wondered why the butler felt it necessary to repeat words he'd heard perfectly well.

'And a scone if there's one knocking about,' Sir Gideon added. 'I'm sure Nurse, er, Wheeler would appreciate a snack.'

'Certainly, Sir,' the butler conceded graciously, 'considering the young lady has spent the morning hard at it on the Commercial Road. I will see what Mrs Shotley has in the tin.'

While they waited, Sir Gideon explained the chart he'd been studying when Grace came in. It showed the English coastline. 'From the Wash to Hastings,' he said, betraying a boyish eagerness. 'These black triangles mark Fighter Command bases. Fear not, I'm not divulging restricted intelligence; the locations are deliberately imprecise. Can't be too careful.'

Grace supposed not and tried to make sense of all the squares and squiggles. 'There's a lot of them. Bases, I mean.'

'We're an island nation, Nurse, with much coastline to defend. These are what I consider our "home bases". Here's RAF Uxbridge.' Sir Gideon pointed to a dot to the west of London. 'Here's Northolt, see? Down here in Kent is RAF Manston, North Weald and Biggin Hill. And here' – he jabbed the top of a finger down hard – 'is RAF Hornchurch.'

'Hornchurch?' The name acted like a mild electric shock. It was where the pilot on her train had been heading, though he must have been going somewhere else first, to be on the Central line. To visit a sweetheart? A little prod in the pit of her stomach made Grace ask, *Am I jealous?* It made no sense, and why should she resent somebody else's happiness? 'Hornchurch is in Essex, isn't it?'

'Correct. I have a special interest in the place.'

'Your son?' she guessed.

'In a manner of speaking.' Sir Gideon looked up as Buckland came in with a tray, and gave a grunt of satisfaction. 'Tea is served. Tell Buckland how you like yours, Nurse.'

Strong with lots of sugar, generally, but as sugar had been rationed since the start of the year, Grace said, 'Just a sprinkle.'

The butler put the tray down and asked if he might 'leave Nurse to pour' while he went up to check on Lady Ventnor.

Once the butler had gone and Grace was sitting down, she said, 'I have to ask, Sir, I hope you don't mind...'

Sir Gideon invited her to 'Ask away.'

'If we were to have an air raid, and I was on duty, what would we do with Lady Ventnor?'

'Do with her?' he repeated, as if Grace had asked him about a box of old books.

She apologised. 'I put that badly. I understand she's not very mobile, and if she sleeps upstairs, there might be an occasion when we'd have to bring her down.'

'I'm with you. When we've finished our tea, I'll show you. Tuck in; one of those scones is yours.'

Grace did so and counted four sultanas. There was a scrape of butter too. The thing about rationing, the smallest treat ballooned into a feast.

Afterwards, Sir Gideon led her down into a cellar. It was musty, but someone had tried to make it comfortable, with chairs and camp beds, lanterns and a paraffin stove. 'The idea is we'll hunker down here. As for getting my wife downstairs, it's brute strength, I'm afraid.'

'You mean, we'll carry her?'

Sir Gideon nodded. 'Let's hope the enemy stays away from Mayfair, eh? Which road did you say you live on?'

Here beginneth the first lie, she thought. Only she couldn't do it. 'I'm between lodgings, Sir Gideon, but I'm staying with family at the present.'

'Jolly good.'

Grace had an idea that Sir Gideon was not all that interested in the human detail. Air bases and gun emplacements filled his mind instead, and that, Grace told herself, went in her favour. She wasn't so sure about Buckland, and Lady Ventnor was still an unknown quantity. Though not for long.

The butler was waiting for them when they'd finished their inspection. Her Ladyship had woken and was ready to receive the new nurse, he informed Sir Gideon. He didn't spare Grace a glance and she returned the compliment by walking straight past him to go upstairs.

Her air of confidence was entirely bogus. The next minutes would reveal if she'd made a shrewd move in a not very illustrious nursing career – or the worst gaffe of her life.

5

Expecting to discover some kind of spitting fury, Grace was disconcerted to find an overweight woman lying in a vast bed, propped up on pillows, one hand reaching out to a box of candied fruit. Lady Ventnor wore a lilac satin bed gown and a knitted turban. Her hair looked dry, like unravelled rope. Her face was pouchy, her cheeks liver spotted. Teeth didn't look so good either. But... in Grace's estimation... the patient looked too worn out to hurl anything. For now.

'You're the new one, then,' Lady Ventnor quavered through a mouthful of candied pear after Grace introduced herself. 'Let me see the black eye.'

Grace obliged. 'I smacked into a lamp post last night, in the—'

'I have no interest,' Lady Ventnor interrupted. 'Kindly keep that side of your face turned away. Buckland says you're common. I hope you aren't. I can't abide slovenly diction or gross manners.'

'Lucky I come out of the top drawer, then,' Grace came back, thinking, *What's the chance I'll kick Buckland's arse before the week's out?* 'You may call me Nurse Wheeler, or Grace, whichever you prefer. Shall I call you "Your Ladyship"?'

'How else would you address me? You will be "Wheeler". Upper servants are always called by their surnames.'

'I am a nurse, not a servant.' Grace spoke clearly. Anxious as she was to make a good impression in this job, it paid to set boundaries right away.

Lady Ventnor seemed not to have heard and motioned towards a side table. 'I'm ready for a glass of water and then you may adjust my curtains. You will have noticed the sun shining into my eyes.'

I've answered my question, Grace thought as she went to pull the curtains across to block out the inconvenient sunlight. *It's a gaffe. The worst kind, since I can't back out.*

Nor did things improve. The snubs and demands kept coming as the clock moved slowly through the hours of the day.

A relief nurse was supposed to take over Lady Ventnor's care at six-thirty, but seven o'clock came without sign of her. She finally arrived at ten to eight, Buckland letting her in. Grace waited outside the door to Lady Ventnor's room and watched the caped figure mount the stairs.

'Nurse Gill,' the late arrival wheezed. 'Are you new?' Dropping her bag, wiping her brow, she gave Grace a fast appraisal. 'What happened to Polly Manning-Smythe?'

'Gone off to join Queen Alexandra's Nursing Corps,' Grace answered. 'Or to hurl herself off Beachy Head. One or the other. You're late.' Apart from a short tea break and a half-hour lunch, she'd been on her feet for over nine hours.

'Lord bless.' Nurse Gill fanned herself. She was short and bosomy, with red-apple cheeks and not from bracing good health, Grace reckoned. She was gripping her sides as if she'd run halfway up a mountain. She'd be a fat lot of help if they ever had to carry their patient downstairs.

'I was expecting you well over an hour ago.'

'It's the buses, you see.' Nurse Gill hung her cape on a hook, lowering her voice as if confiding something delicate. 'I come all the way from Enfield and it's a slog, dear.' She sounded not a jot apologetic. 'Polly never minded.'

That I doubt, Grace privately retorted. There wasn't a nurse alive who welcomed extra hours of unpaid shift at the end of a long day. 'I'd be obliged if, in future, you'd catch an earlier bus.'

Nurse Gill laughed as if Grace had told a corker of a joke, promising, 'I'll do my best, I'm sure. What name d'you go by?'

'Wheeler.' It was a measure of how tired Grace was that she said it without feeling self-conscious. As she walked downstairs to collect her cape, she realised her careful 'Mayfair' voice had lapsed too. Oh well.

She quoted herself, using the plummiest accent in her repertoire, 'Every day offers a new start, don't you know.'

'See you in the morning, Nurse,' came Buckland's sceptical drawl from the shadows. 'Sleep tight. Be sure the bedbugs don't bite.'

6

———————

Saturday 24 August

There was an air raid alert minutes after Grace arrived for her shift the next morning at eight, and though it only lasted an hour, it set everyone on edge. You couldn't trust it to be a false alarm even though, a year into the war, the skies remained pretty clear, bar the occasional stray German plane seen off by the RAF.

At just before teatime, the enemy came back and this time, the alert lasted nearly two hours. As she had earlier in the day, Lady Ventnor refused to get out of bed to go down to the cellar, forcing Grace to stay upstairs with her.

Grace had now survived almost two shifts at Ventnor House. So far without physical injury, but the job was proving relentless. If she suspected Grace was taking a moment off, Lady Ventnor would summon her to carry out some pointless task. Contrarily, when it was time for her medicine, Her Lady-ship would be fast asleep, forcing Grace to wake her, only to have her head bitten off.

At last, the day ended. Later than it should as Nurse Gill

again turned up late. Apparently, there'd been such horrendous bombing on the Kent coast, the buses in north London had developed engine trouble in sympathy.

'Buckland says you live close by,' Nurse Gill commented as she shed her cape and gloves. Grace gave a shallow nod which the other nurse took as concurrence. 'That's lucky, because half the world's trying to get down into the tube stations. I wouldn't fancy pushing through the crush.'

If only I didn't have to, thought Grace. To add to her woes, her black eye was throbbing, bearing out her prediction that it would get worse before it got better. After a stop-start home-ward journey and a trudge in the dark, she arrived home in Dock Street to find washing up in the sink and nothing to eat.

Mam and Ricky were playing a card game, and while her brother looked pleased to see her, her mother immediately began spooling out her worries.

Ricky had seen their landlord go past while he was queuing at the grocer's, she told Grace. 'The way he looked at my boy, it was as if he knew the rent money was gone. It's because we're Irish, Grace, that's what it is. Landlords always think the worst of us. If we're still short in a week, what will we do?'

Grace promised she'd come up with something. She crawled into bed, hungry and bone-tired, thinking, *For now, just let me sleep.*

As she sank into a dream where the RAF pilot she'd briefly met on the train pointed at her eye and shouted, 'Take that thing to the docks where it belongs!' the sirens went off. Grace was out of bed, groping for her clothes before her good eye was properly open. Outside on Dock Street, she could hear whistles as air-raid wardens urged sleepy people to get to shelter. The hooning, undulating wail of the siren never failed to find the thinnest part of your heart.

Shoving her feet into her shoes, she went to the bedroom next to hers. 'Ricky, are you awake?'

A mumble confirmed it.

'Is Cormac with you?' It was highly unlikely as Cormac rented a room near Regent Street, above a seedy club-restaurant, and never slept in the family home. But she'd better check. Much as she hated him right now, she'd not leave him kipping through a possible air raid.

'He's not here, Grace,' Ricky confirmed.

Did that mean Cormac was definitely somewhere else? With Ricky, you had to put exactly the right question. 'You're sure he's not in this building?'

Ricky came to the bedroom door, gripping the frame with a big, blunt hand. 'He's not, Grace. Last time I saw him was when you and him had your ding-dong.'

'You mean, when he thumped me?'

Ricky looked dejected. 'I wish you and Cormac liked each other, Grace.'

'Never mind that now. Get ready to come outside.' Cormac could fend for himself, being smart as a fox, whereas Ricky, the second-born twin and given up for dead after their mother's labour stopped, had to be guided through moments like this. 'Get a coat on over your jim-jams and your shoes on. Don't forget your gas mask, now. I'll check on Mam.'

In another room off the narrow corridor, Grace shook a bony shoulder under the covers. 'Mam, wake up.'

No response, but a familiar smell. Pulling back the coverlet, heaving her mother onto her back, Grace's fears were realised.

'God save us, how are you getting gin when we haven't got sixpence to our name?'

She shouted for Ricky.

Despite his lumbering size, he could move quickly when needed. 'What is it, Grace?'

'Get my torch from my bag – in fact, bring the bag. And my gas mask.' Where was their mother's mask? 'You'll have to help me carry her.'

The siren had wound itself down and outside, the wardens' whistles had a steely clarity, tallying the minutes remaining to get to safety. The goods depot on Commercial Road, where the council had created a cavernous shelter, was too far away.

'We'll go to Peabody,' Grace told Ricky. 'K Block's the closest.'

She got their mother into her coat and, with Ricky's help, pushed Mary Whelan's unwilling feet into her shoes. Together, they got her onto Dock Street and then up Flank Street, which, despite a bright three-quarter moon, was as dark as the inside of a drainpipe. With Grace's torch shrouded in brown tape to conform to blackout rules, it felt like the most hazardous walk of her life.

At the end of the street, the Peabody flats rose up like cliffs, eleven fawn-coloured blocks reflecting moonlight. The sky was latticed with searchlights, swinging to and fro, searching for enemy planes. She thought of the pilot who had made a brief appearance in her dream. Was he one of those brave boys, leaping into his Spitfire or Hurricane, flying on a razor's edge, keeping London safe? People called them Brylcreem Boys, from their habit of greasing their hair to fit under their flying helmets. She couldn't remember if 'her pilot' had been Brylcreemed. She seemed to recall he had dark blond hair, the colour of wet wood shavings.

Her mother chose that moment to become a deadweight.

Mary Whelan moaned, 'Take me home.'

'We'll only be in the shelter a little while, Mam.'

'I won't go into the ground. Leave me here, Immie.'

'It's me, Grace.' Mam had named the wrong sister. 'Immie's not in London, is she? I'm the one you're stuck with. Will you help a bit?' *God save us,* Grace thought, *here's Ricky and me like a pair of sailors, dragging a drunken shipmate back to the boat.* 'How the hell is she paying for gin?' Grace demanded in a hard whisper.

'She borrows off Granny Driscoll,' her brother answered. 'Sorry, Grace.'

It was hardly Ricky's fault. Granny Driscoll was their mother's closest friend, a resident of K Block, and Grace made a note to strangle the woman – until the guns along the docks started firing and an unearthly roar overwhelmed every thought. So, they'd finally come. Who was it who had said, 'The bomber will always get through'?

Looking up, she saw planes caught in the searchlights – four, then five, like the dots on a domino tile.

Grace and Ricky practically carried their mother the last yards. All the Peabody buildings had shelters dug under the lawns, shored up with sandbags and turf. One-handed, Grace hammered on the door of K Block's shelter and screamed, 'Let us in!'

Someone dragged them inside as two almighty detonations shook the corrugated walls.

'That was close,' muttered a croaky East End voice from the darkness. 'No more phoney war, no more bloody make-believe. We're getting it.'

Grace reckoned the explosions had come from the river.

They found a sandbag bench for Mam to flop on. Grace hunkered with Ricky on the floor. Babies howled; small children whimpered. The air in the shelter soon grew thin. Grace moved her torchlight around the space. There must be a hundred souls in here. There was Granny Driscoll, praying over her rosary beads. Other people comforted children or sat with their eyes closed as they waited... for what?

Midnight came and Sunday dawned. Mary Whelan snored, cocooned in gin.

At twenty-five minutes past one in the early hours, the all-clear sounded. Grace had a shift today on Upper Brook Street, but before that, she had a promise to fulfil.

A demon to face.

7

———

Sᴜɴᴅᴀʏ 25 Aᴜɢᴜsᴛ

At a few minutes past six, Grace walked out into an early morning that smelled of smoke, burned brick and spent explosives. She'd left her mother sleeping off her gin, and it wouldn't surprise Grace if Mary Whelan woke up with no memory of London's first aerial attack.

Ricky had joined Grace at the kitchen to drink tea made with slightly off milk.

'Will we be thrown out onto the street, Grace, like Mam says?' He'd made a nervous, biting motion with his teeth, the way he did when he was upset.

'Course not, Ricky.'

'Only, Mam said, the landlord is at the end of his tether with us. We pay late too often.'

'Not this time,' she'd reassured him. 'I'll get the money. Don't I always?' She'd made it sound simple, but there was only one solution, and as she waited for the bus to take her to Liverpool Street station, where she always got on the underground, her heart was beating three times a second. Nor did she feel any braver when she got off the tube train at Oxford Circus.

She struck off down Regent Street, glancing into department store windows, eyeing up the rationed goods behind the criss-crossed gum-tape. From Regent Street, Grace entered a labyrinth that formed a buffer zone between Mayfair, the West End and the shadier corners of Soho. She turned up Brewer Street, passing between iron bollards into an alleyway. Moving like a cat on drawing pins, she knocked on a blistered brown door.

Bolts were shot back and the door opened.

A woman with dyed red hair peered out, clutching a none-too-clean dressing gown to her ample bosom. 'Do I know you?' She had a nasal, cockney voice and she looked Grace up and down, lingering on the bruises.

Whacking a brush over her hair in front of the mirror that morning, Grace had seen that her eye had now reached the tri-coloured stage. Red, black and yellow, like the flag of a distant British dependency.

The woman muttered, 'Another one that walked into a lamp post?'

'You must be psychic.' Returning a cocky remark boosted Grace's nerve and she gave her name without faltering, adding, 'Is my brother Cormac here?'

A thumb indicated uncarpeted stairs across a dingy lobby. 'Be my guest. Rather you than me.'

Grace made her way up, and the higher she went, the more the air smelled of frowsty bedlinen. She opened two doors before locating Cormac's room by the pinstripe jacket draped over a chair. Those squared shoulders, the edge of a red handkerchief in the breast pocket, were engraved on her brain. Her brother had been wearing the same suit when he thumped her.

The curtains were still drawn, a gap between them letting

in meagre light from the alleyway. After giving her eyes time to adjust, Grace saw that the iron-framed bed had two occupants. One was a girl, curled up, holding onto bedcovers that wanted to slide to the floor. Beside her, a man lay spreadeagled on his front, his vest stretched across his broad shoulders. Even in the subdued light, his tumbled hair had a raven sheen.

Confident that both were soundly asleep, Grace crept to the chair and slipped her hand into a jacket pocket. She drew out a wallet. From its thickness, business was booming in Cormac's world. He could pay his family's rent for half a year and not miss it, she thought bitterly. She peeled five notes from the wad.

A muffled groan, a squeak of bedsprings and Grace froze.

Cormac muttered something and the girl gave a sigh that held a piteous note. Grace couldn't resist a closer look at her, and a floorboard creaked beneath her foot.

A figure sat up, rasping blearily, 'Who's there?' Lank brown hair fell over the girl's features. She pushed it from her eyes, asking again, 'Who is it?'

Instinct told Grace to run, but now this girl could give Cormac a description of her, so she'd only be postponing trouble. Making a fast decision, she crouched at the bedside. 'Hey.'

The girl clutched a sheet to her skinny breastbone and the gesture, along with her scared saucer eyes, told Grace that she was young and out of her depth.

Waving the pound notes, Grace touched her bad eye. 'Tell him, five quid just about covers this.'

The girl gave a sideways glance and hissed, 'Are you his sister?'

'Unfortunately, yes.'

'The one he likes, with the children?'

'No, the other one.'

'Oh. The one who stopped him going to school.'

Grace needed to get going, but that comment, sweeping in

out of the blue, made no sense. What on earth had Cormac been telling this kid? 'My brother's four years older than me,' she whispered. 'How could I stop him going anywhere? If he bunked off lessons, that was his choice.' Grace spared a moment to offer the girl a last piece of advice. 'Get out while you can, love. Cormac's a bad apple and they corrupt the good ones.'

8

From the butler's face as he opened the door to Grace's knock, you'd think she was an hour late, not one minute early.

'Bad night, Mr Buckland?'

He didn't dignify the question with an answer, but as Grace stepped across the threshold, she sensed a jittery atmosphere. Sir Gideon was adjusting his Home Guard cap in front of the mirror. He offered Grace a good morning but seemed in no mood for conversation.

Nurse Gill was at the top of the stairs and detained Grace on the landing.

'I could have done with you in the early hours, dear, I can tell you. I hope you got your beauty sleep, because I surely didn't get mine.'

'Course I didn't,' Grace said. 'My part of town got exactly the same treatment as everywhere else.' She hadn't noticed that Buckland had followed her up.

He said in his habitual, uninflected, tone, 'I was under the impression that your, ahem, abode is also in Mayfair, Nurse.'

Drat the man. 'That's what I mean. Whatever you experienced, so did I, with fifteen seconds' time difference.'

Nurse Gill confided that they'd made a drastically late decision to take Lady Ventnor downstairs to the cellar. 'The sirens
were practically in the room with us, and still she refused to
budge, even when the house was shaking. Sir Gideon had to
come up and raise his voice. We got her down between us.'
Nurse Gill made a queasy face. 'She gripped my hair the whole
way and if I'd tripped, I'd have been scalped. All the time we
were in the cellar, she whimpered and found fault with
everything.'

The one positive aspect, Nurse Gill reported, was that the
cellar housed Sir Gideon's pre-war wine collection. 'He had the
foresight to bring a corkscrew. D'you have a cellar at home?'

Did she? There was a basement at Victory Buildings, full of
coal, broken furniture and a population of whiskery lodgers. No
wine, though. Because she found it easier to skate around the
truth than to tell a downright lie, she said, 'We found a public
shelter. Mam' – she cleared her throat – 'my mother has frail
nerves and having people around her helps.'

'You're lucky she can walk on her own,' Nurse Gill said.
'Her Ladyship certainly knows how to be a deadweight. I was
thinking, we need to install a lift...' Giving a glance at the
bedroom door, she lowered her voice. 'Or a block-and-tackle.
Well, I'm off, home to bed to sleep away my Sunday. Want me
to run through the medicine list again?'

Grace said no, thank you. She'd written everything down
clearly. Four pills, two in the morning, two in the evening.
Pretty simple, though as she entered the bedroom and greeted
Lady Ventnor, her brain felt like Piccadilly Circus at rush
hour. Would Cormac have woken and learned of her visit?
She imagined him counting his cash, the wide-eyed waif
looking on fearfully. That poor girl wouldn't be able to keep a
secret long.

One comfort: Cormac couldn't track Grace to this address
as only Miss Root knew she worked here.

'What are you doing, Nurse? Stop dithering,' Lady Ventnor called from her bed.

Turning to say, 'Coming,' it flashed through Grace's mind that Miss Root's observation that Her Ladyship's stroke was mostly in the mind was probably correct. Lady Ventnor was sitting up against her pillows, sipping her second or third cup of coffee. The grip on cup and saucer looked pretty firm to Grace, who had come across hypochondriacs in the hospital wards where she'd trained and recognised there was a grey area between real infirmity and a patient's deep-seated attachment to being ill. Lady Ventnor was unhealthy, that was indisputable. But an invalid? *'I reckon you could get downstairs fast enough if the world's last pot of coffee stood at the bottom,'* she muttered.

She took the morning pills and a glass of water to the bedside. As she leaned across, a blow aimed at her head just missed.

'Think I'm deaf?' Lady Ventnor narrowed her gaze. 'Your agency is one telephone call away, remember that.'

True, thought Grace. *But you'll run out of willing victims one day, then what?*

'Your pills, Lady Ventnor.'

Once they were swallowed, Lady Ventnor waved Grace away. 'Where is my husband? He should have come up for his morning visit by now.'

'I believe he left the house.' Found something more appealing to do with his Sunday, such as inspecting walls and windows for damage from last night's attack. Grace suggested he'd be back for lunch.

'What business is that of yours?' Lady Ventnor snapped.

None, Grace reflected. *I'm just the bloody nurse. I'll do my job, keep my trap shut, take my wages. If it comes to the point I can't stand it anymore, I'll... what? Drink gin like Mam? Join the services?* Neither solution appealed. She'd carry on being her angelic self and one day, maybe, a handsome airman would take her away from all this. Life wasn't *Peg's Paper*, though. It was much nastier.

Mid-morning, Buckland entered with a tea tray and the news that a bomb, last night, had destroyed a church in the City of London, not far from St Paul's. Grace seized the moment, saying, 'Nurse Gill told me you took ages getting Lady Ventnor down to the cellar. If an incendiary had come down on this street last night, it might have been the end of you all.'

'"Might have been the end of you",' Lady Ventnor parroted in the fluty accent Grace used as Nurse Wheeler. 'What would you care?'

'I'd care very much,' Grace retorted, 'though not as much as Sir Gideon would.'

'How would you know what my husband feels or thinks?' The question struck like the sharp end of a pair of scissors, telling Grace she'd hit a nerve.

'Quite so,' the butler echoed. 'How would you know, Nurse?'

Fair enough. Maybe Sir Gideon wouldn't care. If there was any pleasure to be gained from Lady Ventnor's company, she had yet to find it.

She watched Buckland pour tea, noting that he'd brought only one cup.

Sod this, Grace thought. *I'm going down for some.*

In the empty kitchen, she rooted round for a tea caddy. Her feet ached and the aspirin she'd filched from Lady Ventnor's well-stocked cabinet hadn't touched the thumping in her head. And there was another nine hours of this still to go.

She was stirring a quarter-spoon of sugar in her tea when Buckland came in and raised an eyebrow at her. When it became obvious she wasn't going to scurry away, he said, 'Her Ladyship requires the closet.'

By the time Grace had carried out the task and restored her patient to bed, her tea was cold and her back was agony.

'Ring for a brandy,' Lady Ventnor demanded.

'Good God, no. Nurse Gill will serve your nightcap at the usual time.' That being nine p.m. 'Anyway, you shouldn't be sipping the hard stuff, not with your gout. The last thing you need is liquor inflaming your tissues.'

'My doctor sanctions it. I will take his guidance and not that of a jobbing nurse.'

Jobbing nurse. That was the nub of it, Grace reflected. Thanks to Cormac and some ill-timed intervention on the last day of her training, she'd missed her exam and never attained the status of State Registered Nurse. She was a perpetual probationer, deprived of her silver pin and letters after her name. Stuck, like a bent teaspoon in a drainpipe, in a job like this.

At one p.m., Grace went down for her lunch, which was served to her by the unsmiling cook in an airless room off the kitchen corridor. Lettuce, a few slices of tomato and some grated cheese which must have been flung on as an afterthought. A baked spud wouldn't have cost them the earth, since the oven was running anyway.

Lady Ventnor partook of a luncheon of pork fillet in cream sauce with little rosettes of piped mashed potato. Served from a silver platter by Buckland, laid on a table placed on the bed, over her legs. She cleared the lot, then instructed Grace to take the plate down to the kitchen. 'At once. I cannot abide dirty crockery.'

'I'll leave it at the top of the stairs,' Grace said firmly. One sign of weakness, this woman would have her cleaning shoes and hemming curtains.

Lady Ventnor fell asleep soon after and Grace seized the chance to stretch out on a daybed in the room next door.

She drifted off, borne away on thistledown, until a vehicle

backfired in the road. It woke Lady Ventnor, who shouted, 'Nurse, nurse? Where are you? I need you at once.'

At last, the end of her shift arrived, but Nurse Gill did not. Once again, it was nearly eight when Grace heard the front door.

She strode out onto the landing, hissing as a white-capped head bobbed up through the gloom, 'Two hours late?'

Nurse Gill's amiable smile contained no apology. 'Didn't I say, I come all the way from Enfield?'

'Yes, you did. And I have to get back to Whitechapel.'

'Whitechapel? I thought you were a Mayfair rose? You never grew up within the sound of Bow Bells.'

This was what no sleep did for you. Grace performed some quick footwork. 'I'm running a first-aid course there.'

'That's the spirit.' Nurse Gill sounded impressed. 'Tootle-oo, then, dear, but don't overdo it.'

Grace let herself out into a violet dusk. No air raids so far, today. At Marble Arch, she again encountered a noisy scrummage of Londoners swarming into the underground to take shelter. Nurse Gill's warning yesterday had been no exaggeration. All the benches were occupied, with people sitting on the platform itself, on blankets or flattened-out boxes. They were mostly women, old men and children. Some lay full length on makeshift cardboard mattresses, as if they meant to be there all night. A grandfatherly type was playing a squeezebox. Boys rolled knucklebones over squares chalked on the platform.

'Safest place, this,' said a woman seated with four others on a bench, noticing Grace's pained expression. She wore a duster turban on a head of dark curls. Noticing Grace's cape and the remnants of a black eye, she said, 'Bless you, dear, long day?'

'Far too long,' Grace answered. 'I wouldn't fancy bunking down here, though.' Often, waiting on a deserted platform after an overnight shift, she'd seen rats scuttling under the rails. 'I'm too fond of my own bed.'

'Aren't we all. But I'd rather wake up in the land of the living, than outside St Peter's gates wondering what the bloody hell happened. Where do you call home?'

Grace muttered, 'Whitechapel.'

'I hope you've got a good shelter nearby. Jerry's after the docks, that's what I heard. Me and Madge' – she nudged the woman squashed up next to her – 'we work at the Tate & Lyle factory, near Albert Dock.'

'You're Sugar Girls?' Grace asked.

'That's right. I fill tins with syrup; Madge checks it's sweet enough.'

'Surely, Tate & Lyle have a shelter at the factory. Why would you come all the way to Marble Arch?' Grace was genuinely curious.

'We fancied a bit of class,' the woman chuckled. 'If there's a bomb with my name on it, I'd rather be somewhere fancy when it happens. "Mary-Lou Patrick drew her last breath in Mayfair" sounds better than "she copped it on Factory Road, Silvertown".'

Grace mulled this over as she travelled home. If she could get her family out of Whitechapel with its proximity to the river, she'd be improving their odds of survival. Months ago, she'd tried to persuade Mam to evacuate with Ricky to the country, as her sister Immie had done with her kids. Mam had said 'No, I hate fields and ditches.' Like Lady Ventnor, refusing to take shelter in an air raid, Mam was stubborn. Or 'damn self-ish' to put it another way.

Reaching home and yet again seeing lamplight shining between the blackout curtains on the third floor, Grace felt a welling despair. She was like a dog swimming in the water, a rope between its teeth, pulling a boat loaded with people who refused to pick up the oars. An instant later, she was shrieking, 'Oi, d'you mind?'

The street door of Victory Buildings had been flung open,

the knocker striking Grace under the shoulder, sending her gas mask flying. She had a second in which to recognise a well-built figure wearing a suit a little lighter in colour than the night.

Cormac. Off like a hare, his footsteps briefly halting before he made a sharp turn left. More figures came thundering out of the building. Grace flattened herself against the wall.

Coppers. Buttoned-up jackets and reinforced helmets. For a wild moment, Grace was tempted to shout, 'He's gone up Flank Street,' but in the end she let them pound away towards Cable Street, and went inside, securing the catch. A whiff of bay and lemon oil mingled with the odour of cabbage from a neighbour's flat.

Just as she'd predicted, the law was closing in on her brother.

'God help me, he'd better not think it was me who set the police on him.'

9

The first thing Grace did was go into the sitting room and pull the blackout curtains firmly across. The lights had gone out as she'd come upstairs and when she tried to switch them on nothing happened. The meter had run out.

She found Ricky in bed, hiding under the covers.

'What was the unholy visitation about?' she demanded.

'I don't know,' came the muffled reply.

'I was mowed down first by your brother, then almost trampled by two of Cable Street's finest. I'm in no mood for "I don't know", Ricky.'

Ricky eased out from under his blankets. 'They came to ask about Cormac's prescription.'

'His what?' There was never enough money for doctor's visits or special medicines. Aspirin and milk of magnesia were the cure-alls they relied on.

'Cormac should have gone for it,' Ricky continued, 'but he hasn't and the police were going to take him.'

It made no sense to Grace, but there would be a seed of truth in there somewhere. 'I'll ask Mam. She's not at Granny's, is she?'

'No, Grace. In the kitchen.'

She found her mother at the kitchen table with a candle burning in a jar. Or what used to be the table… Grace's knees crashed against something solid.

'What on earth?'

Ricky had followed her and he explained, 'It's a Morrison shelter. Cormac brought it round. He came with his friend, the one who laughs at me.'

'When?' Grace asked sharply.

'At nineteen minutes past seven.' Whatever he lacked educationally, Ricky always knew the time to the minute. 'If there's an air raid, we can get inside it. Show her, Mam.'

Mary Whelan lifted one side of the tablecloth, revealing a steel cage. Grace had read about these shelters, in a leaflet from the council, but this was the first she'd seen close up. Six feet by four, large enough for an adult and a couple of children, it was intended to be used in a raid if there was no chance of getting to a reinforced shelter. It certainly wouldn't fit all three of them. They were a tall family. Someone had laid green baize over the top, spreading the tablecloth over that, and Grace reckoned there were about six inches spare between it, the cooker and the sink.

'Are we supposed to eat our dinner off it?'

'That's what Cormac says,' said her mother. 'I'm not sure I like it. I had a go inside and came over all strange.'

'If we ever have to use it, and we're all at home, we'll have to pull straws to see who gets left out,' Grace said.

'Cormac meant well. Give him credit,' Mam said.

'Mm. I suppose, but unless there's a real emergency we go to the proper shelter. Mam, what was Ricky saying about the police and Cormac's prescription?'

Mary Whelan looked up, the tracks of recent tears illuminated by candle flame. It struck Grace that widowhood and poverty were eating Mam layer by layer. '*Conscription*,' Mary said. 'Ricky got it muddled. Cormac has been called up three times now for his military service, and the coppers want to know why he hasn't presented himself.'

'Is this the first time they've been round?' Grace hadn't seen any official letters addressed to her brother.

'No, the same pair keep turning up, but this was the first time your brother was home.'

Grace patted the Morrison shelter. What an irony, for Cormac to be nearly caught by an act of kindness. Hopefully, he'd know by now that the police had been sniffing after him and it wasn't her tipping them off. 'He didn't happen to mention losing any money, did he?'

'Cormac?' Mary shook her head. 'He was more concerned about getting this thing through the kitchen door.' She meant the Morrison shelter. 'I'll be saying a Hail Mary for those boys, for the language I heard.'

'He didn't mention me at all?'

'No, Grace.' Mam expelled a sigh. 'It all comes at once, doesn't it, trouble? I hate the shadow of a copper on the step.' She pulled her brows together. 'You're late home tonight. Where is it you work now?'

'West, near Hyde Park. I told you that yesterday.'

'It sounds a treat. Nice people?'

'They're fine. There's a butler and a cook.'

'Well, I never!' Mam tapped the rent tin. 'When do they pay you? See, I'm not sure what we do about this.'

Grace took Cormac's five pounds from her purse.

Her mother stared in wonder. 'Wherever did you get it?'

It was on the tip of Grace's tongue to describe Cormac asleep under the sheets with a nameless girl, in the back bedroom of an unsavoury house... but why upset Mam further? 'My new employers gave me an advance on my pay.'

'Bless them, sweetheart, they must be very good people.'

'Kindness itself.' Grace re-pocketed the money. Had Nurse

Gill not turned up so late this evening, she'd have knocked on the landlord's door on her way home. She'd try tomorrow. Meanwhile, this money was not leaving her person.

Grace hunted for signs of left-over dinner, only to be told that Cormac and his friend had finished it off between them. Lifting the lid off a pan on the cooker, she found a scrape of boiled potato, enough to feed a mouse. 'He's not here still is he, Cormac's friend?'

'Frankie O'Halloran? No, he left before the police knocked.'

'Oh, him. I don't like him either. Mam, you need to talk to Cormac about the company he keeps.'

When Grace's dad had been alive, police visits had been a regular thing because Michael Whelan couldn't stay out of a fight. Cormac had taken on Dad's mantle from the day Michael died, but he didn't stop at a fist fight outside the boozer on a Saturday night. Some of the men Cormac associated with had a serious edge of violence, and he could expect more than a fine and a night in a cell if it caught up with him. Frankie O'Halloran. That man, just as much as Cormac, had changed the course of Grace's life.

The morning of her final nursing exam, the one that would have made her an SRN, Cormac had arrived on the doorstep as she was leaving, Frankie with him. Frankie was white pale, clutching his thigh, blood weltering between his fingers.

Grace never had learned who put the blade in or why but Cormac had flatly refused to take his friend to a hospital.

'You're supposed to be a nurse; you can do it.'

Grace had been given an automatic 'fail' for arriving too late to sit her exam. The hospital hadn't let her resit. Two years' slog for nothing. None of the senior sisters had seen the irony of rejecting her as a nurse because she'd saved a man's life. And, of course, not a word of thanks from Frankie or Cormac afterwards.

'Anything else for me to eat, Mam? A slice of Spam, maybe?'

'I thought they fed you at work.' Mary's mind flipped onto another topic. 'I got a letter today from Immie. Wonderful news. She's on her way home with the children.'

'What?' Grace swung round, bumping her hip against a chair. 'She can't. London's not safe now.' Imelda, known as Immie, was the oldest of the Whelan children, married with three little boys. They'd been evacuated at the start of the war, to a village in Hampshire. 'I thought she loved it there, and the boys were being fed milk, butter and eggs?'

'She liked it at first,' Mary said, 'but now she misses her home.'

'Doesn't she read the newspaper?' Immie's house was in south-east London.

'She'll be grand.'

'She will not!' Grace had seen on Sir Gideon's map how close London's outer edges lay to the RAF fighter bases in Essex and Kent, currently the Germans' favourite target. 'Mam, you have to make her go back.'

Mary Whelan couldn't grasp it. 'You try sitting in somebody else's house, minding your manners all the time.'

'I do,' Grace hit back. 'Not that I get to sit much.'

Her mother waved that away. 'I shall be glad of her company. I hate being left on my own, no one to talk to all day.'

'You've got Ricky, and me after work.'

'It's not the same. Immie and I understand each other. We're both mothers, and I miss my grandsons.'

'Tell me she's not bringing the babies with her?'

'Would she leave them behind, you're thinking? Course not.'

'Then she's lost her marbles—' Grace broke off, seeing Ricky chewing his lip anxiously. She leaned across and patted his arm. 'Don't mind me, I'm angry at the world tonight. For the last time, Mam, is there a morsel in this place for me to eat?'

It seemed not. Grace made cocoa with hot water and nothing to sweeten it, taking it to her room. Saying her prayers before rolling into bed, she asked protection for London, Kent and Essex, but most particularly for this part of Whitechapel, and very particularly for Victory Buildings, Dock Street.

She fell into a patchy sleep, one ear cocked for sirens or Cormac coming home, five pounds the poorer and his blood up. She wasn't sure which she dreaded most, her brother or the bombers. As it turned out, she didn't have long to wait for either of them.

10

___

The following night, Grace came home to discover her bedroom door open and the light on. Somebody had dumped a canvas bag in the middle of her floor as well as several wooden crates. Cormac, in shirtsleeves and with his boots on, was stretched out on her bed.

Grace lifted a bottle from one of the crates. Mackeson's Milk Stout. Honestly purchased? Not a cat in hell's chance. 'Get off my bed please.'

Taking his time, her brother swung his legs to the floor and came to stand in front of her. He was as tall as Ricky, but a different build, with his narrow waist and honed upper body. He and Ricky were the dark Whelans, taking after their dad. Like him, Cormac had cobalt-blue eyes which lent him – in Grace's opinion – an air of undeserved innocence. He dressed like the handsome man he was, his trousers and jacket with more fabric, more pockets, more shoulder padding than your average Joe managed these days.

To Grace's relief, she'd caught him in an affable mood.

'Nice to see you, Grace.'

'Nice to see you too, Cormac, but I need my bed.' She held

up the bottle of stout. 'Don't think you're stashing hooky goods in my room. Get them out.'

'Bit late for the lecture, the cops being here just yesterday. Odd that.'

'It wasn't me, if that's what you're implying.'

'Do I believe you...' He adopted a thinker's pose. 'You creep into my gaff while I'm asleep, scare off my young lady, help yourself to a few quid, creep out again and, hey presto, the flat-foots are knocking on the door.'

'I didn't fit you up. And I didn't creep into your room either.' Actually, she *had*. She'd tiptoed about like a pantomime fairy, but she hated the image of herself skulking and afraid. 'Besides, you owe me.'

'Owe you.' He looked at her healing eye and laughed. 'That was your doing. You walked right into my fist.'

'Whatever you say, Cormac. Long story short, you've just paid next month's rent.' On her way home, Grace had stopped at the landlord's dingy offices above a pawnbroker's and handed over the money. September's rent, early.

'I paid...' Cormac echoed, 'because Mam drank the last lot I gave her.'

Grace shrugged. True enough, but the landlord didn't care which Whelan pocket the money was squeezed from. Still, it appeared she wasn't about to be given a second black eye, so she risked a gesture towards the door. 'Will you take your stuff out of my room, please?'

'No, sis.' Cormac turned her around and steered her out into the passage. 'I'm back for a few days. I'll be gone in due time.'

'And these bottles with you, right?'

'What bottles?' He grinned infuriatingly. 'I see no bottles.'

'When did you start believing you were so utterly charming, brother?'

His smile cooled. 'When did you learn to thieve, Grace?

You could have asked me for the money, instead of embarrassing yourself by taking it. It's down to you that I'm here now. Calling for me so early in the morning spooked the establishment, which is why I've had to move out for a while.'

'You've got a bedroom next door.'

Cormac laughed. 'Think I'm going to climb into a bunk bed at my age and listen to Ricky snoring? You'll kip down with Mam.'

'She snores too and I need my sleep or I can't work.'

'I'm the man of the house, I make the rules. Hey—'

She flinched, but he was only reaching to touch her healing bruise.

'That really was an accident, you know.'

'If you say so.'

'Be a good girl and rustle up a bit of supper. And before you ask, there's another five pounds in the rent tin to keep you all in Spam and spuds. Don't let Mam get her hands on it, though.'

'And these bottles, Cormac?' If there was a police raid, she, Mam and Ricky might be charged with handling stolen goods. That would be her career finished for ever. 'Get rid of them, tonight.'

Cormac pointed. 'Kitchen. Go. I'm peckish.'

A tin of sardines between four, some sliced beetroot and mashed potato would be tonight's repast, since there wasn't anything else. Ricky did most of the shopping, queuing at the grocer's and the butcher's on Commercial Road, getting their ration cards stamped, and his food choices were highly repetitive. Grace often wondered what their mother did all day, apart from the obvious. She'd once come home unexpectedly early and found Mary Whelan crying softly over her wedding photographs, with a quarter-bottle of gin on the chair arm.

Ricky came into the kitchen as she finished peeling a

mound of potatoes. 'I helped Cormac bring up the crates,' he said proudly. 'He let me sit behind the wheel of his van afterwards and make like I was driving.'

'He's got a van?' This was news to Grace.

'His own wheels, he calls it. It's a funny colour.'

I'll bet it is, Grace rumbled to herself as she filled a pan with water. Yet again bashing her knee on the Morrison cage, she put the potatoes on to boil. Wanting to check Cormac had told the truth, she took the rent tin from the drawer where they hid it. Inside were three pound notes, some silver and coppers.

'Mam hasn't been out this evening?' she asked Ricky.

'No, Grace. We played Snap.'

Then it would be Cormac coming up short. He always did that, made promises but kept something back so you had to go on bended knee to him. She took the lot, putting it in an empty Golden Syrup tin at the back of the electric meter cupboard, feeding the loose change into the meter itself. Ricky watched and she put a finger to her lips. 'Not a squeak.'

'I won't, Grace, promise.'

The iconic green and gold tin brought back the face of Mary-Lou Patrick, the cheerful woman bedding down at Marble Arch. Mary-Lou had joked about dying 'somewhere posh' though to Grace's thinking, whether a bomb plummeted to earth through the smog of a factory chimney, or the fragrant airs of London, W1, made damn-all difference if you were underneath it. Lady Ventnor would make no more glorious a corpse than an East End factory girl. 'She'd just imagine she would,' Grace said in an under voice. How you viewed yourself affected how the world saw and treated you. Unlike her siblings, Grace had got a place at a good school, but every day had been a battle. She would never forget walking in through the gates, girls snickering, their whispered chants clinging to her back. 'Here's Our Lady, full of Grace. Lice in her hair and a dirty face.'

She'd never had lice. Nits, yes, but then everyone got those as a kid.

The taunts had gone on until Grace had experienced a growing spurt, becoming the tallest, reddest poppy in the class. About that time, she'd discovered the levelling effect of a swift left fist. Cormac had taught her how, give him his due. Her classmates had left her alone after that, and she'd gone right through, passing her Higher School Certificate. Not bad for Mike and Mary Whelan's girl, she told herself as she turned the gas up under the potatoes.

Dinner was tolerably convivial, Mam not slurring, Cormac basking in Ricky's admiration. Grace suggested they leave her to wash up. There wasn't enough room now for two of them at the sink.

Cormac came back as she made a pot of tea with the last dusting of leaves.

'Not a word outside this place about me being here,' he told her. 'Or the bottles.'

'The bottles nobody else can see? Oddly enough, brother, you are not my main conversation when I'm nursing.'

He watched her rocking the pot side to side to coax some flavour out of the tea leaves. 'Any milk?' he asked.

'Nope. Ricky made him and Mam rice pudding for lunch.' She poured tea into two cups. Milk-less, sugarless, horrible. 'Don't turn your nose up, or you'll hurt my feelings.' She handed him his. He'd brought his jacket with him, hanging it on a kitchen chair, as if he didn't like to let it out of his sight. It smelled faintly of cigarettes and hair oil. Grace lifted it up by the collar and looked inside, seeing the name of a Bond Street tailor. 'Made specially?' she asked.

'Course. I have to look the part.'

'Which part, the arse?' That was skirting close to the edge. Sometimes, she couldn't stop herself.

'Give it a rest, Grace. You have your uniform, I have mine.'

'Those coppers would like to see you in a different sort of uniform. You're of fighting age, Cormac, and like it or not, they'll be after you.'

He came as close to her as he could, swearing as he bashed a kneecap on the Morrison shelter. 'Because you bellowed like a fishwife, letting the whole street hear. There's a snitch behind every pair of curtains, but you know that. Sometimes, I think you were born to pull me down.'

He thought that? Dear heavens, another helping of irony.

Sitting down with her tea, she wrote a shopping list for Ricky to hand to the grocer, and another for the butcher. 'If you're staying here any length of time,' she told Cormac, 'we'll need your ration book.'

Cormac was winding his watch and grunted, so she delved into his jacket and whisked it out.

Only it wasn't his ration book, it was his identity card. They all had one of those, issued at the start of the year. It gave personal details and had a registration number. You had to produce it if a policeman asked and Grace kept hers in her work bag. The address inside Cormac's was Anne Street, Plumstead.

That was Immie's house. Around the time she and her boys had been evacuated, her husband, Ted, had been sent to France as part of the British Expeditionary Force. It was suddenly blindingly clear to Grace that while other men were joining up, Cormac had taken advantage of an empty house and passed Immie's address off as his. The police must have called there for a while, but now they were on to him. 'Forging documents gets you a prison sentence.'

Cormac snatched the booklet off her. 'Who says it's forged? I've often stayed round our sister's.'

'Don't I know. You've been hopping here and there like a

flea on a hotplate since you were fifteen. But it's not your address.'

Cormac shoved the ID card in his trouser pocket and picked up his tea, muttering, 'Disgusting muck. Why is there never any milk?'

'Because the fairies forget to round up the magic cows.'

They held each other's gaze. The way her brother waited for her to look away first was never less than disturbing. Just as her vision was blurring, he turned from her and tipped the remains of his tea down the sink.

She followed him to her room, *his* room until he decided to leave, saying, 'Did you know, Immie's on her way home? She's bored with Hampshire and country living, Mam says.'

'Mam told me too.'

'So, you should be worried,' said Grace. 'It means, if the police knock on her door, they'll get an answer. "Good morning, Madam, is there a shirker... sorry, a business gentleman... by the name of Cormac Whelan here?" You need to sort out your story because she can't give them a barefaced lie.'

'Immie won't rat on me,' Cormac said confidently. 'She should have been my twin, and Ricky should have been yours. Now what are you up to?'

She was taking tomorrow morning's uniform out of her cupboard, to hang it up in Mam's room. Afterwards, she went into the sitting room to take cushions off the sofa. Clearly, she'd be sleeping on the floor for as long as Cormac chose to be here.

She discovered her mother and Ricky sitting side by side on the sofa, the wireless on.

'They bombed Berlin last night,' Ricky said. 'That'll show them, won't it, what our lads can do? That's what I said to Mam. That'll show them.'

Grace supposed it would, though she doubted it would deter the enemy for long.

The newsreader was reporting raids on Kentish seaside

towns, 'Diverted there by the fierce resistance of our brave airmen'. Meaning, she supposed, that having been driven off from the airfields, German bombers had offloaded their cargo onto Broadstairs and Margate. It had been Ramsgate just the other day, left with streets of smoking rubble.

'North Weald, Debden, Biggin Hill have sustained bombardment but remain operational,' the newsreader went on, 'with attacks also aimed at RAF Hornchurch.'

Grace felt a slither of anxiety. For a few, brief seconds, her shadow had touched that of a pilot based there and, suddenly, she was alert for every scrap of news. As if her heart was lashed to a Spitfire undercarriage.

She jumped as Ricky rushed to the window. They could hear the drone of an aircraft. 'Don't touch those blackouts till I've switched the light off,' she warned.

When she joined him, she saw the dark forms of aircraft caught in the beams of the searchlights.

'No guns tonight, Grace,' Ricky said, his cheek pressed to the glass.

'You're right. Maybe they know something we don't.' The air raid warning went the moment she'd said it. 'Right, let's go to the Peabody. Mam?'

Mary Whelan shook her head. 'I'll use the Morrison. That's why it's here.'

'The Peabody shelter is properly dug into the ground. We won't be there for long. Yes?' Grace saw her mother's eye nip across to a bookcase whose first shelf stood several inches off the ground. 'Thinking you'd like something to read?'

As she stooped to choose from the small selection of books, her toe nudged the neck of a bottle. London gin. Anger wound her up in loops of barbed wire, but she stayed calm. 'Rotten hiding place, Mam, but if you come to the shelter with me and Ricky, I'll let you have a nip before I pour it away.'

Cormac chose to sit out the raid at home. 'I can stretch out in that bloody cage, if it's just me.'

Grace, Ricky and Mary went to join Granny Driscoll in K Block's shelter, and it was quite convivial, with singing and corny jokes. The all-clear went at four in the morning, making it the longest raid so far. Grace didn't bother making up a bed but snatched a nap on the sofa before it was time to get up and face Upper Brook Street again. This was her life: Cormac, bombs and Lady Ventnor.

'I'm not sure which is worse,' she muttered as she pinned on a fresh cap.

11

———

Bang on eight, having completed the handover from Nurse Gill, Grace checked Lady Ventnor's pills and the dosages. Some medicines had to be taken without food and some should only be administered on a full stomach. Some required equal dosage morning and evening, others seemed random, as if the doctor was hedging his bets.

Lady Ventnor had been sleeping when Grace arrived. She now woke and gasped before grunting, 'Oh, you again. When's the other day nurse back?'

'D'you mean Nurse Manning-Smythe?'

'I don't recall her name, but she had nice manners.'

Unlike you, Grace thought. 'What's wrong with my manners, Your Ladyship?'

'You sound like one of those silly, common girls who work at the telephone exchange.' Lady Ventnor affected a high, strangulated voice. '"Hallo caller, operator speaking. Putting you through." All lipstick and no knickers.'

Grace snorted with laugher. 'No knickers? I shouldn't think so, perched on those stools all day.'

'Where were you dragged up, Nurse?'

Grace knew she was being prodded for a reaction. She couldn't blare out the truth: 'Middle of nowhere, County Mayo' as abandoning the charade was impossible. She was too far in. 'I was born in London.'

'There's a lot of London and most of it is awful. Where, precisely?'

'Here, Mayfair.' She'd said it, fate sealed. 'On the third of May, I emerged into the world...' A new song Vera Lynn had sung on the wireless popped into her mind. 'In Berkeley Square.'

Grace knew Lady Ventnor intended to ask, 'What number?' but fortunately, the rattle of silverware announced the arrival of breakfast.

Grace helped her patient sit up and listened as Buckland cajoled his mistress to tuck into scrambled egg, grilled tomatoes and two rashers of bacon. Her stomach creased. That bacon was half a week's ration for the likes of her, and there'd been two rashers on yesterday's breakfast plate, and on the previous day's.

'Nurse Wheeler claims she was born in Berkeley Square,' Lady Ventnor said between mouthfuls.

Buckland cocked a look at Grace. 'What number?'

Fortuitously, Sir Gideon came in and Lady Ventnor's attention swung away. Buckland served coffee and withdrew.

Grace slipped to the side room. She'd witnessed every day now how Sir Gideon came to bid his wife good morning, and how Lady Ventnor clasped his wrist as if to hold him in place. He would detach himself when a few minutes was up.

'Did Buckland mention we had a visitor late last night?' Grace heard him say now.

'No. Who?'

'Owen, needing a bed again.'

'Owen – he's here still?'

Intrigued by the alteration in Lady Ventnor's tone, Grace angled herself to hear better.

'That's twice in one week,' Her Ladyship continued eagerly. 'I thought he could never get away from his base. How is it he gets up to London?'

'He's on duty without pause; they all are,' agreed her husband, 'but generally, fighter pilots do daytime sorties. They don't fly at night and the boy has to loosen his collar when he gets the chance. Being at Hornchurch, he can roar up on his Enfield after lights-out. I believe there's some girl he's keen on.'

'Girl? What girl?'

Grace placed weights on a set of apothecary's scales, making the little brass pans seesaw up and down. The first medicine of the morning was for Lady Ventnor's gout.

'Search me,' was Sir Gideon's response. 'Turns out, he couldn't remember her address and when he finally got hold of it, there was no answer at the door. He reckons she deliberately sent him on a wild goose chase.'

'Then he should drop her dead.'

Grace flinched at the spitefulness and thought, *I wouldn't like to be her, whoever she is.* She wondered what motorbike-riding Owen had done without a date for the night. Found a bar, got drunk? Or called up another girl and enjoyed a different sort of good time? That's what Cormac would do.

Hornchurch... Thanks to Sir Gideon, she knew Spitfire squadrons were based there, and the squadron numbers too, but this was the first time she'd heard him refer to a pilot by name. The Ventnors were childless, so was Owen Sir Gideon's godson perhaps, or a friend's son?

'Have we given him breakfast?' Lady Ventnor sounded almost frantic. 'Send him up, the darling boy.'

'Gone, I'm afraid. Has to report before nine for duty and needed to drop by home and kiss his fond mama.'

'That woman!'

'Even though it's in the wrong direction,' Sir Gideon finished as if his wife hadn't spoken. 'He was rather too shadowy round the eyes for my liking. What they go through, these young lads...'

'Why didn't he come up to see me?'

'For heaven's sake, Maude.' Sir Gideon's patience faltered, but he thought better of it, saying, 'I didn't hear him go and he must have wheeled his bike to the bottom of the street, not to disturb us. He's a thoughtful lad, my nephew.'

Ah. Uncle and nephew.

Grace came back into the room and saw Sir Gideon edging towards the door.

'Duty calls, dear,' he said. 'Shall I send my newspaper up to you?'

'You always ask that and you know I can't see well enough to read anymore. Oh, don't leave, Gideon!'

But he was gone.

These were the moments her patient was most likely to strike out and Grace approached the bed cautiously. 'I'd like to administer your gout medicine, Lady Ventnor.' She'd measured out fifteen grains of cinchophen.

Lady Ventnor watched her darkly. 'Why didn't my nephew come up to pay his respects?'

'Owen, is it? Is he your nephew or Sir Gideon's?'

'He is my late brother's boy and looks on me almost as a mother.'

Even though he's got one of his own? 'A fighter pilot, I take it. Hurricanes or Spitfires?'

'Supermarine Spitfires. He's a flight lieutenant, but he'll make wing commander in no time, I know it.'

If he survives, Grace thought. The life expectancy of fighter pilots was measured in minutes from the moment they jumped into the cockpit. Taking off at a moment's notice, the alarm jangling in their ears. Flying into the face of oncoming waves of bombers, dropping down on the enemy or outflanking him. Mid-air aerobatics, guns firing. A barrel roll or two. A dog fight. Hopefully, a safe landing followed by a night out, then back on the roulette wheel, hoping they'd make it to the end of another day.

Grace's thoughts swerved to Cormac, who might at this moment be driving a van down a backstreet, running on black-market fuel. Dodging his call-up. Meanwhile, the fighter squadrons flew up to five sorties a day, holding back the Luftwaffe, whose mission was to crush Britain's air defences so their armies could invade. And they'd been doing it all summer long.

'Will you take your medicine now?' she asked Lady Ventnor.

'No. I want more coffee. Go down and fetch some.'

Just as Grace had pretended not to hear yesterday's demand to darn a hole in Lady Ventnor's bed jacket, she ignored this order. 'The doctor was clear, the first dose to be given after breakfast.' She summoned a smile. 'Let's grin and swallow it, then you can ring down for Mr Buckland to bring up a fresh pot.'

'Buckland will be in his pantry, making his lists. And stop saying "mister". You're not a chambermaid.'

Grace couldn't bring herself to call the butler by his surname only. How she wished she could ask for a cup of coffee for herself, and maybe a piece of toast. 'Medicine now, Your Ladyship, or I'll telephone the doctor.'

With a sigh, Lady Ventnor swallowed her cinchophen and water.

Time for her bed bath. Grace swung into a practised routine, while Lady Ventnor made it as hard as she could for Grace to move her and get her nightdress off.

She'd alerted Nurse Gill before she left last night to a potential bedsore. It looked like Nurse Gill had ignored her warning, and now it was a rosy patch the size of a shilling on Her Ladyship's buttock. At the Royal London, it would have been noted in the book, to be kept an eye on. Grace had been taught to treat pressure sores with soap, water and methylated spirits, but in all her training she'd never seen one get better that way. It could also be excruciating for the patient.

'I'm going to help you lie on your side, Lady Ventnor. I'll put pillows behind you, to support your back. In a couple of hours, I'll turn you again.'

'I'm not a mackerel you're grilling.'

Grace explained why bedsores developed. 'We need to get some fresh air to the place. You've got away with it so far, but I've seen cases like this go septic. Better safe than sorry.'

'Leave me be.'

'We'll turn you onto your right side to begin with.'

'Why are nurses such utter-going bitches?' Lady Ventnor made a claw and nicked the back of Grace's hand where the skin was thin.

Grace stifled her instinctive response: a word that would have Mam saying Hail Marys for a month. She limited her response to, 'That hurt.'

'Serves you right because you like it when you hurt me. Put my nightgown on and cover me up.'

It was a battle Grace couldn't afford to lose. 'Shall I tell you about an old lady I nursed once, who had a pressure ulcer so deep, I could have touched the base of her spine through her flesh?' She rubbed her hands together to warm them and placed them under Lady Ventnor's back. 'Help a bit. If I break in half, you'll be on your own.'

'Sir Gideon will find another nurse. You're ten a penny.'

'Oh no we're not.' Now she was doing pantomime. 'Word goes round, you know. You'll be blacklisted, and it'll be Mr Buckland giving you bed baths.'

To her astonishment, Lady Ventnor gave a sniff of laughter. 'That'll be the day. Oh, get on with it then.'

Rolled onto her side, it was impossible for Lady Ventnor to

do anything and Grace suggested she might like to be read to. 'I've something in my bag.'

'What book, who wrote it?'

'*Peg's Paper*.'

'Ugh. Do I look like an imbecile? Cook uses *Peg's Paper* to line her budgie's cage.'

'Fine. Why don't I go down to the library, find something you'd like.'

'You don't know what I like.'

After a wrangle, it was agreed. Grace would select a novel and bring it back upstairs for approval. She went down feeling like a workhouse child let out to play after twelve hours grafting at the wheel – though it wasn't quite half-past eight. She opened the door to the room where she'd first met Sir Gideon. Between its towering bookshelves, the library had midnight-blue walls, and with black velvet curtains drawn, it took Grace a moment to realise there was somebody there.

A man sat at the table, head laid on his folded arms. A light blue shirt collar lay loose across the back of his neck, with a silk scarf pooling on the table either side of his ears. A peaked hat lay beside his elbow. The penny dropped.

The nephew wasn't racing back to RAF Hornchurch on his motorbike; he was here in Mayfair. Fast asleep.

12

———

'Flight Lieutenant?' It took three shakes of his shoulder before he raised his head, and Grace found herself looking into brown, haunted eyes. Dark blond hair carried a gleam, and she noticed a smudge on the surface of the table. Brylcreem, telling tales.

She knew him.

It was him, wasn't it? He'd come to her aid on the Central line when that so-called soldier had been bothering her. He'd thrown her bag to her.

'Hello again,' she said.

He didn't register who she was and it wasn't the moment to remind him because he looked utterly bewildered. 'What... what's going on?'

'You need to get going if you're to be at Hornchurch by nine. Where's your bike?'

'My... Oh, right. Parked outside.'

She'd seen a motorbike by the railings as she arrived and hadn't thought twice about it. 'Where's your coat, your helmet?' He'd have come up for a night on the town in parade dress, or whatever it was called, but he'd have put something on over it to ride here.

'Er... God. Buckland took them.'

'Right, follow me. You need coffee.'

He staggered as he got up and because she didn't smell drink on him, she knew it was exhaustion.

Assuming he knew his way to the kitchen quarters, Grace ran ahead. 'Mr Buckland, Mr Buckland!'

The butler shot out from a room off the kitchen corridor as Grace entered. 'Is it Her Ladyship?'

'No.' Grace indicated behind her.

The butler gaped. 'Mr Owen, you're meant to be back at your base!'

Grace explained how she'd found him asleep. 'He needs coffee, piles of sugar. Toast and jam too, maybe? Is there some of that bacon left?'

'More bacon here than the butcher's. Who's asking?' Glazed double doors at the far end of the corridor swung open, admitting the cook, Mrs Shotley. 'Oh. You, sir. Thought you'd have gone by now.'

Grace explained the urgency.

'I have to sign in by nine.' Owen looked more awake and acutely uneasy. 'Where are my togs, Buckland?'

The butler disappeared, returning a moment later with a set of grey-green overalls that looked like pilot's battle dress. Grace followed the cook over to the range while the change of clothes took place.

'How is it you have so much bacon?' Grace watched Mrs Shotley flip over glistening rashers.

'Not what you know, it's who you know,' came the enigmatic answer. 'Good thing someone found Mr Owen,' she added, 'or he'd be for it. Reduced to the ranks, I shouldn't wonder.'

'I won't be,' came confidently from the doorway. Owen, surname as yet unknown to Grace, had pulled on the overalls. A fur collar cradled the sides of his face and the silk scarf nestled inside it. His hair was hidden under a brown leather flying helmet, goggles pushed up over his brow. Flying boots completed the image of a man ready to vault into his Spitfire. 'I'll crash the barrier if need be.' He grinned.

'You still have to get there,' Grace pointed out. Hornchurch must be, what, fifteen miles off? She admired the way he'd gone from bog-eyed stumbler to fully alert in under five minutes.

'Twenty, probably, but I ride a Bullet, and it's well-named. Thank you, Mrs Shotley.' He accepted a doorstep of a bacon sandwich and drank down a cup of coffee. 'You're a gem. I'll eat on the go. Buckland?'

The butler came in with a hastily wrapped parcel. 'Your uniform, sir.'

'Follow me out; you can lash it to the back of my horse.'

Curious, Grace followed. On Upper Brook Street, she watched Lady Ventnor's nephew mount a black-framed motorbike, kick-starting it as Buckland secured the parcel to the rack over the back wheel.

Owen wolfed down the sandwich before slipping his hands into sheepskin gloves. He glanced over his shoulder to thank Buckland, raised a hand in salute and accelerated away in a billow of exhaust.

What about me? thought Grace. *Aren't I worth a thank you?* Owen hadn't shown her a glimmer of recognition. Still, she'd done him a good turn and maybe when he wasn't bone-tired, he'd appreciate it.

'May the road rise up to meet you and rocks roll out of your path,' she intoned in the voice of her Granny Doyle, laid to rest in Ireland in the village she'd never left.

Buckland sent her a disdainful glance. 'Do you intend to hang around at the kerb all morning, Nurse? Some of us have work to do.'

Grace made her way towards the house and happened to glance up. Good God. Lady Ventnor was out of bed, staring from the bedroom window. 'I wonder if the miracle will last until I'm upstairs again?' Grace murmured.

As she crossed the hall, Buckland blocked her way.

'You're Irish,' he said accusingly.

'Now whatever makes you say that?' she answered in her best impersonation of Nurse Manning-Smythe.

'"May the road rise up to meet you…" I knew anyway. You slip up every ten words. You're no more Berkeley Square than the man who cleans the windows.'

'I haven't the first understanding what you are talking about.'

'If you're Irish, be Irish,' Buckland said, adding repressively, 'Nurse Wheeler,' as if her name was a blot on her record.

She came close to snapping, 'Whelan, for your information,' but something was catching up with her. No, surely not…

She looked at Buckland with dawning realisation, then asked sweetly, 'What was it you said just now? "May the road rise up…"'

'"…To meet you and the rocks roll out of your way."'

Straight into the trap. No doubt about it. Grace laughed. 'You're a Dublin boy.'

Buckland's jaw fell. He recovered and blustered a denial which made Grace laugh all the more.

'You won't be looking down your nose at me any time soon, I dare say, now we both know you're as Irish as I am.' She leaned in and whispered, 'Let's keep each other's secrets, yes?'

13

Had Cormac not been occupying her room, Grace might be enjoying a lie-in on this, her first day off since starting work for the Ventnors. She'd lost count of the number of air-raid warnings that had gone off yesterday, the last day of August. The final one had yanked her out of another blissful cotton-wool sleep.

Wake up, out of bed, the bombers are back! Got your gas mask? Get your coat on. Off to Peabody. Hello everyone, here we are again, we must stop meeting like this. How about a singsong. 'I'm a London lass in love with a London lad!'

Given that her bed was three cushions laid lengthwise on Mam's floor, there was little incentive to stay put. She got up stiffly, going to the kitchen and yet again rapping her knee against the Morrison shelter, and *yet again* opening the tea caddy to find nothing but leaf dust. It was then that realisation parachuted in.

It was high time she left home. Her being here kept Mam in

a state of dependency. Almost like a child and she, Grace, the mother.

Since there wasn't a crust of bread in the flat, Grace decided to make scones. She found a bit of margarine, which she cut up with the last of the lard. No sugar, no currants but there were apples in a bowl, scabby ones from someone's back yard, and she grated one into the mix. Listening to the wireless as she kneaded the dough, she heard that Croydon Airfield had been attacked, as well as bases in Kent yet again. Hornchurch too. Yesterday had been a heavy one for the RAF, Sir Gideon had told her as their paths had crossed in the hall, he returning, she leaving.

'Our fighters tried to take off in the midst of a raid and we lost a few.'

'Just planes?' Grace had sought reassurance, a wobble in her voice.

'Thirteen planes, I understand, and one pilot killed.'

'Do you know who?'

'No.' He'd said it in a way that told her he wouldn't think the worst until he had to.

On her journey home in the dusk, she'd counted the fires that mantled London's suburbs from east to west. One burning so fiercely, it seemed to be trying to incinerate the moon. It was awful to think there must be actual homes, actual people, underneath those flames.

Cormac came home as she put the scones in the oven, looking as though he hadn't slept much either. She described the huge blaze she'd seen and he said it was probably the one near the Woolwich Arsenal, where a bomb had fractured a gas main. 'You should take Mam and Ricky. It's a sight to see.'

'Go sightseeing? The last thing Mam needs to know is that bombs are falling near Immie's place.' Grace shook her head at her brother's unshaven chin. 'What were you doing south of the river, anyway?'

'Never you mind, but I've brought you a present.' He plonked his gas mask case on the Morrison shelter table. Grace knew that whatever the case contained, it wasn't a gas mask. Cormac had made it clear that he'd rather choke than wear stinking rubber over his face. He undid the buckles and presented her with a slab of butter. 'There. Bit of a treat.'

It was wrapped in greaseproof paper, the way old-fashioned grocers did it, scooping the butter out of a barrel, weighing it and knocking it into shape with paddles. Butter had been on ration since the winter and it was the hardest thing for Grace to shake her head and push it away. 'I won't take it because you didn't pay for it.'

'And why would you say that?'

For one, because his ration book was on top of the Morrison shelter with everyone else's. Secondly, this felt like eight ounces and no shopkeeper would sell that much in one go. 'It's black market, Cormac, so don't play silly sods with me.'

'So, it's black market. Mam doesn't deserve a treat on a Sunday, is that what you're saying? What about Ricky? Butter's good for the health. You don't have to eat it.'

'It's wrong, doing what you do.'

'*Wrong?*' He took a step closer which made her feel like she was being slowly squeezed in a vice. She could never forget that swift-moving fist. 'Who is getting all the butter, Grace?'

'Our servicemen and women.'

'Grow up. It's the snobs in Mayfair, the starch-collar brigade who eat their dinners at the Ritz and the Savoy who get all the good stuff. You think the King and Queen get by with a scrape of lard on their toast and a bit of margarine on their potatoes? I don't think so.'

Grace didn't think so either. One week at the Ventnors' had shown her that if you had money and a cook without scruples, getting more than your rations was easy. 'What if we get seen with it?'

He chuckled. 'You mean, by the butter policeman who floats thirty feet off the pavement, staring into kitchen windows?'

'I mean... because Ricky says something, or someone finds the wrapper in the dustbin.'

'That's easy.' Cormac unwrapped the butter and, taking out his cigarette lighter, set the paper alight. It crackled and flared, and he dropped it in the sink.

'You're mad as a goose,' Grace said.

'A goose that's having butter on his scones.' He sniffed the air. 'Are they ready yet?'

He seemed in a stable frame of mind this morning, her challenges landing well and not flipping the lid on his temper.

When she took the scones from the oven, he grinned and took one. 'You're not such a bad good cook when you put your mind to it, Grace.'

Yes, Cormac was all right when the mood took him. Precisely why he was dangerous.

When the table was set, and all but Mam sat round it, Grace gave in. She spread butter on her scone, hiding it under a wave of apple and blackberry jam. Sup with the devil...

'Will you come to Mass?' she asked her brothers. As well as the scones, she'd made bubble and squeak from some left-over mash and cold runner beans. 'Hey, leave a bit for Mam,' she rapped as Cormac tilted the pan over his plate. Their mother was still fast asleep.

'I've work to do,' Cormac grunted, his good mood showing the first dent. 'I have to take those beers to a friend's place, so I need my strength.'

'Oh, yes, knocked-off beer is the heaviest,' she mocked. 'Move hooky goods on a Sunday, you'll be sent to hell.'

'I'll worry when it's time.' Cormac winked at his brother. 'I could do with some help, Ricky. Frankie's not at leisure right at this minute.'

'I'll help carry your crates, Cormac. I'll carry them all.'

It always killed Grace how Ricky came alive when Cormac paid him some attention. Wanting to be included and useful.

'You're coming to Mass, Ricky,' Grace said sharply. 'I mean it,' she said as Cormac started objecting. 'You can wangle your way out of trouble; you have the gift of the gab. Ricky will admit to anything if a policeman gives him a hard look.'

'Take him to Mass, then.' Cormac shrugged. 'It's not a job for boys anyway.'

'I'm not a boy,' Ricky said miserably. 'We're the same age. I can help and go to Mass on Wednesday.'

'You'll stay where you are and Cormac can get those crates out of here the way he got them in. You hear me, son?'

Nobody had seen Mam come to the doorway. She had her dressing gown on inside out and her hair, shoved under a knotted scarf, resembled a mop that had been left out to dry. Grey and faded red strands. 'Your dad would turn in his grave could he see you corrupting your brother.'

'Dad might be doing just that, turning in his grave, seeing as he's in Bow Cemetery.' Cormac poured the last dribble of tea from the pot. 'The Germans dropped a bomb on top of it two nights ago.'

In the end, only Grace and Ricky went to Mass because Mam said she didn't want to face their neighbours asking her why she had two grown sons not in uniform. After the service, on a whim, Grace suggested to Ricky that they take a bus west and stroll in Hyde Park. No sirens had yet marred the Sunday peace, but Grace's ears were cocked as always.

'Will the barrage balloons be in the sky?' Ricky asked as they took a seat on the Liverpool Street bus.

'Over the park? I expect so.'

In fact, they didn't see much until they had grass under their feet. Instead of huge, silvery eggs straining at the ends of their wires, the balloons were grounded, waiting to be reinflated. The sight reflected Grace's spirits: uplifted by going to Mass then brought down again. From the bus window, she'd seen more fires alight on the South Bank and thumbprints of smoke marking the skyline of Kent and Surrey. Until Cormac mentioned it that morning, Grace hadn't considered what happened if an incendiary bomb hit a gas main. She still desperately hoped Immie would delay her return to London and might even be persuaded to stay in the country.

They watched the last balloon being winched down to form a flabby shape on the grass. You weren't allowed to get close, so they found a bench and observed the soldiers manhandling the broad hose that would pump in gas to refill them.

'I'm glad they don't have to blow them up like party balloons,' Grace remarked. 'They'd run out of puff.'

'It wouldn't work. They put hydrogen in, Grace.'

She smiled. Her brother was very literal, but how was it he knew so much? She tilted her face to the sunshine, needing moments like this, though with her complexion, she had to watch for sunburn. She felt in no hurry to go home and said without thinking, 'I need my own place.'

Ricky turned on the bench. 'What did you say, Grace?' He was slightly deaf in his left ear. Some months ago, he'd gone eagerly to his medical appointment, to assess his suitability for the armed services, and he'd had to be called three times before he stood up. He'd been given a 'D' rating, deeming him unfit for military service of any kind. His deafness was the least of his impediments.

'I was saying, I ought to get a room nearer my work, so I don't have such a long trek home every night and morning.'

'Would you live there on your own, in the room?'

'Ideally.'

'What is "ideally"? How do you live "ideally"?'

'I mean, in the best of worlds, I'd live by myself in my own little flat, with a big comfy bed and you and Mam round every Sunday for dinner.'

'But you won't be with us the rest of the week?' Fear coloured Ricky's voice. It was always there, like the tag end of a jumper cuff. Worry, worry. Grace would always rush to reassure him but today was different.

Today, she had taken a step towards a difficult choice. 'I wouldn't be with you all week, that's right,' she said. 'But you'd be fine. Mam's your mam, you know. Not me.'

'She doesn't know how to be Mam since Dad died. The day he went, Mam went with him. I heard Granny Driscoll say so. You can't leave us, Grace. Can't we go on as we are?'

Yes, she sighed inwardly. That's how it would be, because it always was. She would work ten-and-a-half-hour days, be snarled at by Lady Ventnor, then drag herself home and find a sink-full of washing up and nothing worth eating.

Ricky gave her arm a gentle nudge. 'Pinch and a punch for the first of the month, Grace.'

'So it is.' She did it back to him. 'First of September.' In two days, the war would be a year old. She remembered going out onto the street when the news came, to stand with their neighbours, all the women crying. War hadn't come as a surprise, but nobody had foreseen the daily reality. The hardship, the menace that came from the skies.

She told Ricky she'd treat him to tea. 'How about Gunter's on Curzon Street?'

They left by the Stanhope Gate, crossing Park Lane. Grace took Ricky's hand. As they reached the other side, he said, 'Cormac says I'm strong as an ox and twice as stupid.'

Bloody Cormac. 'Oxes have brains, big ones,' she said firmly. 'I mean, oxen. Don't take it to heart, what he says.'

'I don't mind. Cormac has a lady-friend now and he says

he'll find me a lady-friend if I do what he says.' Ricky spoke like a child promised the last cake on the plate.

'Don't listen to him, Ricky. He'll say anything.'

'But I want a lady-friend, Grace. If I could join the army and wear a uniform, the girls will like me.'

She said no more until they reached Gunter's, where she asked if they could sit on the roof garden, only to be told it was full. They might have a table on the ground floor, in a corner. Ricky upended a chair on his way and people stared.

Grace ordered tea and a slice of chocolate cake to share. As they waited, Ricky began listing all the parks in London where there were barrage balloons. Grace was thinking he'd get on well with Sir Gideon, when their tea arrived. She poured and cut the cake, giving her brother the biggest piece. Mm. Real chocolate. She wished she could carry the smell away in a bottle, to waft under her nose whenever Lady Ventnor grew impossible.

'You know what the balloons are for, Grace?'

'To get in the way of enemy planes.'

'No, that's not right.'

'Go on then.'

'The balloons are only there to keep the steel cables in place. If a Messerschmitt or a Junkers or a Dornier fly into a cable, it shreds the plane to pieces. The balloons are the means, not the end.'

'Gosh.' For the thousandth time, Grace wondered what kind of man Ricky would have grown into but for the trauma of his birth. He'd either be in uniform, at a training camp like Immie's Ted, or dead, his spirit haunting a Normandy beach. Or maybe he'd be hand-in-glove with Cormac, two dapper black marketeers, slipping through the night-time streets like a pair of greased eels. 'Here.' She passed him a napkin. 'There's chocolate on your chin.'

She was aware of the smart couple at the next table whispering. The woman pitched a glance at Grace, then at Ricky. It had always been like this, people either amused by Ricky or looking down their noses. Grace curled a fist. *Let them say one word out of place...*

Ricky was staring at the window at something she couldn't see. He would often go off on what she called a mental jaunt, his eyes glazing. She tapped him. 'Come down from the clouds, please.'

Slowly, he turned to her. In a voice that wasn't his, he said, 'Grace, don't leave me alone in the dark.'

A sensation like a penknife in the belly made her put down her cup. 'Oh, Ricky, love, what makes you say that?'

'I'm lost in the dark. I can't move.'

'Don't, you're frightening me.' Some months back, they'd been having Sunday dinner and Ricky had suddenly stopped eating, his fork halfway to his mouth. In much the same voice, he'd told them that his grandfather was standing in the doorway.

Of course, Grandaddy Doyle was in Ireland, never having left the country of his birth. Five days later, hadn't a black-edged letter dropped on the mat?

'Drink your tea, Ricky, and we'll go.'

The woman at the table beside them was clearly earwigging on their conversation, and Grace pushed down her resentment. Whoever she was, she was wearing the brightest red lipstick and a stylish hat that made Grace, in her mail-order Sunday best, feel hopelessly drab. 'Let's settle the bill and go.' Grace opened her purse, and realised the woman was staring directly at her. 'Can I help you?'

'I see the eye's almost recovered,' the woman answered, undeterred by Grace's sharpness. 'Had any hairbrushes lobbed at you?'

'How d'you know about that?'

The woman chuckled and held out her hand. 'Polly

Manning-Smythe. I'm sure it was you caught in the crossfire when I flung my apron at Miss Root. Later, when I went back for my money, she told me you'd taken my job, heaven help you.'

Recognition dawned. 'Oh, right. Sorry. You look so different—'

'Out of uniform? I should jolly well hope so. This is my fiancé, Brian.' Miss Manning-Smythe indicated the man sharing her table. They shook hands and Grace nervously introduced Ricky. You could never guarantee how he'd react.

On this occasion, Ricky shook hands and said 'how d'you do?' to each in exactly the same tone of voice. Brian mentioned the barrage balloons, asking Ricky if he knew they flew over London's commons too. 'At all points of the compass.'

'I didn't know that but thank you for telling me,' Ricky replied. He sat down again and stared out of the window.

Grace apologised to Brian, saying, 'My brother sometimes inhabits a world of his own.'

'Best place, I often think,' said Polly, who then asked Grace, 'Has the cat scratched yet?'

'Lady Ventnor? A couple of times, nothing serious. The worst part is the journey every day and the night nurse coming in late.'

'Oh, you need to get things straight with Nurse Gill. "The buses, dearie, I do believe they go slower every day." She tried that with me twice but never again.'

'I need to be firmer,' Grace admitted.

'How's Buckland, apart from being a ghastly snob?'

'We've reached an understanding. He even brought a cup of tea up to me yesterday.'

'Good God, he must have had a religious conversion.'

'Something like that,' Grace agreed.

'Where are you living – you said it was a long pull into work every day.'

'Oh, yes.' She'd done it again, Grace realised, forgotten she was meant to be Lady Mayfair. 'I'm living near the river.'

'What, Chelsea?'

'Not quite.'

'We live in Flat 3, Victory Buildings, Dock Street, Whitechapel,' Ricky intoned, still looking out of the window.

'You won't get lost, will you?' Polly said, giving Grace a look that implied, *Whoops.*

'I would like a lady-friend,' Ricky said, turning to her. 'Do you know anyone?'

'That's enough, Ricky.' Cheeks aflame, Grace put half a crown on the table and made her apologies to Polly and Brian.

Polly pressed a card into her hand. 'The address on it is where I was living before I quit. There's space, now I'm out of the picture. You could do worse.'

'Thanks, and good luck, both of you.' Grace put the card in her bag without looking at it. Ricky asking Polly if she could find him a lady-friend was the kind of embarrassment Grace had been dealing with for years. It was his earlier comment that tore at her heart. *I'm lost in the dark.* How could she have considered moving out, leaving him on his own with Mam? Escaping Whitechapel was a dream, and like most dreams, it had fallen apart when exposed to the daylight.

14

———

A long late summer dusk was fading as Grace and Ricky walked the last yards home. The journey from Curzon Street had taken them over six hours, as their bus had pulled in when the sirens went. They'd all hurried to a public shelter and waited it out in the foetid and overcrowded space.

'Don't tell Mam how bad it was,' Grace warned Ricky, 'or next time there's a raid, she won't cross to the Peabody shelter. Hey – what...?' A missile flew from the open sitting-room window of their flat. It looked like a paper dart, but when she picked it up, Grace saw it was one of her starched nursing caps, folded into an aeroplane. 'Mam? I don't believe this!'

Behind the window, someone was crooning an Irish folk song.

'That's Mam.' Ricky grinned. 'I think she's on the juice again.'

'I'll give her ruddy juice.' Grace stormed into the building.

Well before she reached the sitting room, she heard her mother's piping voice, '...'Tis off I'm going to *Americay*, my beloved there to find...' another voice joining in with the harmony and what sounded like a child making bomber noises.

Opening the door, Grace's mouth fell open. There was Mam, warbling away in her usual armchair, and at her feet, sitting cross-legged on a cushion, a woman with fashionably curled red-gold hair and a yellow dress.

'Immie!'

Imelda – Mrs Ted Humphrey these days – was singing 'la-la-la' because she'd forgotten the words to the ballad. In the chair that used to be their dad's lolled a suntanned, straw-haired boy. It took Grace a moment to recognise Matthew, her eldest nephew. He'd shot up! A younger boy was launching another of Grace's caps out of the window.

'Vincent Humphrey, don't you dare,' she ordered.

Too late. Her second-eldest nephew turned and gave her a gappy grin. 'It's a Messerschmitt, Auntie Grace, and a Spitfire's going to bring it down. Neeee-ahhh.' He ran around the room with his arms spread wide.

On the cushions Grace had taken to be her bed, Immie's youngest boy, Liam, awoke and began to wail.

Mam, who had been singing with her eyes closed, stopped and saw Grace. 'If it isn't yourself. Where's Ricky? We were just asking where you might be.'

Grace muttered something about the raid, taking stock of a room that had been tidy when she left this morning and now looked like a whirlwind had raced through. Her sister, who was holding out her arms so her bawling youngest could stumble into them, sent a smile, which Grace did not return.

In the back of her mind, a voice muttered, *It'll be like this every minute till they go. You thought you were tired before?*

She asked Immie what time she'd arrived.

'We got back to Plumstead last night, but we didn't get a wink of sleep, on account of the bombing. Is it always this bad?'

'Yes,' Grace said pointedly. 'Last night wasn't the worst.'

That washed over Immie. 'Mam said you were at Mass with Ricky, but you've been hours. What were you doing?'

'We sat in the park, had a cup of tea.' Grace didn't mention chocolate, because she knew what Immie's response would be, and the boys would want to know if she'd brought any back with her. Unfortunately, Ricky had come into the room, and overhearing, put Grace right.

'We went to Gunter's and had tea *and* chocolate cake. It was Grace's treat and we met a nice lady and her friend.'

'Chocolate, was it?' Immie raised an eyebrow. 'Nice for some.'

Mam crooned and stroked Immie's lush curls, 'My angel's come home. Doesn't she look a dream, Grace? Oh, that hair, it's like spun gold.'

Grace tried not to mind, until her mother confirmed what she feared.

'Immie and the boys are staying with us for as long as they want. A terrible thing happened in the early hours – tell her, Immie.'

'A German plane came down in the back garden of a house on my street.' Grace's sister made no effort to lower her voice.

'No,' Grace cried. 'Did anyone die?'

'No. Well, one I suppose. The Messerschmitt pilot. Some lads found bits of propeller and they were selling them to all the sightseers at a shilling a piece.' Immie laughed. 'Matthew was combing our garden for an hour, but all he found were pieces of somebody's garden shed, blown over our wall.'

'So, you're staying here until...?' Grace jumped back as Vincent careered past, emitting gunfire noises.

'Just until,' Immie replied, and Mam wept a little and said, 'I shall sleep better now.'

You might, Grace thought. *Which bit of bedroom floor will I be shoved onto?* 'Anybody thought of dinner?' Cooking for seven would stretch their resources. Eight, when Cormac dropped by.

'Immie's brought a basket,' her mother answered. 'It's in the kitchen. See what you can do with it, Grace, but no more sardines on toast. God love us, if I eat any more of those, I'll turn into a seagull.'

In the kitchen, Grace lit the gas and picked up the teapot. The remnants of its last use sloshed about inside. Straining it into the sink, she kept the leaves for a second go, then removed several carbonised matchsticks from the cooker top. Why was she the only one who ever put them in the bin?

Someone came in behind her and, assuming it was Ricky, she said, 'You'll enjoy showing your aeroplane cards to your nephews.'

'It's me. Why the cold welcome, Grace?'

Grace turned and regarded her sister. Immie looked far more self-possessed than she had the right to, having learned first-hand what an air attack on a city felt like. 'I'm not being cold, I'm just tired. So tired I could sleep for a week with my arms slung over a washing line.'

Immie peered at her. 'I thought those were shadows round your eyes, but you've got a shiner. Who did it?'

'Who d'you think?'

'Cormac? You've been riling him again, then.'

'For pity's sake, Immie, all I did was tell him I was trying for a better job. He lumped me one.'

'He doesn't hit women. At worst, he'll fetch one a slap if she won't shut up.'

'How is that "not hitting"?' Grace tilted her head so Immie could see her eye properly. Even after nine days, traces lingered.

'You look like you've put on your mascara under the bed covers, nothing worse. Anyway, Mam said you crept up on Cormac in the pitch dark and he'd no idea it was you.'

Funny how stories changed in the telling. 'Why d'you always stand up for him against me?' Grace asked.

'Honestly?' Immie smoothed down her dress. The yellow cotton had a silky sheen and a tiny pattern in blue that matched her engagement ring. She wore the dress with an angora cardigan she'd almost certainly knitted herself. Immie excelled at needlework and handicrafts. Despite three babies, she'd regained her waistline and shapely bust. The legs outlined by the dress's economic cut were in good shape too. That was something they shared, Grace thought. Great legs. Shame a nurse's uniform and opaque stockings hid hers most of the time. Immie said, 'I stand up for Cormac because somebody has to. Our dad treated him like scum.'

'That's not true!'

'How would you know, Daddy's little blue-eyed girl? You were too far up your own...' Immie changed tack. 'Too much with your nose in a schoolbook to see what was going on. Cormac needs someone in his corner.'

'You won't be in his corner when you hear how he's earning his living,' Grace hit back. 'Or the way he's evading his duty. The police are out for him, and half of me wishes they'd catch him.'

Burnished curls bounced against Immie's shoulders as she shook her head. 'You'd not do that, Grace. Whelans don't squeal.'

The kettle did. At least, it whistled and Immie stepped forward to take it off the flame.

'I'll make the tea; you sit down.' She poured hot water into the pot. Too much, Grace thought, looking on. Those second-hand tea leaves would drown.

'Does Ted know you've brought the boys home?' she asked.

Immie was opening the cool box and answered without looking round. 'He will if he got my letter.'

'Won't he be angry?'

'Ted's not that kind of husband. He only wants to know we're safe.'

'But you aren't, not here, now.'

'They drop bombs in the countryside too, you know, and

planes crash on villages and farms all the time.' Immie took out the milk and held the bottle to the light, discovering there was only an inch left in it. 'This all we've got?'

'Yes. Didn't you bring some?' Once more, Grace felt resentment rise. Every day, the same blasted thing. 'Don't your boys get extra, being children?'

'A pint or two doesn't go far with lads.' Immie made a face. 'This bloody war. I don't know about you, but I'm always hungry. By the time I've fed my three, I'm looking down at a plate with a slice of beetroot on it and a fish-tail.' She patted her waist. 'Keeps my figure, but some days, I could get down on my knees and chew the rug.'

Grace took potatoes from Immie's basket. Someone needed to start dinner or they'd be still talking about it when the night raids came. 'We're going short so we can feed our soldiers, sailors and airmen, and because our ships keep being sunk at sea.'

'I listen to the wireless too, Grace.' Immie fetched a chopping board off the top of the kitchen cabinet and removed some beans from her basket.

'And because spivs like our brother trade what they steal for profit,' Grace added.

'Cormac's a middleman, not a thief.'

Grace flung down the peeler. 'Oh, come on. He can be your favourite, but doesn't it gall you that he's not in uniform when your Ted is? Don't you hate that your brother is skulking round London in a Bond Street suit while your husband fights?'

Immie managed a shrug. 'Cormac hasn't been called up yet, I suppose.'

'Suppose again. He used your address on his identity card.' Grace began peeling a potato as if it were her worst enemy. 'You probably stepped over his call-up papers when you walked through your door last night.'

'There are no letters for Cormac,' Immie answered calmly.

'When I got home, I opened everything that looked important and everything else, I burned. I don't understand you, Grace. You don't even have a sweetheart, so why are you so angry at our brother?'

Grace wished she could explain how seeing Lady Ventnor's exhausted nephew roiled her guts. How it drained her of tolerance for Cormac and his ilk. She fudged her answer. 'We don't just care about the ones we're married to or related to.'

Immie stopped midway through slicing a string bean. 'Imagine what it would do to Mam if Cormac got sent off and died.'

'Hundreds already have died. Thousands have, and they all had mothers.'

'But this is our mam. Grace, she lost all those babies, the one before me, and the two between you and Cormac and Ricky. Then Dad dying so suddenly. And Ricky being... you know, the way he is.'

Grace knew life had been hard for their mother. The tragedy of stillbirths and being saddled with a husband who had loved her but failed her in every other respect. Except to impregnate her when she could least cope with it... Yes, Mam's state of mind was understandable, if exasperating. Cormac had no such excuse. 'I won't betray our brother,' she said bitterly, 'but if the police come asking for him and I'm here, I shan't lie either.'

'Then you should go, Grace, before you do something we all regret. We got on all right when you were training and in the nurses' lodgings.' Immie rootled in the basket, fetching out a tin. 'Spam with these potatoes and beans?' She didn't wait for an answer but repeated her opinion. 'Honestly, Grace, you should leave.'

'If only.'

But that night, as she lay wide awake on the sagging sofa, Grace remembered the card Polly Manning-Smythe had given her. She'd put it in her bag out of politeness, no intention then of following it up.

In the morning, as she sipped a cup of milkless tea, she read the words printed on it:

Mrs Gloria Kesgrave, Discreet Correspondent, 34 Hill Street, Mayfair.

Grace had no idea what a 'discreet correspondent' was, nor did she care. The address reached out and pinched her. Until that moment, she hadn't realised how much she wanted to be able to say, 'Actually, I live in Mayfair.'

To escape Whitechapel, able to walk to work... have somewhere to snooze or read on her afternoon off... She wanted it so much, but what would Mam do if she abandoned them? How would Ricky cope?

They'll be fine, countered a persuasive voice, *now Immie is here. In fact, it'll be a blessing, as Immie could keep your bed and the boys will stay in your brother's room. One big happy family. A family you've never really felt part of...*

The voice homed in on all her secret griefs, and she felt herself weakening. 'If it doesn't work,' she whispered to Gloria Kesgrave's card, 'I can always come back here.'

15

BETONY

Her mother's bedroom door was ajar and Betony peered in. It was three in the morning, yet Lady Styles was folding something into a trunk and was dressed for a journey.

'What's going on?' Betony went in. 'Why did Wilkins say I had to come and speak with you?'

'Because you weren't at home at a normal conversational time,' Lady Styles answered without looking up. 'You're going to tell me you were caught out in an air raid.'

'I was. We were.' Caught out and kissed very thoroughly when the lights at the Café de Paris went out. Betony could taste the memory, her lipstick, his passion. *Flight Lieutenant Owen Henderson, I believe I'm in love with you.* Thank goodness her mother never looked closely at details like smudged lipstick. 'I take it, you're leaving on a jaunt?' There were hat and jewellery boxes on every surface.

'*We're* leaving and it isn't a jaunt.' Lady Styles laid tissue paper over the garment she'd just packed and finally glanced up. 'Goodness. Whose is that?'

'This?' Betony glanced down at her midnight-blue evening dress. 'It's a Vionnet. It came across the Channel on the last train out of France and has been hanging around the office.'

Lady Styles frowned because the Indian silk shawl covering her daughter's arms did little to conceal that the dress was sleeveless, halter-necked and backless. 'Did you actually go out half naked?'

'London's as warm as the Riviera tonight, and such a crush at the Café, we were all half-suffocated anyway.'

'Who were you with, that Canadian?'

'Not this time.' Her mother was referring to Winter Macpherson, an attaché at the Canadian High Commission who had taken Betony out for dinner twice. Winter was amusing, with the touch of confidence she liked in a man, and her friends gibbered over how good-looking he was. So he was, if you liked thick, dark hair and grey eyes. What Winter lacked was a uniform. A dinner jacket, however well-cut, was trumped any day of the week by a slate-blue tunic. Not that she intended to share these thoughts with her mother. 'You haven't told me where you and Wilkins are going, Mummy.'

'To Styles, where else?' Her mother meant Styles Court, the family's Somerset estate. 'And we're all going. This is an evacuation, you realise?'

'Is Father coming?'

'Of course not. You, me and Wilkins. Go and pack your things, dear. Anything you can't fit into a suitcase can be boxed and sent down. Jeffries wants to set off early, because he says we've only enough fuel to get out of town, and he hates getting stuck in a jam.' Jeffries was their chauffeur, guardian of Lord Styles' Rolls-Royce. 'Your father will arrange a fill-up for us somewhere on the road.' Lady Styles removed another dress from her wardrobe. 'Get to it.'

'To what?'

'Don't be obtuse.'

Betony remained where she was. Leave London, never see Owen again? Never again dance to a swing band and drink champagne? No, no and again – no. 'Is it because the phoney war is over and the bombers have got through?' she asked, adding with a half-smile, 'Not frit, are you, Mummy?'

'Don't use hideous slang. I'm not afraid, but the raids have injected an urgency. Anyway, it's selfish to stay.'

'Surely, the selfish thing is to *vamoose* off to the sticks.'

'Selfish,' Lady Styles repeated, 'as we'll be far more useful in Somerset.' She opened a second wardrobe and reached in to stroke its contents. 'D'you think I should send my furs into storage, or take them?'

'Take them, because by October you'll be freezing.' Styles Court was always six degrees colder than whatever the outdoor temperature happened to be. 'I'm staying in London.'

'I think I'll take them.' Lady Styles removed a voluptuous chocolate-brown mink. 'We have to leave as this house is being turned over to a branch of the Ministry of Supply.'

Betony blinked as her mother's meaning sank in. 'You've given away our home?'

'Your father has. To aid the war effort.'

'Without even mentioning it to me?'

'You're never here, are you? We haven't given it as such, we've *gifted* it for the duration of the war. This is a time for sacrifice, Betony, and you'll benefit from fresh country air and the absence of other distractions.'

Other distractions were what made life worth living.

Glancing down at her bare arm, Betony read the telephone number inked on her skin. Last night, at the Café de Paris, someone had outrageously inscribed it while the lights were out. The memory made her breath quicken. She wouldn't have imagined Owen being quite so daring. It just went to show.

Dancing with him while the band played 'Moonlight Serenade' had finally broken the ice between them. Certainly, the kiss in pitch blackness had felt glorious, and if he'd taken the trouble to leave a number, it meant he'd forgiven her for their first little upset. One swooning kiss and after the lights came back on, he was gone. Probably to roar back to his airbase. Betony could picture him, his Royal Enfield Bullet silhouetted in the flames, a scarf over his mouth filtering the smoky air. All she wanted was to know he was alive and well, and that he wanted to see her again soon.

'Mummy, I can't possibly come with you. Sybil counts on me.' Sybil was her mother's cousin, editor of the magazine where Betony worked.

'I'll telephone her and explain,' Lady Styles answered as if everything was decided and they had moved along. 'She'll find someone else. I won't tell you again – go and pack.'

Betony made a pirouette and blue silk flared out from a nipped-in waist, revealing long legs, pale stockings and evening shoes with a low platform. 'Find someone who fits the designer's sample sizes, puts up with lousy pay and stands for hours without complaining?'

'Very easily, I should think,' her mother replied, adding that Sybil's contacts book had more names than the Westminster telephone directory. 'I got you that job so you could earn pin money and have something to chat about at dinner parties. Anyway, you can't live alone in London.'

'I'll find a flat.'

'Really? The girl who left her National Registration Card in a taxi, twice? Anyway, you won't have a job on the magazine for long. Your father says *Practical Modes* will close.'

'What? Why?'

'Paper,' her mother answered. 'He says it doesn't merit its consumption.'

Up to this point, Betony had felt no more than usually

resentful at being overruled and dictated to, but this made her blood simmer. 'Father's talking out of his hat. The paper stock we use is already one notch up from lavatory roll.'

'Don't be vulgar, darling. Sybil's magazine can't justify the shipping of tree pulp across seas infested with Nazi U-boats. It is a frivolous comic for nonsensical women, your father says. Or was it nonsensical comic for frivolous women...' Lady Styles paused. 'Whichever, it'll close down with or without you.'

'Father's got it in for Sybil because she warned you not to marry him.'

'Now you're being silly.' Lady Styles was packing her mink coat between swathes of tissue. A hardness had crept into her voice. 'We'll find you gainful employment in the country. There'll be evacuee children who need entertainment, and the vegetable gardens will want attention, with the men gone.'

Betony shuddered, seeing a life of wheelbarrows and lumpy tweed. 'I'm not coming.'

'You'll do as you're told. Off you go and pack a suitcase. The car leaves at five.'

Knowing she'd pressed things to the limit, Betony finally did her mother's bidding – except that she packed two suitcases. One with daily necessities, the other with evening dresses, including the Vionnet, several pairs of unsuitable shoes and filmy underwear. She put on a skirt, blouse and a light cardigan, then sat by her open window until she heard the doves cooing in nearby Berkeley Square.

Taking a suitcase in each hand, her gas mask in its chic, silk carrier over one shoulder, she left the house, having put a note for her mother on the hall stand. Betony was not much given to poetic flights, but it seemed to her that a new dawn was unwrapping itself, like a strawberry sweet from silver foil. It was the first morning of the rest of her life.

16

———————

In Hyde Park, Betony slumped down on a bench. Two miles, lugging suitcases, and her arms were dropping off. Having quit the house all but penniless, there'd been no chance of hailing a taxi. Not that there were many around these days.

'I'll learn how to get on a bus,' she promised herself. 'I'm not going back.'

Her most urgent need was finding somewhere to stay. Her imagination reeled out pictures of charming second-floor flats with park views. In each case, with a little balcony where she'd enjoy a drink in the evening, inhaling the scents of grass and blossom. How much would somewhere like that cost?

Sybil would know. Speaking of which... Betony lifted her wrist to check her watch, then forgot all about the time as she saw 'TRA 9876' written in blue on her arm. TRA signified a Trafalgar Square exchange. Wouldn't it be wonderful to be able to whisper to Owen after a night of dancing, 'Come back to mine for an hour or two. I'll mix you a gin-and-whatever.' A tingling, like bottled ginger beer being slowly uncorked, stole into her belly. She desired Owen intensely, which was mystifying as she hadn't taken to him the first time they'd met.

She'd been out with friends, yet again to the Café de Paris, and a cohort of RAF pilots had joined their table, injecting an edgy ingredient that had been missing until then. She'd found herself next to Owen Henderson, who had struck her as a bit quiet. Not in a shy or mumbling way. Just, he was the sort who listened, chipping in only when he had something to say. Not her sort at all. She had worked out quickly, as she always did with a new acquaintance, how his background rated compared to hers. In this case, not much. It wasn't so much the way he spoke, but the fact that his uniform came from a military outfitter and not from an exclusive bespoke tailor. He'd been to grammar school, not Eton or Harrow. Most telling were the silver cufflinks, a birthday gift from his mum. *Mum*. They carried his initials, not a family crest.

'Not out of our drawer, darling,' Betony's mother would say, and it was true. But who wanted to live in a drawer?

At the end of the night, Owen had casually asked if she'd like to go on a date. 'There's a place I know, good music and dinner thrown in.'

She'd said yes, and then, suddenly fearing it was all a ghastly mistaken, had given him a false address.

Unsurprisingly, she'd heard not a word from him after that. Until...

Last night, out with the same friends, there he was. The same glamorous cohort and some WAAFs in tow. WAAFs all looked the same, didn't they? Short, curled hair, confident lipstick, badly fitted jackets. Owen had been distinctly off with her and that might have been that, had Betony not seen him standing alone as the band segued into a slow number. She'd sidled up and asked, 'Foxtrot, or am I in disgrace for ever?'

He hadn't said no, but nor had he smiled. She had moved closer and the music had obliged with a swooping clarinet solo. Somehow, his arms had come round her, and it had felt thrilling, to be in the hold of someone who didn't like her very much.

Betony found Owen Henderson's take-it-or-leave-it style intensely erotic. She'd been certain he was starting to feel the same when the bloody sirens went off. They'd danced on.

Then the lights had failed, the place engulfed in treacle blackness, people tripping over each other's feet. For a minute or so, she'd lost Owen until his arms wrapped around her again.

That was when they kissed and she'd thought she would melt. Compared with Owen, other men simply didn't cut the mustard.

Talking of which... where was the nearest early-morning café? If she could face dragging her suitcases, she could just about run to a cup of bad coffee and a slice of toast.

A thought struck her. Father wouldn't stop her allowance now she'd left home, would he?

'All I need is five thousand a year and a room of my own,' she sighed. 'Not much to ask, is it?'

She must have drifted off to sleep on her bench because she opened her eyes with an unpleasant sensation of being watched. A man in shabby military fatigues was reaching a grubby hand towards one of her suitcases. 'Leave that,' she snapped.

He grinned, displaying teeth in dire need of a dentist. Or a pair of pliers. 'Hope you haven't been here all night, girlie. There are rules against indigents sleeping in the park.'

'I wasn't sleeping, nor am I— Hang on.' She knew him. 'I've seen you going in and out of the Shepherd and Flock.' She named the pub on the corner of Farm Street, next door to *Practical Modes'* office.

He mumbled something and backed away. He had a wheelbarrow with him, the one she'd seen him pushing down Farm Street, loaded with vegetables purloined from local allotments. Today it was empty and Betony saw a way to save herself effort.

'Two shillings if you wheel my suitcases to my office.'

He weighed up the offer. 'Three.'

'Not a chance.' She didn't have any shillings. She'd have to borrow from Sybil. 'You only get paid if I find them sitting, unmolested, on the top floor where I work.'

He shrugged. 'All right.'

'And if you so much as peek in either of them, my father is a government minister who knows every chief of police in London and they'll all come after you.'

17

———

Betony's workplace was a three-storey red-brick town house with Georgian windows and a door painted lamp black. A brass plate screwed to the side stated: 'Practical Modes. Proprietress Miss Sybil March'. A note on the door advised visitors to 'Walk straight up.' A second note added, 'There is no lift. Direct complaints to the architect.' Betony had worked at *Practical Modes* for over six months before she cottoned on to the fact that the architect had died in 1754.

Her suitcases weren't in the downstairs lobby meaning the man with the wheelbarrow had either run off with them or lugged them upstairs. She supposed it depended on how much he'd wanted his fee.

A glance at her watch brought a gasp. Where had the time gone? She was two hours late for work.

She climbed three steep flights, at one point catching her foot on a loose brass stair-rod. *Practical Modes* wasn't *Vogue* or *The Tatler*. It was a tabloid journal on yellowish paper, all sketches, no photographs, with editorial that told its readers what they ought to wear and why. No frills. It was bi-monthly, though Sybil had been heard to mutter that they might have to go quarterly. If Betony were honest, she wouldn't want to be seen reading it on the train, but it was cherished by many. It certainly wasn't the garbage her father declared it to be.

At the top of the building, she entered an attic studio that was stifling, despite windows being open at both ends. Sybil, cool in trousers and a blouse, was conferring with a heavy-set man in shirtsleeves who slouched at a tabletop easel. Betony greeted them in her cheerful manner. 'Reporting for duty, Madam Editor.'

The Honourable Sybil March regarded Betony critically. 'You certainly didn't spend two hours at the dressing-table this morning.'

'It's jolly hot out there,' Betony said defensively. Sybil was right, of course. Her skirt was sticking to her thighs and she'd knotted her cardie round her waist.

'You should wear these.' Sybil patted her linen slacks. 'It's far too hot for garden-party dressing.'

'I know. Sorry to look a fright, but I left home this morning.'

'Left home this morning *without...*?' Sybil prompted.

'No, just... "I left home this morning." I expect Mummy will ring, when she realises I mean it.'

'Gosh, is that wise? Flying the nest, I mean.'

'Probably not, but I've done it all the same.'

'Well, it's your life,' Sybil said in her easy fashion. 'I ran away too at your age. At least you're in time to hear the bad news. I was telling Ambrose that last week, I gave Marjorie and Alison their notice.' That was when it dawned on Betony that she hadn't heard the clack of typewriters as she came up the stairs, nor for the last two days.

It boded ill. Marjorie and Alison were staff writers, *Practical Modes'* entire journalistic division. 'Aren't they somewhat essential?' she asked nervously.

'Of course,' Sybil agreed. 'I didn't do it lightly. Alison's getting married,' she went on, 'so she was philosophical, but Marjorie said, "Right, I'll go and join the Wrens and if I die at sea, it's your fault."'

'Oh, Sybil.'

'I know. I hated doing it, but I simply can't afford them.'

Father was right, Betony thought. 'Does this mean we're closing?'

Sybil denied it. 'But we're in survival mode. Go and drink a glass of water and let's get some work done.' She clapped her hands at Ambrose, still sitting morosely at his easel. 'Don't look so depressed.'

'Why not?' Colin Ambrose muttered. 'Writers out, the artist will be next. You're cutting things to the bone.'

'True, but you, me and Betony are the skeleton. No more cutting.'

Ambrose, always known by his surname, gave a sceptical 'Ha'.

Sybil went to open a window as wide as it would go. Like Betony, she had long arms and was tall. Unlike Betony, energy zinged from her, even in this heat. Grey-blonde hair hung over a shoulder in a pigtail. Sybil March was a fashion editor who ignored fashion.

'Good morning,' Betony said to Ambrose, who so far had not acknowledged her.

Ambrose glowered. 'What morning are we referring to? The one long passed, or one yet to dawn?'

'He's right, you're grossly late,' Sybil translated. 'What's today's excuse?'

'Apart from running away and dedicating last night to cheering up one of our RAF heroes, I have spent the last four hours visiting accommodation agencies.'

'And?'

'Nothing. There's hardly anywhere vacant and everyone wants money up front. I even called on an old schoolfriend— Oh, speaking of money, did my suitcases arrive?'

'Ambrose put them in the stockroom,' Sybil said. 'I paid your unsavoury porter. Three shillings, he wanted.'

'*Two.* I made it very clear.'

'Not clear enough. I'll take the money out of your wages. Now get your togs off so Ambrose can start.'

Behind the screen, a rack of clothes waited for Betony and the sight of them almost gave her heatstroke. As they were putting together the October issue, she was modelling autumn and winter fashions. She stripped to her slip and, minutes later, was standing on a square of white cloth, posing in a town suit of Harris tweed, suede gloves, a fox-fur hat and stole. Ambrose lined up his pencils and stared at her with his head tilted, as though summoning the creative juices.

'Ambrose, darling, if I abase myself for being late, will you get on with it?'

At last, he put pencil to paper. Betony counted backwards from ninety-nine to stop herself passing out.

During a break, she asked Sybil if she could use the telephone. A man didn't write his number on a woman's arm if he didn't expect her to call. Though she preferred never to come across as too keen, the fact was, as a Spitfire pilot, Owen might not have the luxury of time.

'Two minutes max.' Sybil one-handedly liberated a Russian cigarette from its packet. Betony had interrupted her writing a letter. 'You know how much calls cost. I shall be timing you.'

In a niche next to the editorial office, Betony asked the operator to put her through to TRA 9876. She felt ridiculously nervous, though she'd been rehearsing what she'd say while Ambrose sketched. Keep it simple: 'Betony Styles, wishing to speak with Flight Lieutenant Henderson.' She couldn't wait to hear Owen's laconic, 'who cares' voice coming at her through the ether. It had got under her skin and started a blaze.

The operator connected the call.

'Canada House, who is calling please?'

Canada House... the Canadian Embassy... Winter's place of work? What was going on?

The polite Canadian voice prompted, 'May I help, ma'am?'

'Um, yes. Is Winter Macpherson available please?' What else could she do, slam the phone down?

The call was put through. Betony answered Winter's opening comment, 'Are you OK, Betty?' by saying, 'Perfectly, thank you, except that some chancer scribbled his phone number on my arm.'

Warm laughter rippled through the wires. 'Give me his name; I'll have him shot.'

'That means you were at the Café de Paris last night.'

'I guess it does.'

Which left one great, gaping question. If Winter had written the telephone number, who had kissed her so passionately in the blackout?

Sybil mashed out her cigarette as Betony came out of the telephone nook and said, 'Date for tonight?'

'On Friday. Oh dear. Sometimes I wish I hadn't been brought up to be polite.'

'You'll grow out of it; one does. I've just written Marjorie's letter of reference. She's deadly serious about joining the women's navy. It's given me a flash of inspiration. You need somewhere to live, so what about their place?'

'Marjorie and Alison's?' Betony had an idea they shared rooms, though she was vague about the location. 'Won't they still be there?'

'Nope, cleared out and gone. Since they had no job, they didn't want to pay another month's rent. Unless their landlady has found new tenants—'

Betony didn't wait to hear the rest. 'What's the address?'

'It's a hop and a skip from here and if you get the place, no more excuse for rolling up late.'

18

———————

GRACE

The woman who opened the front door of 34 Hill Street was swathed in a floor-length, floral brocade dressing gown. It was the kind of garment Grace imagined the Chinese ambassador might wear for entertaining at home. This was her third visit to the house. Previous times, nobody had answered her knock.

Fearing she'd interrupted an afternoon nap, she was about to apologise when the woman pre-empted her.

'Do I know you, darling?'

'I'm Grace, er, Wheeler.' She pronounced the name as if Buckland was announcing her arrival at a ball. 'Here for the flat.'

'Flat...?'

'The apartment. The accommodation. Lately occupied by Miss Manning-Smythe?'

'You're a friend of Polly's? I was so sad to see her go. Do come in. Grace, did you say? What a pretty name. I'm Mrs Kesgrave, Gloria Kesgrave, and before we go any further, let me tell you I am probably ten years older than you might imagine me to be.'

'Gosh. Right. Sorry.'

'No need. Shall we go straight up?' Ushering Grace along a passage made narrow by bookcases and potted plants on stands, she asked over her shoulder, 'Are you married, by chance?'

'No, I'm single.' Grace hoped that was the right answer.

Mrs Kesgrave led the way upstairs, the Chinese robe sweeping each tread in a way that seemed to Grace both queenly and dangerous. 'Single,' the lady reflected. 'Wise you. One more flight to go. We are heading for the top. You could imagine yourself as Miss Honeychurch and I your cousin, Miss Bartlett.'

'I will,' said Grace, eager to comply though having no idea who they were. She couldn't fathom Mrs Kesgrave, though she'd liked the house on sight: mellow brick, rectangular windows and a door with a fanlight. The street was perfect too, not grand but elegant. Better yet, she'd timed the journey from Upper Brook Street. Eight minutes door to door. No more slogging back and forth from Dock Street. No more sleeping on Mam's draughty floor. That she was being shown upstairs suggested the flat was still available. In her grasp...

At the top of the next flight, Mrs Kesgrave flung open a door, announcing, 'East-facing with a view, though I fear you will have no sight of the Arno.' Going to the window, she lifted down a blackout of baize cloth stretched over a frame, held by brackets screwed into the window recesses. 'Clever, don't you think?'

'I'll say.' At Victory Buildings, the blackouts were made from worn-out coats or flattened cardboard boxes. A pest to remove in the morning and put up again at night. More often than not, they stayed in place all day and the family kept the lights on or sat in darkness when the electric ran out. *Will Ricky remember to keep some pennies by to feed the meter?* Grace had to remind herself that Immie was there now, steering the ship.

By letting in the daylight, Mrs Kesgrave had revealed pinprick moth holes all down the front of her dressing gown.

And now, Grace could make a better judgement of her age. Somewhere in her fifties, but did she have to add another ten years to that? Though it was early afternoon, Mrs Kesgrave was heavily, *cleverly*, made up. Her distinguishing features were her eyebrows, an aristocratic nose and a wide mouth punctuated by a beauty spot which crumpled when she smiled.

'Hill Street has some fascinating characters,' she told Grace, pointing to the street with a cigarette holder that she'd removed, like a hat pin, from her extravagantly upswept black hair. 'Some days, I fancy I glimpse Admiral Crawford peering through the window at me, from number 35, directly across.'

Scandalised, Grace forgot her polish. 'The bugger tries to see you into your bedroom?'

Mrs Kesgrave looked momentarily nonplussed. 'Henry and Mary Crawford's uncle, the admiral, from *Mansfield Park*. Jane Austen? He lived on Hill Street.'

'Oh. Course. I remember now.' Liar, liar. At school, Grace had preferred maths and science and, with five of them crammed into a small flat, could never find anywhere to read her set literature. Cormac hadn't helped, with his habit of snatching whatever she was reading and chucking it out of the window. 'You'll get an ugly squint, Gracie. One eye in a book, the other up the chimney.' Desperate to make up ground, she said in her most refined voice, 'I presume the Arno is a cinema? I don't think I've seen one of that name hereabouts.'

'The Arno is the river that runs through Florence.' Mrs Kesgrave scrutinised Grace thoroughly. 'I was quoting E. M. Forster earlier. *A Room with a View*. The heroine, Lucy Honeychurch, visits Florence chaperoned by Charlotte Bartlett. Are you not a reader?'

'I haven't much time for it.' If you ignored the *Peg's Paper* in her bag. 'I'm not dim, though. I did quite well at school.'

'Indeed, you appear quite the opposite of dim. Forgive my habit of parroting literature; I tend to assume that if I've read something, everyone has. And now, dear one, before I tell you more about the accommodation, tell me *everything* about you.'

That was the last thing Grace wanted to do and she began with the least contentious fact. 'I'm a nurse.'

'Like dear Polly! You work privately? Polly had a terrible time. An unspeakable ogress of a patient who liked to hit her, if you please. Don't go near that one.'

Too late. 'I work for a titled family here in Mayfair,' Grace continued, 'who have urged me to settle close by. I trained at the Royal London Hospital and was educated at a girls' school establishment.'

'A school establishment? What is that?'

'It's a school,' Grace said limply.

'And your family?'

Grace teetered on the rim of an outright lie and settled for a half-truth. 'They hail from a different vicinity of London. My father passed away and my mother... she, er, keeps house for my brothers.'

'Excellent. So – what d'you think?'

Now at leisure to look around, Grace discerned a large, square room with an ornate fireplace on one wall and three single beds spread with quilted salmon-pink eiderdowns. Two beds stood side by side, separated by veneered nightstands. The third occupied a niche beside the chimney breast.

She searched for a door leading to a kitchenette and, hopefully, a private bathroom. Having her own kitchen and bathroom was the pinnacle of a dream. There were no other doors, other than the one they'd come through.

For some reason, Grace had assumed that Nurse Manning-Smythe would live by herself. 'Um, Polly lived in this room... just her?'

'Not at all. She shared with Alison and Marjorie. What a shock, losing all my dear boarders at the same time.'

Grace took a second look around, adjusting to the new reality. 'I take it, the apartment is to be shared?'

'Apartment... it's a room, Grace. What you see is the entirety of the offering.'

'The bathroom?'

'On the floor below, and the hot water ration is as generous as I can make it under the given circumstances. How fortuitous you should come just as I was thinking I should put a notice in the *Morning Post*, or the grocer's window. Will it suit?'

It would have to, because having made the critical decision to leave home, Grace couldn't afford to dither or delay. Anyway, one more disappointment in life shouldn't embitter her soul. It was just... well... disappointing. 'May I ask how much you're asking?'

Mrs Kesgrave was peering through the window and seemed not to hear. 'There he goes,' she murmured.

Grace looked too. *Him.* The blighter on the train who had mocked her accent. Still wearing his fake uniform.

'I call him "Lurking Larry",' said Mrs Kesgrave. 'He moves from pub to pub, doing a bit of washing up, emptying the glasses, mostly down his own throat. He thinks we don't know he raids the Berkeley Square allotments.' She drew her eyes away and said, 'Nine pounds a month.'

'Nine?' That was way more than Grace earned.

'Between three of you, I should say.'

Oh, relief. Three pounds was still a chunk from her wages, though.

Mrs Kesgrave smiled, shooting her beauty spot sideways. 'As the first taker, you would have prime choice.'

'Of?'

'Bed. But you'd share the wardrobe.' The cigarette holder indicated a piece of furniture whose dark veneer matched everything else in the room. 'Putting another one in would spoil the aesthetic, don't you think?'

'I suppose it would. So, who are the other two lodgers? Boarders, I mean.'

Dark lashes made sweeping beats and faint frown lines appeared. 'That is the crucial question. As I said before, the previous three decamped at the end of August, which is why I'm eager to re-let. If a room's empty, our government billets its own waifs and strays upon one. I'd rather choose my own. Not that I'm suggesting you are either a waif or a stray. I have one "possible" lined up, a girl named Jess. If you'll take the room, it means one more to be found.'

'For three pounds a month' – Grace wanted to be sure she'd got it right – 'sharing with two others, I could move in?'

Gloria Kesgrave clapped her hands, as if Grace had given the answer to a fiendish riddle. 'You will be provided with breakfast and dinner too.'

'You give us dinner?'

'House rules are that everyone takes a turn at cooking. One night in four, once we have our full complement, you will cook and wash up. You will hand over your ration book and I will do the shopping and queuing. I charge a flat fee of seven shillings each per week. We muck in and eat together, like a peasant commune. Or a nunnery. It's fun.'

'Fun' would depend on much.

'The other girl you mentioned,' Grace said, 'the "possible". What does she do?'

Mrs Kesgrave had absolutely no idea. 'I'm not even sure her name is Jess, as I met her at the bottom of an escalator in the underground. She'd just fallen the whole way down.'

'Heavens, what happened?' Grace had seen escalator injuries ranging from severe bruising to fingers ripped off from being caught in the mechanism.

'She'd had a drink,' Mrs Kesgrave said. 'She strikes me as a lost soul.'

That didn't sound encouraging.

A loud knocking from below interrupted them. Mrs Kesgrave went to see who it was, inviting Grace to take a look around.

Left alone, Grace sat on the bed that was separate from the others and gave the mattress a bounce. Seemed all right. The satin eiderdown would have to go or be covered up. That shade of pink anywhere near her hair brought on a migraine. She could faintly hear Mrs Kesgrave speaking to someone in the hall.

The toilet also must be on the floor below. There wouldn't be one up here. Awkward if you were caught short in the early hours. Running her fingers along the stitch lines of the bedcover, Grace made some calculations. Wages, six pounds, twelve shillings per month. Take out three pounds for rent and, say, three pounds ten shillings for food and necessaries, that left... 'Two shillings to send home. It can't be done.'

Unless Immie and Cormac stumped up for Mam, Ricky and the rent.

Almost in tears from frustration, she listened to the returning footsteps on the stairs. Mrs Kesgrave was bringing someone with her.

Grace got off the bed as Mrs Kesgrave entered with a blonde girl in her wake. Willowy, her hair in careless curls, a few damp tendrils sticking to a high forehead. The newcomer's mouth was a fashionable shade, lipstick perfectly applied.

'Isn't this wonderful?' Mrs Kesgrave's smile spread joy. 'Grace, permit me to introduce Miss Betony Styles. Betony, this is Grace... I'm so sorry...?'

'Wheeler,' Grace answered and experienced the same dispiriting plunge she'd felt looking at Polly Manning-Smythe in Gunter's tearoom. The new girl's dress fitted perfectly on the waist and hips. Silk, too. Oh, for the love of God, a green taffeta bag instead of a cardboard gas mask case. *I hate you already.* What did you have to do to be called 'Betony Styles'?

Stroll across the room, it would seem, peer out of the window and say, 'Isn't that Viscountess Wharton's house? She's a friend of Mummy's.' Then turn around and survey the room with a distant smile and ask, 'Is that the only wardrobe? I have rather a lot of things, you see.' And when told yes, and it would have to be shared, raise an eyebrow in a manner implying refined astonishment.

Grace saw Betony's gaze pass over the twin beds and alight on the one she, Grace, had been sitting on. The glossy mouth formed a steely smile. 'I will claim that one, as I simply can't sleep cheek by jowl with someone I don't know.'

Until that moment, Grace had been wondering how to break it to Mrs Kesgrave that, on second thoughts, she couldn't take the room. She couldn't afford it. But this Styles girl, lady-ing over her in her silk and taffeta, turned a dial and changed her mind.

Grace sat down on the bed *she* had claimed already and said with flinty sweetness, 'Sorry, but this one's got my name on it.' She flashed Mrs Kesgrave the sunniest smile she was capable of. 'I'll take the room, thank you, and move in as soon as I may.'

19

JESS

Homeless, sleeping in any shelter she could find – and once in somebody else's bed – it was blissful to be in hospital, being cared for. The feeling lasted until Jess remembered she was here because she had fallen while drunk.

That'll teach you, said the judgemental voice she carried in her head. *Warned you, didn't I? Men like to corrupt innocence. Well, yours has gone, as your sister's went.*

The staff had asked Jess repeatedly if she wanted them to call anyone. The nurse who had woken her for the day's first cup of tea now tried again.

'You've had no visitors, love; there must be someone.'

'There isn't.' Nobody Jess would share her predicament with, at any rate.

'What about the lady who came in with you?'

Jess shook her head, as much as her painfully stiff neck allowed. Who *had* brought her in? Her last memory before she fell was of seeing Charlotte, and the emotion pushed everything else aside. Either she'd conjured a vision of her dead sister, or Charlotte was alive.

'I don't want you to call anyone,' she insisted, but seeing the nurse shake her head in a way she didn't trust, Jess discharged herself at once. She limped the two miles from Barts Hospital to Gower Street, entering Senate House, headquarters of the Ministry of Information, dead on eight-thirty. The muscles between her ribs were so sore and tight, she couldn't expand her lungs properly. Under her torn blouse, she was dappled with bruising. The prospect of a day at a desk, leaning and stretching, was miserable.

But inescapable.

Mr Brinkworth came up as Jess sat down. He watched her take the first letter off her pile.

'Good to see you back, Miss Gresham. I understand we are lucky to see you at all. I've always detested escalators. Monstrous objects.'

Jess gazed anxiously up at her supervisor. Had details of her mishap leaked into Senate House? 'I'm fine,' she whispered. 'It was frightening but, um' – she swallowed – 'over quickly.'

'Good, good. What's that you've got there?' He nodded at the letter in her hand.

Jess sliced into the handwritten envelope and took out a sheet of note paper. It seemed to be a harmless message from a mother in London to her daughter in Plymouth. Oh. Perhaps not so harmless, as the mother was 'once again' begging her daughter 'not to do it'.

Conscious of Mr Brinkworth waiting, Jess read to the end. The daughter had a fiancé in the navy but had fallen for another man. She gave the gist to her supervisor.

'And what will you do now, Miss Gresham?'

'I will put the sheet back in the envelope, like so.' She did just that, adding, 'It's sad, but not a threat to national security.'

'I agree.'

Jess sealed the letter with the gummed strip identifying her as Censor No. 765. Which summed her up, she thought as she bumped her rubber stamp down on the envelope. A lowly civil servant among hundreds, scanning other people's private correspondence in the hope of catching a spy. Though, more often, they caught ordinary members of the public inadvertently passing on information that could help the enemy.

Passed by Censor. The letter went into her out-tray. On to the next.

At lunchtime, she went out on her own, through habit separating herself from her chattering colleagues. After buying food from a café, she made her way to nearby Bedford Square and eased herself painfully onto the grass to eat. Bread-and-margarine and carrot sticks, costing threepence.

Afterwards, folding her paper bag and stowing it in her pocket, she closed her eyes and summoned back the minutes before she'd passed out and knocked herself unconscious. She'd been feeling bad as she approached the underground and had feared she was going down with flu. Hardly surprising after ten days in London without a proper roof over her head. She remembered gripping the escalator handrail as her vision blurred. A few stairs down, a girl had turned as if she sensed Jess's crisis. What had she been wearing? Jess racked her brain, but nothing had stuck other than the face.

Charlotte's.

The need to learn her sister's fate had brought Jess to London, drawing her into danger. The same obsession might easily have conjured Charlotte's image. 'That has to be it,' she muttered as she got awkwardly to her feet and shook the crumbs off her skirt. The only other explanation was that her sister was alive and her father had lied.

That was, quite simply, unthinkable. Yet think it she must, leaving her with no choice. She had to ask her father the truth or be haunted for the rest of her life.

. . .

When the day's work was over, Jess trudged to Marble Arch underground station, where she was currently bedding down at night. In the foyer, she joined a queue for the public telephone and when it was her turn, asked the operator to connect her to St Saviour's Vicarage in Ramsgate.

Expecting the parish secretary to answer, her father's voice on the line panicked her momentarily.

'Hello? This is Reverend Gresham. Who is calling please?'

'Daddy, it's me.'

'Jessica? At last. How are you, what news?'

She knew if she hesitated, she'd pour everything out. How the room she'd paid for had turned out not to exist. How a grimy man pretending to be a soldier had stolen her purse within hours of her arrival. How she was surviving on a few shillings' advance on her pay, and then her fall... 'It's all fine, Daddy. I'm doing well. Mr Brinkworth, my supervisor, called me a bright spark.'

'And so you are. What else?'

What else... a man I bumped into outside a pub bought me an orange squash, only he put something in it. The nurses call it 'spiking'. She didn't say that, of course, and with only one minute left of her call, moved to her purpose. 'Daddy, I want you to swear on the Bible that Charlotte died.'

'I beg your pardon?'

'When I found her on the bathroom floor, she was ice cold. You went with her in the ambulance and said she passed away on the journey. But if she didn't, you need to tell me where she is.'

The crackling silence that followed felt like judgement. Vital seconds passed.

'Daddy? I saw her.'

At last, the Reverend Gresham answered. 'That is impossible, Jessica. Your sister is dead and how dare you abuse our kinship with questions like this?'

'Please, Daddy—' The pips went, demanding more money. Jess dug for another penny, but it jammed in the slot. Shaken by her father's cold fury, she hung up, and muttered apologies to the people waiting behind her. Tears welled. He'd accused her of abuse, but wasn't her enduring love for Charlotte the purest show of kinship?

'I won't be shamed into silence,' she said out loud. Then, faced with a descent by escalator to the deep platforms amid the gathering crowds, Jess went back out onto the street, watching a policeman directing cars and buses between Cumberland Gate and Park Lane. 'I can't do it. I can't go down.'

She put her hand in her pocket to see if she had enough for the cheapest cinema ticket – a way of passing the evening – and felt the edge of a card. She stared at it, first in puzzlement, then in vague recognition. It must belong to the lady who had summoned help when Jess had tumbled down the escalator, who'd stayed with her.

MRS GLORIA KESGRAVE, DISCREET CORRESPONDENT. 34 HILL STREET, MAYFAIR.

20

GRACE

Thursday 5 September

'Do I have a nurse, or am I paying for a bedroom ornament that mutters?' Lady Ventnor, sleep-deprived and more than usually caustic, cut through Grace's thinking.

'I'm repeating the drill for your bedsore, Lady Ventnor,' Grace answered as calmly as she could. The sore had got worse because Nurse Gill had bathed it with methylated spirits, and a wound had opened. She and Grace had exchanged strong words and the family doctor had been drawn in. He had backed up Nurse Gill's method.

'Methyl alcohol, massaged in with soap, is the tried-and-tested method,' he'd informed Grace in the way of someone aiming an apple core at a wastepaper bin.

Tried, tested and shown to be ineffective. Overruled she might be, but nothing would induce Grace to put raw spirits onto a sore and she was diluting it with four parts of cooled, boiled water. She lit the baby camping stove that Sir Gideon had provided to save her traipsing down to the kitchen whenever she needed hot water.

She was out of sorts with the world because last night, she had moved into 34 Hill Street. She'd first gone home to Dock Street to pack and break the news. And, honestly, you'd think from the way Ricky and their mother had wailed that a death had been announced. It had sounded like the keening at a wake until Immie, God love her, had intervened.

'Grace can't sleep her life on a bedroom floor, and I won't either. We'll get by. We'll pool our money, two pounds a month into the kitty from me, three from Cormac and two from Grace. Right?'

Grace had agreed, though where on earth would she get an extra two quid from?

She'd arrived at Hill Street with her worldly possessions in a kitbag her dad had brought back from the last war, only to find Miss Betony Styles had nabbed three quarters of the wardrobe *and* the best bed. Grace's bed. She'd found the bloody creature arranged on the satin eiderdown, curling rags in her hair, stripped down to a peach-and-lace under-slip, reading the latest copy of *Vogue*. Looking up to find Grace at the foot of the bed, red-faced from the effort of lugging the kitbag up the stairs, she'd said, 'Awfully sorry, but I have to have this one. Anything else is simply impossible.'

'Simply impossible'. What a wonderful motto for a self-entitled cow. What would hers be? Grace wondered. 'Keep slogging on' mounted over crossed bedpans and a downturned mouth.

And another thing... Mrs Kesgrave, putting a plate of tomatoes on toast in front of her at breakfast, had jauntily called her 'Nurse Wheeler' and it was too late to correct her. When she signed the rent book, she'd be there under false pretences. And it would be blindingly obvious when she handed over her ration book, in the name of Whelan. What a tangled web.

Still, she had a bed, a home and a quarter of a wardrobe, which would shrink to one eighth when the other girl – Jess, was it? – turned up. Let's hope Jess had few clothes and didn't snore.

'You haven't given me my medicine for my condition,' Lady Ventnor complained.

'I'm just putting it up,' Grace said. *Condition be damned. Call it by its name: gout.*

How many grains of cinchophen? Her mind was blank. There'd been sirens last night, though no bombs nearer than the Thames estuary. Trouble was, Grace was now so primed to wake on full alert, she'd forgotten how to switch off. Miss Betony Styles didn't snore, but she talked in her sleep, exactly the way she did when awake. It made Grace anxious what voice might come out in her slumbers.

Think, Grace. Five grains or ten? Why was it that being a nurse, with life-or-death decisions to make, came packaged with so few hours of rest? The likes of Lady Ventnor, with twenty-four hours of leisure every day, ought to be the nurse. Where was she... Oh yes. Fifteen grains of cinchophen in a glass of water.

Grace tapped powder into a tiny measuring scoop and repeated the actions she knew by heart. *Check the water is cool enough. Stir well to create a suspension.*

She took the medicine to the bed. 'Here you are, Lady Ventnor, for your, um, condition.'

'Don't be pert with me, girl.' Lady Ventnor allowed Grace to tuck a napkin into her nightdress frill.

Leaving her patient to gulp the mixture down, Grace went to turn up the flame on the camping stove. Now for the bedsore. She reminded herself, under her breath, 'Half a gill of methylated spirits to a half pint of warm, boiled water...' Grace would say afterwards how the cuff of her sleeve caught the pan handle as she poured the spirits. She jumped aside to avoid a scalding as the pan flipped, and raw spirit ignited. Lady Ventnor screamed. Grace moved quickly, grabbing something lavender coloured from the end of the bed. She burned her fingers smothering the flame and shutting off the fuel.

Shaking out the lavender folds, she discovered she'd put out the fire with Lady Ventnor's favourite dressing gown. Her Ladyship would not be wearing it again.

21

'You have to find me another job.' Grace had dashed the short distance to the Root Agency, her ears raw. Lady Ventnor had spewed fury until her vocal cords failed.

Rather than be sacked on the spot, Grace had run.

'The woman's impossible and I'm exhausted because the night nurse is late every time, so I end up crawling home in the blackout. If there's a raid, I end up sitting on a coal sack in their cellar, while Lady Ventnor complains about me to everyone else. This is not why I became a nurse.'

'Why did you, as a matter of interest?' Miss Root enquired.

'Train as a nurse?' At her original interview at the Royal London Hospital, Grace had unfurled her girlhood dream of gliding through quiet wards, a Nightingale in starched poplin. The reality was very different, of course. 'What else is there for a girl of my background that provides a steady salary and the chance of getting somewhere in the world? It was that or teach.' A teaching diploma had been out of her reach. She'd needed to earn a living straight from school, so nursing was the obvious choice.

Miss Root took all this in. 'Go home, Grace. You've taken over Miss Manning-Smythe's room, I believe?'

'How d'you know that?'

'Mrs Kesgrave and I are registered at the same grocer's.'

'I won't be there long if I'm sacked. I won't be able to pay the rent.'

For once in their acquaintance, Miss Root seemed sympathetic. She peered into Grace's face. 'I know that look. I'll call Sir Gideon and mention the night nurse's timekeeping. It is unacceptable that you should be on your feet all day and half the evening too.'

The unexpected kindness was Grace's undoing. She began to sob. Miss Root sat her down and made her a cup of tea, adding an entire spoonful of sugar.

By lunchtime, Grace was putting her key into the lock at 34 Hill Street, an afternoon nap ahead of her.

Mrs Kesgrave came to the door of her sitting room as Grace went to the stairs.

'Early today, dear one.'

'Yes. The family had visitors and I wasn't wanted.' Grace wasn't going to admit that she might be jobless.

On the first floor, she washed her face and hands at the bathroom sink, then traipsed up the last flight to her room. It was empty, thank the Lord, but look at that... Miss Styles had plonked a vanity case on the centre of her bed, the way bossy women put towels on deckchairs at the Chingford lido.

As Grace unpinned her cap, she planned ways of turning the tables. A wriggling Thames eel under Betony's sheets was the favourite, but that would probably get her thrown out. She brushed out her hair, making sparks. Easing off her shoes, climbing out of her tunic, she went to the wardrobe in her white cotton slip.

Pushing hangers aside, she scrutinised her off-duty clothing. Her two 'best' dresses stood out, one made of plain green cotton, and one which Immie had given her before leaving for the country last summer. Immie's hand-me-down was calf-length, artificial silk. Amethyst in colour, with a silk peony sewn into the point of a sweetheart neck. The peony was the shade of pink known variously as 'hot', 'shocking' or – in Grace's opinion – 'hideous'. She ought to do something about it, because if she got a date to go somewhere smart with... *Come on, imagination...*

Owen's features stayed stubbornly blank in her mind's eye. Not surprising, really, as the last time she'd seen him he'd been more interested in his bacon sandwich than in her.

He wasn't the only fish in the sea. London was humming with men in uniform, on leave and looking for love, or a good time at any rate, but they'd soon get sick of her having almost no time off. That was the thing that killed her romances.

Undecided what to put on, she went to the window and pushed up the sash to let in some breeze. Her new bed was the closest to the window. Sitting on the edge, she hitched up her slip and unsnapped her suspenders, rolling off her stockings, then lay back. Bliss.

I nearly burned down Lady Ventnor's bedroom. Had she done something similar at the Royal London, she'd have been frogmarched to Matron, then hung, drawn and quartered on the hospital lawns. She loathed Lady Ventnor – only, she desperately, desperately wanted to keep this room. Which meant she had to keep her job. Besides, if she didn't go back to Upper Brook Street, she'd never lay eyes on Owen again.

How would she find her share to keep Mam and Ricky afloat? A bit of barmaiding? God, she'd die on her feet. Night shifts as a private nurse, moonlighting? It might come to that.

Now thoroughly ruffled, she took *Peg's Paper* from her bedside cupboard but couldn't focus and it came to rest on her stomach as she fell into longed-for sleep – only to be woken by someone shutting the door hard.

Grace sat up and saw Betony slipping off her shoes while taking the pins out of her straw hat.

'Slam the door, why don't you?'

'Oh, sorry,' Betony said, as if she hadn't noticed Grace was there. Her glance went straight to the wardrobe. 'Sorry to be a nag, but would you mind shutting it after you've done? Otherwise, the clothes fade in patches. You end up with one sleeve a lighter colour than the other.'

'Dear me, reach for the smelling salts.' Grace swung her legs off the bed and *Peg's Paper* fell to the floor.

Betony came and picked it up, making a face. '"*Oh, Reginald, my one true love, how stern you look in your uniform!*" You don't, surely?'

Grace snatched it back. 'Snobbery is the last resort of the stupid.' She'd heard a down-and-out man hunched on a park bench shout that at a passer-by and had stored it up. It felt good to finally make use of it. 'And you've got a nerve, laying down the law about the wardrobe when you've annexed it like bloody Hitler.'

'Like – now just a moment—'

Betony's outrage had no chance to express itself as Mrs Kesgrave tapped and came in. 'Sorry to barge, but Grace dear, you have a visitor.'

Grace imagined Mam or Ricky downstairs, pleading with her to come home because they couldn't find a tin opener or had run out of matches. 'Who?' she asked. Blasted Betony was all ears too.

'Sir Gideon Ventnor, and I've put him in the drawing room. Apparently, something awful has occurred and they need you.'

Grace dressed as fast as she could and ran down. Sir Gideon was on his feet and she had the impression he'd been pacing.

'Is it Lady Ventnor?' Grace asked.

'No, my nephew, Owen. He's had the most dreadful accident and is in hospital in Kent.'

The news hit like a boxing glove to the stomach, but what could Grace do?

'My wife is insisting on going down to see him,' Sir Gideon said helplessly, 'and I cannot possibly take her without your help. Would you consent, if I ask you most humbly, to come back to us?'

'D'you mean tomorrow?'

'Today, now. Without delay.'

22

———

It was less of a surprise than it might have been to see Lady Ventnor downstairs, in her coat and hat and seated on a hall chair, because Sir Gideon had pre-warned Grace as they returned at a jog from Hill Street.

'You must have realised by now that my wife can walk when the need takes her. She's fixed on going to Owen's hospital bedside.'

Grace wanted nothing more than to race there too, to learn the worst. If it was 'the worst'. However, the nurse in her had explained how unwise and, frankly, unwelcome their presence would be. 'At the very least, Owen will need peace and quiet. The ward sister won't allow you in.'

'You've met my wife,' was all Sir Gideon had said in answer to that.

At their appearance, Lady Ventnor asked eagerly, 'Well, do we have transport, Gideon?'

'In a bit. Say good evening to Nurse Wheeler, Maude. She's been good enough to give us another try.'

'Back like a bad penny, more like. I want the other nurse, the one who knows how to behave and speak.'

Sir Gideon ignored this and turned to Grace. 'Might I impose on you to fill a bag with whatever my wife will need for her journey?'

'Of course. Lady Ventnor will need her evening medication, but I suggest we administer that before we leave.'

'I'm not a dog or a lunatic,' Lady Ventnor hurled. 'You don't "administer" to me.'

Words weren't all the woman had hurled, Grace realised as she stepped over broken porcelain. A matched pair of Japanese vases on the hall table were reduced to one. A shame, but unimportant compared to Owen's situation.

Sir Gideon had told her what he knew. Following what sounded like a crash landing, Owen had been taken to Shorncliffe Military Hospital on the Kent coast, but the extent of his injuries was unclear.

Buckland stepped forward, giving Grace a dry smile, suitably concealed behind his hand. 'How are you intending to travel tonight, Sir?'

Sir Gideon explained that he'd talked one of his Home Guard volunteers, a greengrocer, into loaning his van and petrol ration for the journey. 'He'll look the other way for a day or two.'

It was all Grace could do not to shout, 'You have to be joking!' The greengrocer might have fuel, but non-essential motoring was a violation of rules. He might lose his ration, or even his licence. She made the point that since they'd be setting off as it grew dark, with minimal headlamps and on unfamiliar roads, they might easily come to grief on the way. 'And what if there are more bombing raids? That part of Kent has been hammered almost every day since the end of August. The Germans shoot at civilians. We could all get killed.'

'I didn't take you for a coward, Nurse.' Lady Ventnor's lip curled.

'I'm not a coward, but my life isn't for throwing away, and

the last thing your nephew needs is you bursting in on him, in hysterics.'

'Hysterics? How dare you.'

'If his injuries are severe, or, heaven forbid, he's been burned, you won't be allowed near him, for fear of spreading infection.'

'I am not infectious and I dare you to stop me!' Lady Ventnor got to her feet, batting away Buckland's attempts to support her.

'You've never met a dragon of a ward sister whose patients are her first concern,' Grace hit back. 'You'll be out on your ear, and your feet won't touch the ground.'

'Brava,' whispered Sir Gideon, behind her.

'If anyone should visit your nephew, it should be his mother.' This journey was entirely Lady Ventnor's madcap idea, and Sir Gideon was trying to appease her. It had to stop.

Grace addressed him. 'How far is Shorncliffe from here?'

'Oh... sixty, seventy miles, perhaps?'

'A one-hundred-and-twenty-mile round trip at the least, risking our lives only to get there and find there's no visiting allowed, or that your nephew is too ill to be seen. Does that make sense to you, as a military man?'

Course it didn't, but Sir Gideon sighed.

Grace turned on the butler. 'What about you, Mr Buckland. Do you think it's a sensible plan?'

Buckland gave her a look that said, *Don't push it.*

'I'll assume the answer is "no".' Right. Time to put the plan she'd formulated during the last minutes into action. 'I'll prepare Her Ladyship's medication. May I suggest, Sir Gideon, you put a call through to the hospital and establish their protocol for visitations.'

Protocol for visitations. Where the devil had that come from?

She went up to the bedroom she thought she'd seen the last

of and measured out fifteen grains of cinchophen. Instead of dissolving it in water, she tipped it into the wastepaper basket. That way, nobody would think she'd missed a dose. First rolling up her sleeves, she lit the spirit kettle and boiled water. From a second medicine bottle, she measured out five grains of Veronal on the scales. Five grains were minimum, fifteen the absolute maximum. Among nurses, Veronal was known as the 'suicide's friend'. Still, she knew her stuff and Grace added more, making seven grains in all. She dissolved the substance in hot water, added a shot of cold, mixed it well, and took it down on a silver tray.

'I wonder if Her Ladyship wouldn't be more comfortable in the drawing room,' she suggested to Buckland. Sir Gideon was presumably making his telephone call.

When Lady Ventnor was seated on a Chesterfield sofa, Grace gave her the glass, saying, 'Down in one, ma'am.' She felt not a shred of guilt. This woman's selfish obsession with Owen could bring real harm.

By the time Sir Gideon found them, Lady Ventnor was placid and her eyelids seemed heavy.

'Did you get through to the hospital?' Grace asked.

'Er, no,' he said after a moment of abstraction. 'They're calling back.'

'Sir, I hear a van.' Buckland was at the window. 'Do you wish me to go out and speak with the driver?'

'I'll do it,' said Sir Gideon. 'Nurse, would you go and stand by the phone?'

Grace went willingly. The instrument rang as she reached the library and her head felt light. How many times a day did a hospital like Shorncliffe make telephone calls and how often was it dreadful news?

She took deep breaths as she lifted the receiver. 'Sir Gideon Ventnor's residence, Nurse Wheeler speaking.'

A brisk female voice came down the line. 'Staff Nurse

Williamson here, how can I help?' She sounded impatient, as might be expected of a nurse in a front-line military hospital.

'We're calling for news of Flight Lieutenant Owen—' Grace broke off. She didn't know Owen's surname. Nobody had mentioned it, and she'd never dared to ask. 'Um, the Owen who was brought in from RAF Hornchurch yesterday. Spitfire pilot.' She made a face as Staff Nurse Williamson replied that she needed a surname. 'I can find out,' Grace said. 'Please hold the line—'

'It's Henderson,' said a high, precise voice from the doorway.

Grace turned, expecting to see that Lady Ventnor had somehow risen from her couch, and almost dropped the phone.

What the hell was *she* doing here?

23

'You've got a bloody nerve,' Grace hissed.

'Yes,' Betony agreed, 'when it concerns the man I love.'

'The man you...?'

'Love. Who loves me. Tell her his name. It's Henderson.'

Grace repeated it into the phone, her voice splitting under the weight of shock. 'I believe he was brought in—'

'He's gone,' interrupted the nurse, over a buzzing phone line.

'Gone?' Grace glanced at Betony, who gripped the door frame, her face a mask.

'You mean he's died?'

'What? No,' said the staff nurse. '*Gone*. Discharged himself. You know what these boys are like. They'd get back in their planes with one leg hanging off if they could.'

The sound of a door swinging shut prompted Grace to end the call and push past Betony, who immediately elbowed past her, almost tripping her up. In the hall, they saw Sir Gideon holding the arm of a young man in slate-blue uniform. It was Owen, a bandage around his forehead. He was limping badly.

Sir Gideon was smiling so hard, his moustache stretched to

his ears. 'Operation Shorncliffe called off, all personnel stand down,' he blared thankfully. 'Here's my boy, right as rain. All but, anyway. And who've we got here?' He peered at Betony, who raced to Owen, taking his other arm.

'Owen, darling,' she gasped, 'thank God, I was heartbroken and now I'm the happiest idiot alive.' Betony flung back her head and her blonde curls danced.

Grace saw Owen's arms curl around Betony's slender back. He looked towards Grace, then away.

Buckland came up to her, saying under his breath, 'I understand the young lady to be the Honourable Betony Styles, daughter of Lord and Lady Styles, of Bruton Street, Mayfair and Styles Court, Somerset. Surely, as an avid consumer of *Peg's Paper*, you love a romance?'

'Who cares what I think?'

Buckland agreed. 'Lady Ventnor, who adores the genuine aristocracy, will crow from the treetops. When she wakes up. *If she wakes.*'

They went to the drawing room and watched the patient breathing deeply under her blanket.

'I take it, there'll be no nip of brandy in bed tonight, Nurse.'

'God, no. You need to hide the bottle.'

Buckland observed, 'You're crying, Nurse Wheeler. It never pays to show too much of yourself. I learned that a long time ago and it's saved me from a lot.'

Grace retired upstairs until Nurse Gill arrived. Between them, they got Lady Ventnor into her bed. Handing over, Grace explained the dose of Veronal so there was no room for doubt. No more must be administered and absolutely no alcohol to be given.

Sir Gideon met her as she came downstairs, saying, 'All's well that ends well.'

'Is your nephew all right?'

'I think so. He asked after you, but that young lady —

Betony, is that her name? – said you were shy and preferred your own company.'

I bet she did. 'Is she still here?'

'She is, and I've slipped away to give them time together. I' – Sir Gideon gazed at Grace, whose uniform was crumpled and her cap askew from helping get Lady Ventnor up the stairs – 'thought you handled that situation jolly well.'

I did, she agreed silently. *And you don't know the half of it.*

Grace continued downstairs. Sir Gideon followed. Pausing in the hall to put on the cape she'd flung on two hours earlier, she heard voices from the drawing room. The soft trill of laughter, a deeper voice murmuring. A remembered scene came back: herself as a little girl, spending all her money at the coconut shy at the fair, her dad saying, 'You won't win anything, don't waste it.' Course, he'd been right. The wooden balls had gone in every direction and the coconuts had stayed on their posts. That feeling of one chance, taken and wasted, overcame her now. She didn't even say good night to Sir Gideon, though he hurried to open the door.

'I'm not sure we pay you enough,' he said gruffly.

Any other time, Grace would have laughed it off, but with her guard down and emotions scraped raw, she agreed. 'You don't, and you know what? I need an extra two pounds a month or I'll have to leave. I've taken a room nearby, but I'll still have to send money home.'

'Right. I see.'

Now I've embarrassed him, she thought. *Time for a swift exit.* 'Sleep well, Sir Gideon.'

'Two pounds, eh?' He came out with her, detaining her with a touch. 'From me, into your pocket once a month, no pack drill, is that what you're saying?'

'I don't understand, pack drill?'

'No fuss. We don't tell Miss Root. Or Lady Ventnor, for that matter.'

'Oh. Do you mean it?'

He tapped his nose. 'Leave it to me.'

Grace walked home, taking care where she put her feet in the twilight. That time at the fair, her dad had gone back to the coconut shy and had three goes himself. He hadn't won either, so he'd bought a coconut off the man and given it to Grace. She remembered her delight. Life wasn't all bad. She had her job back and if Sir Gideon kept his word, she could stay at Hill Street. *If* she could stomach Betony Styles mooning over Owen Henderson. 'The happiest idiot alive!'

Whereas, she was just an idiot, Grace told herself. Who had been firmly put in her place.

24

———

Friday 6 September

Tonight, it was Grace's turn to cook and she made rissoles with corned beef and onion, coated in breadcrumbs and fried. Mrs Kesgrave complimented her, saying, 'Isn't it wonderful how food shortages make us so creative?'

Grace didn't mention that corned beef and breadcrumbs had, one way or another, kept her family going for years.

All three sat down to eat, Grace and their landlady tucking in. Betony tried a mouthful or two before putting her knife and fork together with a murmured, 'Very nice.'

'You haven't finished,' Grace accused.

'Not because they aren't delicious,' Betony insisted. 'Just, I'm out on a date later.'

'Owen Henderson?' Grace blushed the moment she'd said it.

Betony also coloured up. 'No, someone else.'

'Not playing fast and loose, surely?'

'Not at all. It's a pre-arranged thing that I can't escape, but I shall tell the chap I won't be going out with him again.'

'You and Owen are serious?' Grace wondered why she was picking this particular scab, drawing blood from herself.

'*I* am. I hope he is.' Betony gave her impish smile, the one that annoyed Grace because it made her look normal, good-natured. Fun. Grace much preferred the supercilious 'let's be nice to the peasants' air Betony displayed the rest of the time. It allowed her to keep hating the woman.

Betony delicately dabbed her mouth with a napkin. 'Would you mind if I get down from table, Mrs Kesgrave? I need to make myself decent. Can't break a man's heart looking like a scruff.'

Since Betony already looked as if she'd stepped from the pages of the magazine she apparently worked for, 'scruff' was galling to Grace.

But not to Mrs Kesgrave, who said, 'Off you go, poppet, I'll help Grace clear up. If you really are breaking some poor fellow's heart, do it with poise. It shows respect.'

At the sink, as Grace washed the dishes and her landlady dried, an air of camaraderie blossomed. Sustained air raids were chipping away at habits of formality and deference and there was something about being two Cinderellas doing the washing up while the beautiful sister gets ready for the ball that encouraged intimacy. As she scrubbed a plate, Grace asked the question that had been in her mind since first seeing Mrs Kesgrave's calling card. 'What is it you do, exactly?'

'I'm a liberator of the oppressed, dear one.'

'A journalist?' If asked to place a bet, Grace would have had Gloria Kesgrave down as an actress or fortune teller, or both.

'Journalist? Not at all. I've met a few, and they're cross-grained women. Foreheads permanently grooved with sarcastic thoughts. Why did you imagine so?'

'Your card says, "Discreet Correspondent".' Grace put the

plate on the drainer, adding, 'Sorry if I'm being nosy, but what is one of those, if not a journalist?'

'Firstly, you're pronouncing it wrong. I am a discreet *co-respondent*.' The emphasis was on 'co'. 'I help women get divorced – or men if I believe their motives to be pure. The system is so archaic, no woman can free herself from a miserable marriage unless she can prove her husband is either violent or adulterous.' Stepping back from the drainer, she cracked her tea towel like a whip. 'A man may divorce an adulterous wife with impunity, but if he is a gentleman, he will take the social stigma on himself and allow himself to be discovered in a hotel bedroom with a woman of ambiguous virtue. I am that woman.'

'Gosh.' Grace stared. Nothing about Mrs Kesgrave struck her as ambiguous. Never in her life had Grace met a woman so completely comfortable with her own unique style. Was she saying she slept with those divorcing gentlemen? All of them?

Her reaction wrung a warm chuckle from Mrs Kesgrave. 'Nothing of a physical nature takes place. Did you imagine it did?'

'Not at all.' Grace blushed solidly.

'Generally, I and the gentleman play cards or wrangle with *The Times* crossword. I invariably get their life story, and tales of woe, and I return the compliment, and tell them mine. In the morning, we are encountered by a chambermaid who, like me, is paid. My name is entered into the divorce petition as "the other woman", the chambermaid gives evidence, as do I, saving the man's wife indignity and notoriety. That's what a *co*-respondent is and that, my dear Grace, is why I consider myself a freedom fighter. Liberator of the enchained.'

'Gosh.' Grace knew she was repeating herself. 'That is quite some job.'

Gloria Kesgrave's laughter rang freely. 'Isn't it just? And so much more rewarding than begging for bit parts in third-rate plays and out-of-town repertory theatres.'

'Ah, I thought you were an actress.'

'Ex, darling. The parts dry up when you fall into the pit of forty.' Mrs Kesgrave turned at the sound of footsteps. 'Here she is, Fair Helen, child of Zeus, whose beauty will bring men to war and heroes to their knees.'

'Oh, stop it.' Betony was wearing a midnight-blue, floor-length dress and a white, quilted velvet shoulder shrug. In under half an hour, she'd redone her make-up and put her hair up.

Oh, stop it. Grace absorbed every inch of the vision that was her roommate, while the dishcloth in her hand seemed to twitch from a desire to go *splat* in the sweetly self-deprecating face.

'Will I do?' Betony giggled.

'Very well indeed, my dear.' Mrs Kesgrave's smile turned a little sad. 'What a shame you have to choose.'

'Choose?' Betony echoed.

'Between your two beaux.'

'Oh, I see. Winter will be all right. All he need do is look sad and lost, and he'll have fifty women trying to mend him. You don't think the dress is too much? Only, I wore it to go out with him before. I thought, wearing it again would be a subtle message.'

'That you've stopped caring?' Grace translated. The way the silk cleaved in butter-soft folds to Betony's legs, her date was unlikely to give a whistle if he'd seen it on her ten times. What he'd care about was that some other bloke would get the benefit once he'd been given the elbow.

'Better dash,' Betony said, with a glance at the frail gold watch on her wrist.

'Where is it you're going?' asked Mrs Kesgrave.

'Only the Savoy.'

Slumming it, Grace thought sourly.

'Good choice,' said Mrs Kesgrave. 'It has a bombproof ballroom.'

It flickered through Grace's mind that if Owen heard about this escapade, he'd drop Betony Styles flat. There might be a way of telling him... Buckland might help... Only that would make her a rat.

Betony left in a whirl of blue silk and perfumed smiles, asking them to add their prayers for a taxi to get her to the Strand.

Grace and Mrs Kesgrave put away the crockery, and in a spirit of self-flagellation, Grace insisted on cleaning the cooker, even the gas jets. As the clock struck ten, they retired to the sitting room for what Mrs Kesgrave referred to as 'a furtive glass of port'. Grace was savouring her first sip when the air raid warning rang out.

25

'These blasted sirens have sounded every night since the last week of August,' Mrs Kesgrave complained as they gathered themselves to get to the shelter.

'Not quite,' Grace said, reaching for her cardigan. 'There were two nights when we actually got some sleep.'

'I didn't. I sat up with my Thermos at the ready, and ears on high alert. Well, dear one, are you ready to go subterranean?' Mrs Kesgrave took a lipstick from her bag and applied a slick of plum. Seeing Grace's amusement, she offered the stick. 'Go on. Imagine, if one died with pallid lips. How about you make a Thermos of tea while I do some sandwiches.'

A thought struck Grace as she filled the kettle. 'I hope Betony knows what to do.'

'In a raid? If she doesn't, she's the sort of girl who dates men who know exactly what to do on such an occasion. Do you play rummy? I'll find the playing cards.'

Grace didn't answer. She was imagining Mam and Ricky hearing the sirens in Whitechapel. Which one of them would say, 'Let's get across the road to the shelter'? Neither would, but Immie would take charge. They'd be fine.

Her mind veered off to Upper Brook Street, to Sir Gideon, Nurse Gill and Buckland trying to get Lady Ventnor down to the cellar. Owen doing his best to help, and in no way fit enough. It was on her mind to run over and help, but the whistling kettle brought her back to something she'd said yesterday. *My life isn't for throwing away.* Empty heroic gestures did no good and besides, she'd be more interesting to Owen alive than dead.

Stop it. Despising her obsession with a man who saw her only as a nurse if he saw her at all, she flung tea leaves straight into the Thermos flask. She added sugar, boiling water and a splash of milk, gave the whole lot a violent shake, then followed Mrs Kesgrave to the back-yard Anderson shelter.

Sunk two feet into the ground, the shelter was damp and claustrophobic. All that lay between them and falling bombs was a curved, corrugated steel roof and a foot of soil and turf. Both Grace and Mrs Kesgrave had to bend double to get through the low doorway.

'It'll be a squeeze when it's all three of us in here together,' Grace said, arranging a blanket around her shoulders.

'Three shall soon become four, as I'm still expecting little Jess... Oh dear.'

'What is it?' Grace asked. 'Jess?'

'No. My girls. I hate leaving them unprotected.'

Grace realised Mrs Kesgrave was referring to the chickens she kept in a coop in the yard, three buff Orpingtons and a little black Dorking. She liked the creatures, and certainly appreciated their eggs, but if Mrs Kesgrave was about to suggest what Grace suspected—

'I'm desperately allergic to feathers, Mrs Kesgrave. Tell you what, tomorrow I'll help you make a bombproof hen coop.'

26

BETONY

The siren sounded at a few minutes past ten, bringing silence as if time itself hiccupped. Then, as everyone in the Savoy's famously bombproof ballroom wondered what would happen, the *chanteuse* walked up to the microphone. The Carroll Gibbons band began 'In the Still of the Night' without irony or a note out of place.

Minutes later, the first incendiaries fell.

Winter held her in a relaxed embrace. He was telling her about a new secretary who'd been allotted to him, a lightning-fast typist who could take shorthand in three languages, including German.

'Which means she's probably a spy. What d'you think, Betty?'

Winter was the only person who ever called her that. Friends were permitted to use 'Betts', but to the rest of the world, she was Betony. No trimming or pet-naming.

'I have no idea,' she said. For all this was her last night out with Winter, and the 'Dear John' speech was looming, she wasn't thrilled to have him praising another female directly into her ear. Particularly not one he shared an office with.

'Go on,' he said. 'You always have an opinion.'

'All right. She's a spy, transmitting highly sensitive information to Berlin as we speak. You should inform SIS.'

'Wouldn't it be more useful to watch her, see where she goes, who she talks to. Where she posts her letters?'

He was adept at teasing, having exactly the right kind of voice. Deep, a tad sardonic. The Canadian accent added a layer of ambivalence. With her own set, she could easily calibrate the extent to which she was being taken for a fool. With Winter, she was often at a loss.

'Do as you like,' she answered sharply, 'but, seriously, if you have doubts, Secret Intelligence will want to know. Don't get dragged into some Nazi plot.'

'And be sent back home to Vancouver? God, no. Think what I'd miss.'

The band played the last notes of 'In the Still of the Night' and flowed into 'Moonlight Serenade', which was everybody's favourite. Winter's hand moved to the part of her back where the V-shape began, bringing a treacherous flash of desire. Blast her animal nature. Things would be so much easier if Winter weren't athletic, with the hair and eyes of his Celtic legacy. And damn nice, too.

Until the all-clear sounded, she spent the time deliberately cataloguing all the young men in uniform. Army and RAF officers, Senior Service in full dress, comparing them to Winter Macpherson in his well-cut suit and black bow tie. She didn't care that he noticed, because it would make the next part easier.

It was as they drank a final glass of champagne that she finally blurted out, 'I'm so awfully sorry, Winter, you're an absolute dream and I'm an ungrateful wretch, but...' She took a breath.

'You've met someone else.' He put down his glass. 'I'm not blind. Just tell me this. If you're not interested, why come out with me tonight?'

'Oh, you know.'

'Actually, I don't, and I didn't have you down as a girl who'd string a man along just to get a slap-up meal.'

'I haven't! I mean, I didn't! I mean...' She was stuttering because Winter had hit a truth. She could have finished with him over the telephone. So why agree a date? 'It was nothing to do with food. I wanted to do this nicely. The fact is, I have only one heart to give and it seems to me, with a war on, I should bestow it on a man in uniform.' She reached out to touch his arm. 'I don't want you to hate me—'

He didn't let her finish and got to his feet. 'I don't either. Come on. Let's see if there's such thing as a taxi on the Strand and if one will consent to pick up a man not in uniform.'

'You mean, you're still—'

'Going to get you home safe? Sure. What d'you take me for?'

27

Along the Strand, abandoned cars reflected a gleam that owed nothing to the moon or an untimely sunrise. Behind St Paul's, the sky shimmered red. The cathedral dome made an eerie silhouette.

'What district has been hit tonight, d'you think?' Winter asked, as they paused to look.

'Um... I'm not sure.' The geography of London beyond the West End and Mayfair was *terra incognita* to Betony. It didn't stop her thinking that there must be people trapped under that burning cone. Families, solitary old folk, pets... little birds in cages. Her thoughts soared into the velvet dark, imagining Owen in his cockpit, firing rapid rounds, turning, climbing or dropping a wing to avoid return fire. Of course, he was grounded until his injuries mended, and he'd told her last night in his aunt and uncle's drawing room that fighter squadrons only flew daytime sorties. Night flying against incoming bombers was like trying to find black cats in the dark. Moved by his offhand tone, she'd raised his grazed and bruised knuckles to her lips, begging him to stay safe. He had detached himself, presumably because it hurt, and said, 'Noted. Do my best.'

Ought she drop in at Upper Brook Street and see how he was doing? The last thing she wanted was to appear clingy. Then again, he mustn't think she didn't care. She'd made that mistake once already.

She was now convinced beyond doubt that it was Owen who had kissed her in the darkness, at the Café de Paris. Only he could have acted so decisively. Saying and asking nothing, the soul of restraint.

She realised she was biting her lip and that Winter was looking at her. 'I expect the Germans were aiming for the warehouses and the East End docks,' she said, in an attempt to appear well-informed. 'The flames seem to be along the South Bank.'

'Then they missed,' Winter said drily.

They walked in silence towards Trafalgar Square. Though she hadn't come out for a good meal, despite what Winter thought, the Savoy kitchen had excelled itself. She thought of Grace's hideous-looking offering at supper. Corned beef rissoles were what they'd force-fed her at school. With Winter, it had been lobster cocktail, then French onion soup, pork cutlets in cream sauce, a *delice* of iced coconut and chocolate truffles for dessert. No rationing at the Savoy, no shortage of waiting staff either – though she'd noticed Winter didn't consume his food the way the boys in uniform did, as if any plateful, drink, dance or kiss might be his last.

That was the problem, squeezed into a nutshell. That taboo kiss, the night the first bombs fell, was branded onto her soul, ineradicable. Unlike the telephone number Winter had scrawled on her arm, which had come off with soap and water the following night.

'Slow down,' she said because he was walking as if he wanted this evening over. Not that she blamed him. *If I were out with me, I'd feel the same.* 'Remember, I'm in heels.'

He suggested they head to the Embankment. 'We can beg a

cup of coffee at a cabman's shelter and wait till a driver turns up. Will your new landlady be wondering how you are?'

'I doubt it. She said herself, the Savoy ballroom is bombproof.'

'Nothing's bombproof,' Winter came back, 'until it gets tested for real.'

'True. She won't worry, anyway, and that's such a relief. You won't understand, being a man.'

'What won't I understand?'

'How tedious it is when you're grown up but you still can't go out at night without there being somebody waiting at home, clock-watching. I'm free. It's glorious.'

It might also be short-lived. For the past two years, her father's secretary, Miss Allsop, had paid four pounds each month into Betony's Post Office account, on Lord Styles' behalf. September's money had arrived as normal, as at the time, Betony hadn't left home. But what would October bring? If Father saw fit to cut her off, liberation would come to a crashing end. Her rent and contribution to meals came to four pounds, eight shillings per month, and she only earned five pounds. You didn't have to be a mathematician to see the gaping shortfall.

'You like being a bachelorette?' Winter slowed his pace to match hers.

'Bachelorette,' she echoed. A new word. 'I *do* like it.' Though not as much as she'd like being 'Mrs Owen Henderson' which sounded both exciting and complete. 'The Hon. Mrs Henderson...' That would make her friends sit up. 'Flight Lieutenant and the Hon. Mrs Henderson' sounded pitch perfect.

They were passing the Hotel Cecil, behind which stood Shell Mex House, where her father worked in an office overlooking the Thames. Father might be holed up there even now, dictating memoranda. Miss Allsop was one of the faithful, who would stay at her post while the bombs fell. Would it be any use, Betony wondered, to suggest Father take her out for lunch, and bring up the subject of her allowance while he was feeling mellow?

I'm living as a bachelorette, Father, until I marry, of course.

Out loud, she said, 'I may have to get a better-paid job, Winter. Any ideas?'

'Can you type?'

'No.'

'Answer telephones nicely?'

'I expect so. How much does that pay?'

'Depends who's employing you. Are you fed up, working for that magazine, standing around in nice clothes?'

'It's always been boring, but I'm not trained for much. I suppose I could become an auxiliary firewoman or something. Hey.' She didn't appreciate Winter's laughter. 'I could.'

'Course you could. Sorry. But, you know, you're better employed doing what you do. Women still need to dress and feel good about themselves, and *Practical Modes* – have I got the name right?'

'Yes.'

'It's as much part of the war effort as, I don't know, reporting from the Front or repairing barrage balloons.'

'Thank you, Winter. When I see my father, I'll tell him that. I've never heard him question the validity of his morning paper, or the salmon fishing magazine he gets sent from Scotland.'

'Your father's a different generation. The world's changed around him. It must be like waking up and finding someone's painted the sky a different colour.'

'Very diplomatic. You'll go far.'

'Maybe.' Her glib answer had clearly troubled him. Didn't he like being in diplomatic service? She knew he'd been plucked from some other career to join the embassy staff, and that his family was behind the decision. Maybe that was it. He'd folded in the face of parental pressure and disliked himself for it. Unlike her, marching towards an uncertain future, unfurling the banner of liberation.

They got a cab on the Embankment. The few miles to Mayfair passed in silence, Winter keeping to his side of the cab, she to hers. Betony was familiar with the male habit of sliding a hand along the back of the seat, to 'accidentally' rest on her shoulder. That Winter didn't do it was a gold star to him but also discouraging. Her choice of dress might have been intended as a hint that she hadn't taken the trouble to select anything new to impress him, but it really ought to produce something more from her date than, 'Hill Street, please, driver,' and 'Are you comfortable, Betty?'

At their destination, Winter told the driver to wait, he'd be right back. 'Got your key?'

'I do.' Betony showed him. 'Thank you, Winter. Good night, what's left of it.'

He bent and kissed her cheek. 'Night, Betty. See you around.'

She replied, '*À bientôt,*' as if being non-committal in French was less final than saying goodbye in English. She didn't entirely understand her reluctance to let him go. Because she'd always hated goodbyes, she told herself.

He walked her to her door, where, seized by an impulse she couldn't explain, she put her arms around him. She didn't kiss him, but leaned her lips against his, making him choose.

For a moment, it seemed he would pull her against him, but he stepped back. 'So long, Betty. Keep safe.'

He turned on his heel, leaving her with the sense that hers was the greater loss.

28

GRACE

SATURDAY 7 SEPTEMBER

A long night it had been, the all-clear only sounding in the wee hours, but exhausted as she was, Grace was eager to get to Upper Brook Street. The only thing she had over Betony was that she could legitimately ask after Owen. And perhaps see him.

Breakfast was over, medicines had been given. Grace approached the bed where Lady Ventnor lay on her right side, airing the stubborn bedsore on her left buttock, and a similarly worrying patch on her right heel. 'Anything you'd like me to do?'

'Yes. There's a letter on my bedside table. Read it out to me.'

Grace picked up the sheet, and her eye fell on the signature at the bottom. 'Prim'. Short for? Nothing came to mind. The letter had been written yesterday, in Ealing, London W5. Ealing was a few stops along the Central line. A memory flowed in:

'You're on the wrong train, mate.'

'I'm on the right one, but thanks for the advice.'

'Hurry up,' snapped Lady Ventnor. 'You can read, can't you.'

'"Dear Gideon,"' Grace began. 'Wait a minute, this is addressed to your husband.'

'That doesn't matter. Reading each other's mail is what husbands and wives do.'

Uncomfortable, Grace continued. '"Dear Gideon, I hope you are well. I understand from my son's squadron leader that Owen sustained an accident, was hospitalised only to discharge himself prematurely. Is he with you? I am out of my mind with worry."' Grace broke off. She had no right to be reading this.

Lady Ventnor snatched the page and finished reading it out loud. 'Dah-di-dah... boo-hoo. "If he is with you, urge him to telephone and to come home as soon as he is fit to travel." Oh, you'd like that. "As his mother, I would prefer to be the one tending to him. Yours—" Primrose.' Lady Ventnor finished with a sneer. 'Such a below-stairs kind of name.'

That explained 'Prim'. *But God, if Owen's mother was 'below-stairs'*, Grace thought, *I'd be in the basement.* 'She's concerned about her son. Can't you see that?'

'She married my brother John,' said Lady Ventnor, as if that answered everything. 'She should have stuck to her own level in life.'

Angry as she was, it pained Grace to think of Owen hurting his mam. Mum. Mother. He'd spent the summer battling an enemy who wanted to destroy him, his friends, his country. Day after day, death after death, Owen had climbed into his cockpit. Now, forcibly grounded, he seemed to be avoiding the one who had brought him into the world. The parallels between them were striking, and unsettling.

You can love someone and not want to live with them, she reassured herself. *It doesn't make you a horrible person.*

It didn't make you a good one, either.

A vision of Mam struggling to boil a pan of potatoes shot

through her mind. She deliberately placed Immie in the picture and again reminded herself that her sister would take charge.

As for Owen, once he recovered, he'd be calling on Betony, and Grace wouldn't be able to escape them. She might answer the door to him at Hill Street, and have him say, 'Hello, Nurse, is she ready?' How would it feel to be the one going out with him, to dance in his arms, just once?

Lady Ventnor came in like a demolition ball. 'Can you write?' She waved a hand at the door. 'You will find pen and paper in the library. Bring some up and I will dictate a reply to this woman.'

In the library, Grace found Sir Gideon and Owen poring over the charts. Owen was telling his uncle that RAF Tangmere had fallen off the edge.

'I haven't missed it,' Sir Gideon insisted. 'My map only goes as far south-west as Brighton.'

'The Germans bloody well won't. You need a bigger chart.'

Sir Gideon noticed Grace. 'Yes, my dear?'

What on earth could she say, with Owen in the room? She explained that Lady Ventnor had opened a letter, 'Addressed to you, Sir. You might want to read it before I take down Her Ladyship's reply.' Her vocal underlining was lost on Sir Gideon, who pointed to a bureau.

'Help yourself to writing materials.' As she searched for a pen, he asked, 'What d'you make of my nephew today?'

Grace faltered, as it forced her to look directly at Owen. He was wearing his uniform trousers and a jumper over his shirt, no tie, his collar loose. He'd taken off his head bandage. Bruises and contusions discoloured his forehead.

'Think he's on the mend?' Sir Gideon prompted.

'Well...' Her heart was beating the way it used to when she was summoned to Matron's office. Owen was standing with one shoulder notably higher than the other, suggesting he'd torn muscles and tendons. Grace assumed her professional persona. 'Bruises heal, and rest is so important. You were wearing your flying helmet when your head met something solid, Flight Lieutenant?' She summoned a smile.

Owen returned the smile. 'Some would say the solid object was my head. My plane flipped on landing and I'm told I'm lucky not to have broken my neck.' He put a hand on a point on his left shoulder, pressed down and tilted his head, his teeth clenching. 'This is the painful bit.'

'You need a good massage,' she said, then blushed in case he thought she was offering.

He did think it. 'I'm all yours. It's giving me the most fearful headaches.'

'Take an aspirin.' She grabbed what she'd come for and hurried away, thinking, *Dear God, Grace Whelan, some nurse you are.*

Owen called to her as she mounted the stairs, telling her he was coming up to see his aunt shortly.

'Tell her not to go to any trouble. I'll see her as she is.'

You'd better not; her backside on show.

Lady Ventnor was in the same position as Grace had left her. She gave Owen's message, at which any plans to write a reply to Primrose Henderson flew from Lady Ventnor's head.

'Bring my hairbrush and a mirror. And my jewellery. And get me sitting up. Hurry, hurry. He can't see me like this.'

29

Grace helped her patient into a clean dressing gown and brushed the wispy hair. She laid out make-up to Lady Ventnor's precise instructions and held a mirror for her. Her Ladyship creamed, powdered and daubed like a nervous debutante off to a ball.

'My complexion is like death. It's the medicine you're giving me.'

'The medicine your doctor prescribes,' Grace replied. 'You could always ask him to reduce the dose. Anyway, Owen won't care.'

She was told not to be fatuous. 'The day a woman ceases to care is the day she may be laid in her coffin. And kindly refer to my nephew as Flight Lieutenant Henderson.' Lady Ventnor waved two fingers towards the dressing room. 'There's a jet brooch in my satinwood box. Fetch it.'

When Grace brought it to her, Lady Ventnor pointed to an area above her left breast. 'Pin it here and don't jab me.' She sent Grace back for earrings. 'Diamonds, but not the sparklers.'

After a search, Grace found pear drop earrings that

answered the description, only to be told they were opals. 'I suppose you can't be expected to know. Bring the whole box.'

After another trip, Grace sat on the side of the bed to clip teardrops that looked like bits of dirty glass onto Lady Ventnor's earlobes, after which she was told she could go.

'You girls can't keep your eyes off a man in uniform, though I believe the Styles girl conducts herself better. It's unfortunate I was too tired the other evening to receive her. Her mother is a member of the Mayfair Preservation Society and highly thought of.'

'Will you be showing Owen... Flight Lieutenant Henderson... the letter from his mother?' Grace asked.

'Don't be ridiculous. Why would I heap more distress onto his shoulders?'

'If you told him, he could at least phone her and allay her fears.'

'Fears! She throws hysterics and stages illnesses to play on Owen's heartstrings, and who asked your opinion?' Lady Ventnor's lips twitched sourly. 'I did everything possible to stop my brother marrying her. He knew it was a mistake before the wedding but was too honourable to pull out. What would you expect of a woman named Primrose.'

'I think it's a pretty name. What are you doing?' Lady Ventnor was pushing a ruby dress ring onto her middle finger. Straight away, Grace could see the skin puffing up around the band. 'That's too tight. It needs to come off.'

'Don't fuss.'

'I'm paid to fuss.' Getting off the bed, Grace filled a bowl with warm water and dropped a bar of soap in it. 'Hold out your hand,' she said when she returned.

'Oh, really.' Lady Ventnor reluctantly extended her fingers.

The ring was stuck fast. Grace slid the edge of the soap under the band and tried to wiggle it loose.

'Ow, that hurts.'

'It'll really hurt if your finger swells much more.'

'*You're* making it swell.'

'No, it's the ring cutting off your blood supply.' Grace dried her hands on a piece of lint. 'Let's try castor oil.'

That got the ring as far as the knuckle, but Lady Ventnor kept pulling her hand back, making Grace hurt her even more. Castor oil dripped onto the dressing gown.

'Stupid, stupid!' Lady Ventnor snatched her hand away and Grace, worried about oil marks on satin, didn't see the slap coming until it caught her face side-on.

Grace lurched back. The rose-cut ruby had snagged the side of her eye, just missing the eye itself. 'You evil old besom, you've drawn blood.'

'Serves you right.' Lady Ventnor sounded pleased at having finally landed a blow.

Grace stood over her, making no effort to contain her fury. 'It'd serve *you* right if I locked you in here when the bombers come and pray for a direct hit. No, don't you dare!' Lady Ventnor had raised her hand again.

'That's enough.'

The order rang out from the doorway. With blood trickling down her cheek, Grace straightened up. Owen walked into the room. He'd heard her threatening his aunt, but hell would freeze before she apologised.

30

Lady Ventnor reached out beseechingly. 'Owen, get this ring off my finger before it has to be cut off. This imbecile nurse is making things ten times worse.' She snarled, 'Go,' at Grace. 'I don't wish to see you again for some time.'

'The feeling is quite mutual.'

Grace was mortified at being caught verbally abusing a patient but had reached the end of her patience. Lady Ventnor had crossed a line.

Professional dignity made her pause at the door and say, 'Flight Lieutenant Henderson, kindly inform Nurse Gill when she arrives that your aunt will not have been given her five o'clock cinchophen.'

'Leave it to me.' Owen was sitting on the bed and had taken his aunt's hand. Using the soapy water Grace had left by the bed, he was working the ring over Lady Ventnor's knuckle and she was leaning back against her pillows, quiet as a lamb.

Grace went downstairs, every vein thudding. Obviously, Owen thought she was a foul-mouthed tyrant. She met Sir Gideon coming out of the library.

'Your nephew's upstairs,' she said curtly.

'Yes, I saw him go up.' Sir Gideon peered at her. 'There's blood on your cheek. I hope...?'

Grace's face conveyed enough. Sir Gideon sighed miserably.

'What's it all about, Sir?'

He indicated for her to come into the library and shut the door. 'It started about ten years ago. We'd long given up hope of having children, and then Maude fell pregnant. She was forty-six and her doctor was horrified. With reason.'

'She miscarried?'

He nodded. 'Maude suffered...' He gathered himself. 'A breakdown. On doctor's advice, I sent her to Switzerland for a rest cure. But she came back home convinced she was a bedridden invalid.'

'The gout is real,' Grace said. 'And that is an awful condition.'

'But if she ate less and moved about... Apparently, swimming is beneficial.' Sir Gideon gave a hopeless shake of the head. 'She shouldn't keep to her bed, all day, every day.'

'I agree. But you'll have to find someone else to help with that, Sir. I'm sorry, but I can't stay in a job where I constantly fear I'll be assaulted.'

Sir Gideon tugged on a rope, making a bell clang deep in the servants' quarters. A minute passed, but nobody emerged. 'Must be taking a break before the next onslaught,' he said gruffly. 'Would you mind finding the first-aid box on your own? It'll be somewhere adjacent to the kitchen.'

'Did you not hear me, Sir?'

'Brew yourself a cup of tea while you're there. There'll be some cake lurking, I don't doubt. And, er...' Sir Gideon fished a hip flask from his pocket, passing it to her. 'Single malt. Good for shock.'

A five-pound note had somehow got itself attached to the hip flask. Grace took a swig from the flask, then handed it and the note back to Sir Gideon. He looked self-conscious, but somehow, the gesture had changed the balance between them, showing Grace how much she was needed.

'I'll clean myself up,' she said, 'have a cuppa and go back into the fray. But please tell your wife she must never hit me again. And while you're there, ask your nephew to phone his mother.'

31

In the kitchen, Grace lit the gas cooker and, while the water boiled, had a snoop around. Damn right she'd have some cake.

A minute's hunting turned up the first-aid box, but nothing more appetising than a tin of cheese biscuits. Grace crammed a couple into her mouth. There was cotton wool and surgical spirit in the first-aid box and the underside of the biscuit tin lid made a good mirror for cleaning the cut to her eye. Once again, she looked as though she'd crawled away from a dockside brawl. 'First the fist of Cormac, now Her bloody Ladyship. Bastards both.'

'Who is Cormac?'

Owen strolled into the room. He'd taken off his jumper, possibly having got his cuffs wet, and she saw his trousers were held up with cream-coloured braces with leather button ends. He came to her and inspected her face.

'Your boyfriend?'

'No, he's, um, just someone I know.' Feeling some reference must be made to the scene upstairs, Grace said, 'Nursing's hard enough without the patient striking out.'

'It's what my aunt does.'

'I bet she never hits you.'

'No.' Owen pulled up two chairs, one for him, one for her. 'I saw her throw a tray at Buckland when he was a footman. She wouldn't do it now.'

'Naturally. One can't have one's butler answering the door with half-healed cuts to his face.'

'It's more if he leaves, she won't get a replacement.'

Grace looked more closely at Owen. He'd sounded angry when he'd shouted 'That's enough!' and she'd assumed it was aimed at her. Perhaps she'd misread him. 'Somebody might suspect you don't like your aunt.'

'I wouldn't say that.'

'I know you wouldn't say it, because you're well brought up and wouldn't want to upset your uncle.' Devilment made her add, 'And then there's the money.'

'What money?'

'The fortune she's going to leave you.'

'I don't know anything about that.'

'Garn with you, you're heir to all she has, meaning you've got a lifetime ahead of grinning and bearing it.'

Sounding a touch put out, he asked, 'Are you always this blunt?'

Generally, at work, Grace kept her thoughts to herself. But with that slap still ringing in her bones, she didn't care if she broke the social taboos. Sack her again, see if they could keep a new victim more than a week. 'Are you aware that your mother is waiting for a call from you?'

'I called her from the hospital, Thursday afternoon, but she wasn't in.'

'And you're only allowed one telephone call, right?'

Owen was riffling through the first-aid box and didn't answer. He held up a tube of calendula ointment. 'Let's slather some of this on and, hopefully, your face won't swell up. Stay still.'

'No, it's fine.' The idea was disturbing. She'd offered to massage his neck, but with her in control. 'I'll do it myself.'

Owen was untwisting the cap. He squeezed some onto his finger.

She flinched at the first contact. Not that it hurt. After that, she couldn't help thinking how nice it felt, a gentle massaging and the concentration in Owen's eyes. She'd already discovered that, though he was fair, his eyes were deep brown. Shadows deepened the sockets and, along with the bruises and welts on his forehead, there were marks on his chin, and down the side of his neck similar to carpet burn. He'd obviously had a bad time, flipping his plane. Even so, the agitated air that had made him seem almost wild the morning she'd woken him in the library was less. He must be catching up on sleep.

'There, done,' he said, sitting back and putting the cap on the ointment. 'Are you going to stay?'

'Till six-thirty, when my shift is supposed to end, though it finishes whenever Nurse Gill gets here.'

'I meant – will you stay after what Aunt Maude did to you?'

'What did you see, exactly?'

'I saw her hit you and I know she did something similar to the last nurse.'

'She hurled a hairbrush at the last one,' Grace said.

'She can be sweet too.'

'To you! I judge people by how they treat their staff.'

'I always say "dogs". I judge people by their attitude to dogs.'

'Dogs and nurses. Well,' she said in a tight voice, 'now I know where I stand.'

He laughed and it was a warm sound, not cruel, the way Cormac laughed, or snide like Lady Ventnor. Owen Henderson was obviously well-educated, and no doubt cultured, but he wasn't plums-up-the-arse-posh like Betony. He'd become so, she thought sadly, if he and Betony made a match of it. He'd iron his voice and starch his soul to keep on the right side of her. Just as she was doing with this Mayfair nonsense.

'I am staying on,' she said, 'partly for your uncle's sake, but mostly because I need the salary and this job is fine when I'm not being used as a punchbag. It's a bore trying to find a new one.'

Grace winced. 'It's a bore' had slipped out in that hideous 'Lady Muck' voice she couldn't seem to get rid of. Maybe she'd betrayed herself because Owen asked her where she came from.

For a simple question, it was complex. From Ireland. From County Mayo. From Whitechapel.

'From hereabouts,' she said.

'Mayfair?'

'Pretty much.'

'What made you choose nursing?'

'You all ask that.' She put the surgical spirit and ointment back in the first-aid tin and replaced the lid on the cheese biscuits. 'Nursing is a good option if you don't mind the hours, the pay and the patients.'

He frowned, unimpressed by her joke. He'd been watching her hands as she re-packed the tin, and she wondered if he was noticing that her nails were filed short, that she wore no jewellery, or any adornment other than the fob watch on her apron. He said, 'Girls from round here go to finishing school, don't they?'

'Do they?'

'They take secretarial courses or flower arranging classes and work in smart offices for about a month before being whisked off to get married.'

'Well, that's not me.' Though it sounded quite nice, really.

Owen got up, saying, 'I admire you.'

Lovely, she thought. *That's all I want in life, to be admired. Respected. Relied on to be a true brick.*

'What are you up to?' She'd thought he was going, but

Owen fetched two sherry glasses down from a cupboard. From his pocket, he took a hip flask Grace recognised as his uncle's. He poured a finger of whisky into each glass. 'I shouldn't drink on the job,' Grace said.

'Today is not an ordinary day.' Owen handed her a glass. 'I asked where you came from, because I had an idea you might be Irish.'

'Why is that?' She tried to sound amused.

'The colour of your hair, the blue eyes, the shape of your chin. There's a man in my squadron name of Keating, from Tipperary. You look a bit like him.'

'A minute ago, I was being compared to a dog. Now I'm a man?'

He gave a bent smile. 'You aren't either. Will you go upstairs and make peace with Aunt Maude? She's embarrassed about what she did.'

'I doubt it. If she were embarrassed, she'd make more effort to find out if I was all right.'

Without considering how a delicately bred Mayfair Miss would approach a shot of whisky, she knocked hers back in one, the way her dad used to.

Owen Henderson blinked. 'Impressive.' He picked up his glass. 'Here's to you, Nurse... Sorry, I've forgotten your name.'

Didn't that just say it all?

'Wheeler. Grace Wheeler.'

He downed his shot.

'Did you get the ring off?' Grace asked.

He nodded. 'Once Aunt Maude relaxed her fingers. I don't fawn over her, by the way. I keep the peace for Uncle Gideon's sake, but I have no desire to be left this mausoleum, or whatever money they have.' He looked down at his hands and Grace saw marks over the knuckles. Cuts and friction burns. 'I don't think that far ahead,' he went on. 'None of us do. You said I have a lifetime ahead of me of kowtowing, but actually, I don't know if I have any time at all.'

Grace took one of his hands, with the excuse of inspecting his injuries. She regretted the dig about him being his aunt's heir. 'I hope these cuts were disinfected straight away?'

'Thoroughly. They wanted to keep me in hospital, but they need the beds for the chaps who are really hurt.'

'You must have whacked your head hard.' She still held his hand.

'Medical diagnosis?'

'I'm not qualified for that.' Time to let it go. 'Call it nurse's intuition.'

Something was nagging him, though she only realised it when he said in a rush, 'You're right about my mother. Mum deserves a call, but it is so difficult.'

'What is?'

'Hiding it all,' he said. 'The one thing she needs from me, I can't give.'

'And what's that, Flight Lieutenant?' Though Grace suspected she knew and when he didn't answer, she said it for him. 'You can't promise your mother that you'll come through. And so you stay away, sleep here in Mayfair and hit the town at night.'

He flinched, as if she'd touched him with a live wire.

'Love is hard, Flight Lieutenant.'

'For God's sake, call me Owen. And you're wrong. When you're living on your nerves all the time, falling in love is the easy option. When you're in the air, everything's a blank except what you're seeing from the cockpit. The moment you touch down, you're awash with uncontrollable feelings all looking for a target. A smile from a sweet pair of lips, and in you go, headlong.'

'You sound like the man who can't resist a drink.' Was this wild abandonment what he felt with Betony? If Betony hadn't been in the right place at the right time, would it have been another woman... such as her?

'It's not dissimilar to drinking,' he agreed. 'But daring to love just one person in perpetual fidelity, that's like taking on a debt you know you can't ever pay and so you don't.' His pupils darkened, emotion concentrated in their centre as he willed her to understand. And she so wanted to... and not make it about herself or Betony.

Grace spent too long grappling in silence. Somebody was coming into the kitchen; a door opened and the air raid sirens bled in.

'Here we go.' Owen got up, and the mask came down.

Grace got up too. 'Right. I'd better measure out your aunt's medicines and take them down to the cellar.'

Owen followed her out. 'When this is over, I'll walk you home.'

That brought her up short. He had no idea she and Betony lived in the same house. She had to tell him.

'You and Betony know each other?' He looked appalled.

'We share a room. But if you're imagining we discuss love affairs, think again. What you said just now will never pass my lips.'

She left the kitchen before she could see the effect her comment had.

32

The air raid was done by six, and Nurse Gill arrived an hour and a half later. Grace delivered a fast debrief and headed for the door. Owen, presumably having forgotten his pledge to walk her home, had left a few moments before, wearing his RAF greatcoat and cap. He'd looked to be on a serious mission. He shouldn't be going out as the light faded, so soon after a head injury. She was going to follow him with her nurse's cap on, physically and figuratively.

Stepping out into a glossy sunset, she blinked like a mole from the hours spent in the cellar. Lady Ventnor had monopolised Owen, chirping incessantly at him like a budgerigar. Nobody else had spoken much, and Grace had kept company with her fear of being entombed should a bomb hit them. The sky to the east, glowing orange, showed that, for some, fear had become the reality.

I'm lost in the dark. I can't move.

Grace stopped and looked around, as if the words had been spoken behind her. What if one of today's bombs had dropped on Mam, Ricky and the others? It could have happened, and she'd know nothing about it. She had to rely on them doing what she told them they *must* do every time – get to shelter.

She walked down the east side of Grosvenor Square without catching sight of Owen. She turned into Carlos Place, then took a short cut through Mount Street Gardens, where she was deafened by starlings circling and chattering as they seized a last lungful of life before the guns sounded again. Oh, for a night's peace.

Where South Street merged with Farm Street, she glanced towards the Shepherd and Flock pub and there he was. She saw him stop at the building next door.

She'd rather suspected that was his mission: an evening call on Betony Styles. She watched him bend to read a nameplate, then walk inside.

Grace had been past Betony's workplace a few times but had given it no more than a glance. After letting a couple of minutes pass, she crossed over and, on impulse, went inside too. Up a flight of stairs whose worn carpet was fixed with brass stair rods in need of a polish. It pleased her, to discover faded grandeur rather than manicured elegance.

As quietly as she could in her sensible lace-ups, she went as far as the second half-landing. There, she lost courage and crept back down. A taxi had drawn up at the kerb to allow a tall man in a broad-shouldered coat and homburg hat to alight. Grace heard him say through the window to the driver, 'Put the fare on the usual account, and wait here ten minutes, OK? I may ask you to take me and a friend to the Connaught.'

American? Grace stepped aside.

Seeing her, he tipped his hat. 'Good evening, Sister.'

It was like being addressed by a film star. Surely, it wasn't legal to do this to an innocent girl, leave her mumbling incoherent rubbish?

She watched him walk up the stairs she had just come down, then glowered down at her sensible feet. Sister. Nurse.

When was the last time a man had noticed she was a woman, under the blue tunic?

She'd bet her back teeth the Handsome One was also in search of Betony. He'd meet Owen.

'I hope they don't punch each other's lights out,' she said to nobody in particular.

Except, chances were, they'd be *terribly, terribly* polite.

Grace stumped homeward, hating herself far more than she did the star-crossed trio on Farm Street. She was turning into a jealous woman. *If I'm not careful, I'll end up resembling a cross between Lady Ventnor and Miss Root.* She wondered what the chances were of a hot bath tonight.

Zero, it turned out. She arrived at No. 34 Hill Street as the sun dipped down between Holland Park and Ladbroke Grove. On cue, the dog-howl of the siren ripped over the rooftops.

Mrs Kesgrave was waiting at the foot of the stairs.

'Grace dear, thank goodness. Would you pop upstairs while I make a Thermos and gather the necessaries. Jess has arrived, and she's asleep. Wake her gently.'

Grace hurried upstairs, thinking, *Now there'll be even less wardrobe space.*

The new girl lay under the covers, dark hair as straight as pump water spread across the pillow. She must be sleeping like the dead as the siren hadn't woken her. Despite the urgency of the moment, Grace couldn't hold back a grin. Jess was in Betony's bed and an enormous suitcase was parked right next to it.

'This promises to be fun,' Grace murmured and shook the newcomer awake.

The girl turned over with a groan before sitting up with the speed of someone attuned to danger. Her hair flopped over her face.

'Get up,' Grace chivvied. 'Siren's going.'

The girl jerked as if she'd just that moment heard it, but still didn't know where she was. Pushing the hair from her face, she revealed pale cheeks and dark, scared eyes.

Grace gasped because this was the second time she'd woken this person from sleep. The last time, the girl had been curled up in Cormac's bed.

33

Three of them in the Anderson shelter was a predictable squeeze. How they'd do it if it was ever all four of them...

Mrs Kesgrave was setting out a board game on an upturned milk crate. 'It's called Monopoly,' she said, 'and we go round buying up bits of London. Such fun.'

As the deep-throated guns were now firing from all sides, the ground shivering, Grace couldn't decide if the game was an ingenious diversion or depressing. Jess, poor, scared rabbit, was obviously struggling to follow the instructions as Mrs Kesgrave read them out by torchlight.

This child-woman, Cormac's bedfellow. How had that happened? The odd thing was, Jess hadn't recognised Grace yet. Perhaps she'd been too frightened the first time to absorb any detail. Grace wasn't going to say anything. With a bit of luck, it had been a one-off encounter and Jess had since come to her senses.

Innocent as Jess seemed, she carried the marks of the accident that had hospitalised her. Drunk, apparently, at Charing Cross station at seven in the evening. Observing the nervous, close-handed way Jess shook the dice, getting the story out of her would be like cracking a walnut with your teeth.

Grace's thoughts edged back to Farm Street. She burned to know what had happened after Owen called on Betony, only for Admirer No. 2 to walk in on them.

She's got a flaming nerve, though, Grace seethed. *Two men, both knock-out handsome, and me with nobody. Playing Monopoly in a blasted Anderson shelter.*

Still, it had its upside. At least she wasn't in the cellar in Upper Brook Street, with Lady Ventnor wailing, 'Where's Owen, where's my boy?'

As they shook the dice in turn and moved their different-coloured buttons, Mrs Kesgrave chatted away about her life as an actress during the 1920s and early '30s. 'My shining moment came as understudy to Irene Eddrich, as Titania. Irene was a peerless performer with but one fault.'

'What was that?' Jess sounded almost mesmerised, as if she'd never met anyone like Gloria Kesgrave. Chances were, she hadn't.

'Robust health. Irene didn't miss a performance and I never got to go on. Ah, but to watch from the wings. To see Patrick Carnforth as Oberon in tights was to witness the divine. I married soon after that run and Mr Kesgrave demanded I give up my career.'

'Where is Mr Kesgrave?' Grace expected a tale of widowhood.

'Up a gum tree with a sharp stick up his backside, I hope,' barked Mrs Kesgrave. 'He was a tyrant and refused me a divorce. After months of misery, I took matters into my own hands and tumbled into the arms of another man. We were found out.'

Jess gasped, 'How dreadful for you.'

'Not in the least, my pet. It was all cleverly staged. I got my divorce.'

Grace said, 'If I marry, I want to be glad I did so every day of my life. You don't mind being a...' Even saying the word was difficult. 'Divorced woman?'

'At the time, it was most unpleasant,' Mrs Kesgrave acknowledged. 'My former husband named me the guilty party, the utter-going rotter.'

'Well, I suppose you were,' Grace ventured.

'A gentleman would take the rap, whatever the facts.'

'You didn't fancy marrying the fellow you got found out with?' Their landlady was still 'Mrs Kesgrave', so Grace presumed the answer was no.

'One marriage is sufficient. I am free and single, as are you, dear Grace and Jess.'

Grace flicked Jess a sly glance. Jess looked more sad than self-conscious.

Mrs Kesgrave saw it too. 'I do hope I haven't shocked you, dear one.'

'A little,' Jess admitted. 'My father's a vicar. Obviously, he likes marriage to be permanent.'

'And I'm Roman Catholic,' said Grace. 'And that's like tea stains on white cotton. It never comes out. Why do you keep "Kesgrave"?' Grace reckoned, if she'd been named in court as an adulteress, she'd have given herself a new identity.

Impossible, Mrs Kesgrave explained. 'My former husband is guarantor of this house. It's rented from the Grosvenor estate, and they won't let a divorcee put her name to a contract. I pay all the bills, but *his* name is on the legal papers.'

'Does he mind?'

The answer was simplicity itself. 'He doesn't know. While I pay the rent on time, nobody asks questions.'

'Now I know why you were so keen to get three of us in the room,' Grace said. Maybe everyone fiddled the facts these days. Cormac's identity card carried the wrong address. What about herself, swanning around as Nurse Wheeler?

Her thoughts tracked back to Farm Street and Owen. Was he sitting out the raid with Betony? If so, Lady Ventnor would be beside herself, and it would be Grace picking up the pieces tomorrow.

She wished she hadn't let Owen think her name was Wheeler. If he rumbled her, he'd despise her for lying. There was nothing wrong in being Irish or living in the East End. God love them, if any populations were to be celebrated, it was the Irish surviving everything thrown their way, and the East Enders being hammered by the Luftwaffe. Maybe she should just own up.

She took a deep breath, and dived in. 'Wheeler isn't my real name.'

'I wondered when you'd mention it,' Mrs Kesgrave said placidly. 'I feared the name in your ration book must be a misspelling.'

'I'm Grace Whelan. I was born in the West of Ireland.'

'I realised that the moment you first spoke. You emigrated during your childhood, I apprehend?'

'We got on the boat when I was five. You guessed at once?'

'Instantly. Don't be downhearted. I have perfect pitch and at RADA, where I studied, we spent a whole term perfecting "Round the Rugged Rock, the Ragged Rascal"—'

A prolonged detonation made the shelter vibrate.

'That feels close,' Grace muttered.

Jess curled like a dormouse, visibly shaking.

Mrs Kesgrave suspected it was further away than it sounded. 'The docks again. The fires there will be burning from the daytime bombing, so they'll know where to open their hatches, the fiends.' She was fretting about her hens. 'Did I mention, Jess helped me stretch tarpaper over the top of their coop to create a cave effect, so at least they're spared the searchlights and the flares.'

Nothing would save the creatures from a direct hit, Grace thought. But then, they'd all be gone anyway.

The loudest detonation she'd ever heard in her life had her shining her torch at the shelter's rear escape hatch, checking there were no obstructions. Right this moment, people were dying and some might not be so lucky, surviving the impact only to have a crushing weight descend on them, and be forced to listen to the fires raging above.

Lost in the dark. Can't move.

Grace exhaled a silent prayer.

Please let Mam, Immie, Ricky and the little ones have got themselves to shelter. Let them be safe.

34

———

BETONY

Betony cleared specks from the surface of her glass. It was the dead of night and there were five of them in the Farm Street cellar. Only in wartime and under attack could this group have formed. Sybil March, Colin Ambrose. Winter Macpherson of the Canadian High Commission and Flight Lieutenant Henderson. Oh, and herself, of course.

The crump of a massive bomb striking its target made everyone sit up. Winter looked her way, giving her time to flash an awkward smile before detaching his gaze. He'd seemed amused at first, finding himself sitting on an upturned tea chest in his evening clothes. Now, not so much.

It had been the worst moment of her life when he'd walked into the editorial suite and found her with Owen. Her hand had been on Owen's blue serge shoulder, her eyes half-closed in anticipation of a kiss.

Owen's arrival had been completely unexpected, but after recovering, Betony had dared to believe he intended to propose. Two of her friends had got engaged after knowing their fiancés less than a month. She longed to be able to show off a ring, to be kissed every night the way Owen had kissed her that memorable time, safe in the knowledge that he was hers and nobody could tear them asunder.

Except that Winter had managed to do just that.

They'd sprung apart as he appeared in the doorway. Owen, give him his due, hadn't stammered or made excuses and the men had shaken hands. Deadly civilised. In fact, Winter had come across so nonchalant, so, well, bloody amused, she could only conclude that he'd never been the least bit in love with her and had sought her out one last time as a way of proving it to her.

He had a table booked at the Connaught. Did she fancy joining him?

The sirens had gone off, sparing her the need to answer.

Another bomb fell nearer than was comfortable and the ack-ack guns coughed in reply. More plaster dust floated down, this time settling on the lined pad Betony had placed over her champagne. Sybil had done her best to transform the cellar into an emergency office-cum-entertainment space, with chairs, blankets and cushions. She'd built a desk from an old door and had the handyman buttress the ceiling with wooden posts. Hurricane lamps illuminated all but the deepest corners and though the air smelled of the coal that had been shoved to one side, one could breathe. There was a spirit kettle and ersatz coffee in an alcove. And a rack of Moët & Chandon.

Betony marvelled at her boss's ability to make a to-do list and work down it. Sybil had brought her typewriter and was rattling out copy as the world exploded around her. In a lull between detonations, she eyed Betony.

'Did I say, one of Rubenstock's girls brought over a day dress with a clever little belt and a *soufflé* of an evening gown. Yellow chiffon.'

'Sounds charming,' Betony said. More fairy dust spiralled down.

'Is the chiffon a Molyneux knock-off?' Ambrose shifted his chair to look at something Sybil had written.

'It is, but he'll never find out.'

'Course he'll find out, and he'll sue. Tell Rubenstock to send something else.'

Listening to them bickering, Betony felt a stab of envy. Sybil and Ambrose had been working together through these disturbed nights, him creeping home at dawn to snatch a few hours' rest, returning before the first raid of the day. Sybil hardly left the office at all, often sleeping on the floor by her desk. Betony couldn't help worrying that if things got worse, and money tighter, she'd be out of a job, whatever Sybil promised to the contrary. Which meant she'd be out on the street. Her monthly allowance would not be paid henceforth. A telegram from her mother had made that clear: 'Money stopped. Stop. Re-instate when BDS arrives Somerset. Stop. Reply with intention. Stop.'

BDS was Betony Dorothea Styles. Betony hadn't replied. What could she say, knowing her parents would only accept total capitulation?

It was so much more inviting to lean into a conversation going on between Owen and Winter. Owen was describing the flight that had ended badly for him. He'd been flying back towards Hornchurch after a sortie off the Belgian coast.

'It came over the radio that our base was being bombed, but I couldn't turn away. I hadn't enough fuel to make it as far as Northolt or Manston. Anyway, Manston was being bombed too. I had to tuck in between waves of Messerschmitts blowing craters out of the runway as I came in to land.'

'I guess you went into one of those craters, from the way your face is messed up,' Betony heard Winter say.

Not exactly. Owen described spotting red danger flags on the runway, swerving to avoid them. 'The plane flipped.'

'What – turned over?' Winter sounded impressed. 'You got out? Well, obviously.'

'I was *got* out. There's always ground crew around who'll run through the smoke. Flipping is a Spitfire hazard; they're nose-heavy, see.'

'Sure. I get it,' said Winter. 'I was in the RCAF – still am technically. Our lot's flying Hurricanes.'

Betony's ears pricked so hard, she felt them twitch: RCAF, Royal Canadian Air Force. Winter was trained to fly? He'd never said a word! Or was he making it up, so he didn't lose out to a real pilot?

'Your lads fly out of Digby in Lincolnshire, don't they?' Owen had been there briefly, he said, after he first got his wings. 'The crosswinds over the fields I will never forget. A hell of a thing on your first solo.'

'Damn right,' Winter agreed.

Either the man was a total charlatan, or he'd been hiding the most important thing about himself. Betony could hardly credit it. Had Winter Macpherson quit the Royal Canadian Air Force, thrown off his wings, for a job at his country's embassy? She was speechless. Choking with anger.

Everybody's got a story, she thought. *All except me. I work for a publication that tells the female population how to turn an old coat lining into a fetching hat. I don't even write about it, I just stand still with it on my head.*

To salvage some pride and show the men that their conversation wasn't passing, unhindered, through the air vents in her brain, she called across to Owen, 'What luck about the red flag, otherwise you'd have gone in the hole. Crater, I mean. Wouldn't that have been worse?'

'Probably,' Owen acknowledged. He didn't attempt to come over to her. 'Hit anything as you touch down, it can rip out your undercarriage.'

'Thank heavens for ground crew,' she said, matching his laconic tone.

'It was a WAAF from the control tower who saw me coming in and dashed out with the red flags.'

'What a girl,' cheered Winter.

Owen agreed, 'Under enemy fire too. She ought to get the George Cross.'

'That's it,' Sybil shouted, catching the tail end of this. 'Forget Molyneux. Next edition, we'll do a spread on military-style tailoring. "Quick march, button up your jackets for winter warmth, and celebrate our Royal Air Force heroines." Good idea?'

Ambrose was enthusiastic. 'My neighbour's niece is a WAAF, and pretty too. I could see if she's got any leave, and sketch her in uniform, making a salute or scanning the horizon...'

Terrified that the only job she was any good at was being snatched from her, Betony chipped in, 'Could we wangle an actual visit to a base. Hornchurch, say?' She smiled hopefully at Owen. 'I could meet the other boys.'

Owen answered quickly. 'It wouldn't work. Everyone's too on edge.'

'Wouldn't it raise morale?'

'No. It would be a distraction.'

That's me snubbed, Betony thought.

All-clear came around three a.m. and they made their way upstairs on stiff legs, and with nerves rubbed raw. Sybil made coffee and offered cigarettes. The least affected appeared to be Winter, who had carried Sybil's typewriter upstairs and now spread his coat out on the studio floor and went to sleep. Owen raised the window in Sybil's office and smoked while staring out at the night. With the blinds up, they couldn't put the lights on, but Betony didn't mind because it allowed her face to fall into a despondent mask.

Yesterday, she'd have confidently asserted that two men were in love with her. Now, she wasn't at all sure either of them was.

35

GRACE

Sunday 8 September

Coming down the stairs from Lady Ventnor's room intending to ask if she might use the house telephone, Grace heard subdued conversation behind the library door. Owen must have come back at some point as, on her arrival this morning, she'd seen his greatcoat draped over the stair post.

Using the ruse of tying a shoelace, she bent close to the door and heard Owen stating his intention to return to his base.

'I'm itchy, Uncle Gideon. I need to sign back in. The squadron's being pulled back to Catterick. I don't want to miss the move.'

'They're sending you up to North Yorkshire? You're not fit yet,' she heard Sir Gideon protest. 'Give it another twenty-four hours.'

Grace didn't catch Owen's reply, but after another exchange, she heard him say, 'I can't risk losing my nerve. Every day for months, I've slithered out of the cockpit thinking, "Survived another one. What about next time?" It's like backing ten horses in a row, and they all win. You can't help wondering on what day the luck will run out.'

He was speaking his fears out loud, as he had yesterday in the kitchen. Not of love this time, but describing a fatalism that scared her so much, it brought a physical pain to her heart.

'Everything goes so fast when you're chasing the enemy,' Owen was saying. 'The day I crash-landed, I downed a Junkers 88, saw it go into a dive and burst into flames, then over my left wing, two ME 109s were coming for me—'

He described the dogfight that had led him out over the sea, to the point he almost ran out of fuel and had to return to his base, despite it being under attack.

'You were lucky, m'boy,' his uncle growled gently. 'We're all lucky, those of us who care about you.'

'But how much longer? Sorry. Sorry.' Grace pictured Owen reaching out to his uncle. 'Don't mean to talk like a flying logbook. Thing is, I've got a projectionist in my brain, replaying the same frames over and over. That's why I need to go. Idleness makes it worse.'

Grace heard a chair scrape and stepped back – onto the polished leather foot of Buckland, who had approached stealthily with a silver tray bearing coffee pot and cups.

'Checking the door frame for draughts, Nurse Wheeler?'

'I need a word with Sir Gideon,' she improvised.

'Through the keyhole?'

'Cut the blarney, Mr Buckland.'

The library door opened, and Sir Gideon looked out and saw them.

'Ah, coffee time. Bring it in, Buckland. Nurse, something amiss upstairs?'

'No, Sir. Lady Ventnor is sleeping. I wondered if I might use your telephone, because last night's bombing scared—'

'The bejaysus?' Buckland inserted quietly.

'The living daylights out of me. I need to know my family is all right.'

'Mayfair hasn't been hit, far as I know,' Sir Gideon said as Buckland, pouring coffee, gave a snort. 'Of course you may make a call. Buckland, show Nurse Wheeler the more private telephone.'

'Certainly, Sir, only...' Buckland paused and Grace knew he was fermenting something. Since catching him out as a Dublin native, their mutual dislike had modified. They were now locked into a competition. Who could deliver the most subtle snub and get away with it. 'Wouldn't it be simpler for Nurse to nip home, since her family are virtually our neighbours. In Mayfair,' he added for emphasis.

Sir Gideon looked at Grace. 'Makes sense. We wouldn't mind.'

Buckland turned the screw. 'A mere five minutes.'

Grace had grown up thinking on her feet. 'I'd rather phone, because if I turn up on the doorstep, someone will think it's bad news.'

'Your family has a telephone?' inquired Buckland.

Course they didn't. If the Whelans needed to contact anybody urgently, they nipped to the Hearts of Oak, next door. Grace was intending to call the landlady and only if there was no answer would she fear the worst.

'Will you show Nurse Wheeler where ours is?' Sir Gideon prompted. Grace felt he wanted to finish his conversation with Owen and drink his coffee.

'Unfortunately, Sir, the house telephone is presently out of service.'

'How?'

'Mrs Shotley tried it this morning to call the butcher. No dial tone, she says.'

'You'd better use this one then.' Sir Gideon picked up the receiver of the library phone, frowned and said, 'Dead too. I suppose a line has come down.' He cast Grace an apologetic look. 'Looks like you'll have to nip home after all. We'll hold the fort with Lady Ventnor.'

Got you, said Buckland's smirk.

Grace didn't know how to handle this situation. One didn't 'nip' to Whitechapel after a night of heavy bombing. Buses got cancelled, roads closed, the tube trains diverted. She was ready to sink down and confess, 'All right, you've got me,' when Owen said, 'I'll take you.'

He gulped his coffee, reached into his pocket and took out a key on a leather fob. 'If you don't object to the back of a motorbike?'

She had never in her life sat on a motorcycle, but she nodded. 'If you're sure?'

'I want to get back to Hornchurch, so now's as good a time.' He extended his hand to his uncle, who gave it a hearty squeeze.

'You'd better put something warm on,' Owen told Grace. 'Got a coat?'

'I've got a cape.' She fetched it while Owen went to kick-start his bike. She removed her cap, or it would end up decorating a branch or a railing once they picked up speed. From the street came a gruff roar.

Owen had parked a short way up the street and was edging the Bullet to where she stood waiting. He was wearing a belted leather coat and had crammed a leather and sheepskin cap onto his head. He looked the part, but how would she retain her dignity, riding pillion in a nurse's tunic and black stockings? Trust bloody Buckland to come out with Sir Gideon to watch.

Pretend you do it every day.

Walking up to the bike, she hitched up her dress and swung a leg over the back wheel, placing her bottom on the bit of seat between Owen and the rack, which had a bag lashed to it over the mudguard. 'Oops, tight fit,' she said.

Owen looked over his shoulder. 'Hold round my waist and please, please relax. When I lean, lean the same way. When I start up, press right into me. Don't want you flying off the back.'

'Got it,' she muttered. 'Pressing close' was a given, since she hadn't the sylph-like dimensions of Betony, presumably the female shape he most appreciated.

The bike started moving, a smooth getaway which boosted her confidence. She even managed to give Sir Gideon and Buckland a cheery goodbye wave.

Owen stopped at the junction with Grosvenor Square and turned off the engine.

'So, where to?'

She sucked in a breath. 'Dock Street.'

'Dock Street, Mayfair?' He was craning over his shoulder, which meant he couldn't look her right in the eye. But she read the tone of his voice. Like Buckland, he had rumbled her.

'Dock Street, Whitechapel.' For the first time within the precincts of Mayfair, Grace let her real voice ring out. 'Head east to where the sun rises each morning.'

She was tired of pretending. It was stupid, being anybody other than yourself when any time, day or night, you could die.

36

Her face mashed into Owen's shoulder, and the pungent smell of leather in her nose, Grace couldn't decipher the route they were taking. Only when Old Street underground station flashed past did she realise that he was making for Bethnal Green. So, he had been listening.

They were stopped at Shoreditch by ARP wardens, who directed them down towards the river, saying they could link up there with Whitechapel High Street. A brazier glow over the docks had turned the sky to the colour of violet creams.

They passed the Royal London Hospital, where she counted six ambulances in the road, others nosing past to get in. That meant casualties, lots. One of the ARP wardens had muttered that yesterday and last night had been the worst of the war. Hundreds dead.

Grace had to resist the urge to tap Owen on the shoulder and make him stop, so she could run into the hospital and offer her services. Only the certainty that she'd be sent packing deterred her. Wait, though – if they'd passed the hospital, they'd gone too far. She poked him until he pulled up.

'We need to turn around,' she told him. 'Back towards Aldgate East.'

'Sure?' Owen brushed away a strand of her hair that blew against his face. The netting holding her bun had come adrift.

'I know this area,' she assured him. 'I trained here.'

For the last few miles, she'd seen no damaged buildings, no burning piles of rubble, but she could not feel easy. The sensation she'd had walking home yesterday, and again in the Anderson shelter, of being trapped in the dark, kept sliding over her. She forced herself to breathe slowly. Seeing a sign for Leman Street, she prodded Owen's shoulder and made jabbing motions to catch his eye. 'That way. Left. Nearly there.'

Leman Street merged with Dock Street and seeing the familiar facades, the church and the gables of the seaman's mission, drab as ever but intact, she tapped Owen in the middle of the back.

He drew up and turned off his engine. Grace eased herself off the seat, staggering as she put both feet to the ground. Her backside was numb. Propping the Bullet on its stand, Owen got off too and drew off his gauntlets and leather cap. He glanced at the building next to the pub and asked, 'Home sweet home?'

She returned his look. 'It is. I'm not a child of Mayfair, in case you hadn't guessed. I was putting on airs.'

'Then what are you?' He sounded genuinely curious.

'Irish. And an East Londoner. Proud to be both.'

'It must be a relief to drop the act.' Owen raked his hair off his forehead and caressed a wayward strand of hers. He seemed fascinated by its golden-red colour against the undersides of his fingers. The brown eyes had a troubled expression and a fear she'd had, that he'd been driving through the streets in a mesmerised state, felt valid. The way he was looking at her... it didn't bode well, so she got in first.

'Your aunt loathes the Irish, I was warned, but I needed the job, so I pretended to be lah-di-dah Miss Wheeler, when, actually, I'm Grace Whelan from right here.' She pointed up to the third-floor flat with its drooping blackout curtains. Grace couldn't help thinking they resembled an old widow's cast-off drawers. When Owen failed to answer, she filled in again. 'You must despise me as I do myself, though for different reasons.'

'Why should I despise you?' He snapped out of whatever thinking he'd fallen into, tucked the lock of her hair behind her ear. 'We all pretend.'

'I don't think you do. What you do every day can't be faked. It defies the blarney.'

That brought a dry chuckle. 'You should be a fly on the wall in the officers' mess at Hornchurch, us commissioned grammar school boys talking as if we're all on a jolly day out, playing at war. The ones who don't come back have "bought it". Nobody dies. The names are rubbed off the board for the next sortie. Nobody mentions it.'

'You make me feel so petty, pretending to be what I'm not.'

'Who wouldn't? Aunt Maude is a snob, but she's nothing to Buckland. Have you rumbled him?'

'I, er, might have.'

'Have you noticed that though he calls me "sir", he leaves an infinitesimal pause, so I know he's making the effort. In his eyes, as well as my aunt's, my mother lets the side down.'

'You love her though, your mam?' It was so important to Grace that he did.

'I adore her. Prim's the best, but didn't I tell you, she's scared. Terrified I'll die and I can't afford to soak up her doubts on top of mine. I know every time I fail to visit I'm putting the knife in, but...' He tailed off.

'You have to survive. I understand. I left home too. It's why I'm here, why I'll have to keep running back to make sure my family is all right because I couldn't live with myself if anything happened to them. They are God's most irritating creations, but I...' Grace tucked her hair into her collar, as her voice wobbled.

'You love them.'

'So very much. Ah, God, look at me.' Her tunic skirt, creased from being hitched up, made her think of a music hall concertina. She didn't want to know what her hair resembled. Betony would probably step off a bike with not a tress out of place. She, Grace, leaned towards chaos, Betony towards perfection. Yet, Owen Henderson was looking at her as if he found something to like.

'Sorry I accused you of being after your aunt's money the other day,' she said.

He shrugged, implying he'd already forgotten. 'The first thing we trainee pilots do, after getting our wings, is write our wills. All I have worth passing on is this bike. I don't know who to leave it to, but I'm glad it's all I have. I'd have hated choosing who to make rich when I'm dead.'

She told him not to talk like that. 'You said yourself, we have to believe we'll get through, don't we? With a bit of luck on our side, so we will.'

'I like you better as an East Ender. Mayfair girls always sound as though they're sucking oysters out of a half-closed shell.'

'Your friend Betony doesn't sound like that. She's nicely spoken, a bit superior, but then, she's the true article.'

'She ought to be,' he said. 'Lord and Lady Styles' daughter.'

Grace wondered if it impressed him the way it did Lady Ventnor and Buckland. 'Should I be calling her "Lady Betony"?'

'No. She's the Honourable Betony Styles, but that's a courtesy title, and never used except on very formal occasions.' Owen looked bothered suddenly and asked her exactly how well she knew Betony.

'Not very well at all. I mean, I lodge with her in a rented

room, her bed so close I could throw a stocking and it might land on her pillow. Not that I would,' she added hastily. Betony would pick it up with a crooked finger and tell her it had a hole in the toe. 'You don't need to worry that we talk. We're not on those terms and her business is her business.' Gesturing at the blacked-out window behind which her family were still, presumably, slumbering, she said, 'This was my home for nearly fifteen years. It's not that Betony and I aren't out of the same drawer – we're not out of the same piece of furniture.'

Owen stepped back, and she thought – *I've offended him, talking like that about his girlfriend.* In a bid to salvage something, she asked if he'd like her to give Betony a message. 'Anything you want me to pass on?'

He ran a hand through his hair which the helmet had flattened. He must have spent the night in a cellar, or a shelter, as she had. Certainly, he hadn't shaved and his beard formed a clear shadow, shades darker than his hair. Though not black like Ricky's or Cormac's, who, if they hadn't seen a razor by midday, looked as though they'd stumbled out of a coal mine.

Why was she holding her breath? Because she'd offered herself up as the messenger between two sweethearts, which was a form of self-torture.

'There's nothing I want you to say to Betony,' Owen said slowly. 'But there's something I want to say to you.'

He was going to tell her it was time to confess her charade to his aunt Maude. Or apologise, or both. 'Say it.'

He dipped his head and kissed her on the mouth. Grace gave a smothered gasp, but rather than push him away, or stiffening in shock, she rose up on her toes so as not to break his hold, or his concentration. Whatever this kiss meant to him, to her it was a beautiful thing. It was hope coming to life in broad daylight and she didn't want it to stop.

But stop it did, as a pair of sailors coming out of the Mission building offered them the use of their beds for a couple of shillings.

'I have to go,' Owen whispered. He touched her cheek, below the last fading mark of her black eye. 'Can I see you again?'

She nodded. 'But what about Betony? I thought—'

'Sh,' he said. 'That's for me to worry over, not you. I'll phone you at my uncle's.'

37

Grace found Mam, Ricky and Immie in the living room, Granny Driscoll with them. All in one piece. Though her head was reeling, her mind all colours of candyfloss, a quiet alarm rang inside her. Something was off.

Immie's two older boys were on all fours, pushing tin trucks around on the carpet, but with no sound effects, as if they'd been warned to say not a word. Little Liam was asleep on his mother's lap.

It was Granny who said, 'Grace dear, isn't it a treat you look in your uniform. All in your lipstick and your hair... well, you always have lovely hair. Does my heart good.'

Grace asked falteringly, 'Who's died?' Not Cormac, her mother would be hysterical if it were.

'Have you not heard?' Granny's voice, always husky, seemed to claw out of her throat. 'A bomb fell on the Columbia Road, right on the market.'

'No.' Columbia Road was where they always shopped. A sprawling, Gothic building in Bethnal Green, it housed families, shops and storehouses, as well as the huge, covered market. Grace remembered the massive explosion last night that had made Mrs Kesgrave's Anderson shelter shiver. 'People wouldn't be shopping so late,' she said. Had the housing block been hit?

'It was the shelter under the market that took the blast,' Granny explained. 'Hundreds inside.'

Ricky took up the story. 'A bomb fell through a ventilation shaft, Grace, and went off where all the people were sleeping.'

Grace shut her eyes. That explained the congestion at the Royal London. If she'd finished her training there, she'd have been on one of the wards, helping the injured: people she had seen week-on-week for as long as she could remember. 'How many?' she asked.

'Dead?' Granny mouthed because the little boys were staring. She shook her head. 'I was saying to your mam and Immie, I shan't know whether to run down to our shelter now when there's a raid or hide under the dinner table.'

'The shelter,' Grace said firmly. 'They're designed to withstand blast, and even the Germans will know that the Peabody estate is just homes, no industry, no shipping.'

'That hasn't stopped them flattening dozens of houses so far.' Immie spoke for the first time since Grace had walked in. She looked strained, and Grace wondered if she was regretting her return to the city. 'If a plane's shot down, it comes down anywhere. If the plane that crashed on the street next to my house had come down ten seconds sooner, you'd be strewing flowers on the ground for us. I've told Granny she should stay put and get under the table.'

Taking a breath, Grace spoke slowly. 'If a bomb comes through the roof of one of the Peabody blocks, anyone inside will be buried under floors of rubble.'

Immie copied her look. 'Last night, we trooped to the Tilbury shelter on Commercial Road. It's horrible, it stinks and it's brought Liam's bad chest back.' She dropped a kiss on her son's downy cheek. 'Me and my boys will take our chances in the Morrison, in the kitchen. You know what they say – if a bomb has your name on it, it's your turn anyway.'

Nights without sleep, and sandpapered emotions, triggered the Whelan family temper. Grace yelled, 'God love us, Immie, d'you think the Germans wrote the names on a bomb of all the people who died last night? Don't be an idiot. They just drop the bloody damn things and fly away, hoping to get home. So they can load up and drop more. Take your boys to the shelter and rub some Vicks on Liam's chest.'

Bristling, Immie asked her where she'd spent last night.

'In the back garden where I'm living, in my landlady's Anderson.'

'How very nice for you,' Immie trilled. 'We don't have back gardens round here, do we? What if half a ton of high explosive had landed smack on top of you?'

'I wouldn't be here talking to you.' Grace went to her sister and crouched down. Her lips still felt raw and swollen from Owen's kiss. None of them had seen it happen. None of the neighbours. Only those sailors, who, by the looks of their bulging kitbags, were on their way to rejoin a ship. Cormac must not discover this fledgling love. Dear God, no. 'I don't want bad things to happen to you.'

'No. Well. Likewise.'

A truce.

'Any chance of a cup of Rosie Lee?' Grace asked.

Apparently not. The water was cut off, because so much had been used to douse the flames on the Columbia Road. Tea was off. But gin, it seemed, was not. When Grace went to kiss her mother goodbye, anxious to start the bus journey back to Upper Brook Street, she got a fine whiff of it. It seemed to Grace that, once they'd got over the surprise of her arrival, her family forgot she was there. Only Ricky came down to the street with her when it was time to leave.

'You will be all right, Grace, won't you?' he said as they hugged.

'I'll do my best.' She asked him if he'd seen Cormac lately and Ricky said no, not since the police had chased him out of the flat.

'I think he likes it better with his lady-friends, Grace.'

As she walked up Dock Street, she thought of Jess, though it wasn't long before the destruction on Columbia Road caught up with her again and images of bodies on stretchers filled her mind. Thousands of children and other vulnerable people had been evacuated to the countryside in the summer of '39 and not only for their safety, Grace reflected. They'd left so others, like herself, could get on and do essential jobs without the crippling worry of knowing loved ones were in danger.

After he'd finished kissing her, Owen had said into her hair, 'They'll keep coming. A thousand every night and so few of us. We can't get them all. We can hardly make a dent. I cannot see the end. I just know, one way or another, it'll come.'

Even knowing that, he'd got back on his bike, headed back towards danger. *What am I doing?* she asked herself as she joined a morose queue waiting for the Liverpool Street bus. Tiptoeing around Maude Ventnor, bathing bedsores, when hundreds lay injured in London's hospitals.

Something had to give.

38

In Upper Brook Street, Grace interrupted Lady Ventnor writing a letter. From her bed, Her Ladyship glanced at Grace and said, 'You're back, then.'

'I am.' *And how kind of you, to ask how my family are.* 'Can I get you anything?'

'I'm writing a reply to that woman, and when I'm done, you can take it to the post box.'

'That woman' being Owen's mother, no doubt. Grace felt a creeping anger. Today, Owen had revealed intensely private feelings about his love for his mother, which felt at times too heavy to bear. Emotions Lady Ventnor was too full of prejudice to grasp.

Grace went to the medicine table and, for a second, was tempted to sweep the bottles to the floor. The sight of Lady Ventnor scribbling spiteful lines to a woman whose son was in hourly danger made her want to scream, 'Do you have nothing to spare for anybody but yourself?'

'What's biting you, Nurse? Or did a ride on a motorbike shake your brains loose.'

It wasn't much of an insult, compared with the many she'd

put up with, but it cut the fine wires holding Grace's temper down. She said harshly, 'Are you aware that our fighter pilots fly up to six sorties a day?'

'It's what they're trained to do.' Lady Ventnor, writing again, did not look up.

'Really?' Grace knew a bit about the Spitfire squadrons, thanks to Ricky's obsessions and his enthusiasm for repeating what he knew. 'Some fly their first missions after a few hours' training and they're the ones most likely to be killed.'

Lady Ventnor looked up from her page, pen suspended. 'What are you saying?'

'On their first tour of duty, before their reactions are honed. The other lethal point in a fighter pilot's career is at the end of a tour, when they scent freedom or they're numb from exhaustion. What I'm saying, Lady Ventnor, is that maybe your nephew needs to say how he feels and be listened to. And maybe his mother is the best person for that job.'

'Are you suggesting my nephew is asking to be let off from his duty?' The frigid question matched the look of loathing Lady Ventnor sent Grace.

'No. Just to be heard.' Grace turned away and found some bottles to rearrange. How much longer could she stand this woman? It was only eight days into the month; she couldn't afford to throw in the towel yet again. Earlier, she'd given Ricky all the money in her purse, in case Mam was seriously on the gin, and they were going short. 'I won't post your letter. Take it yourself.'

She strode downstairs with no particular idea of what she intended to do, except that the pin-sharp memory of stretchers being offloaded at the Royal, and Owen's comment that he'd left hospital early because 'they need the beds for the chaps that are really hurt' was knocking hard at her conscience. He'd meant the ones who came down in burning planes, or were dragged out of crumpled wreckage, their lives in ruins. She was treading water in Upper Brook Street, wasting her training, and one day Owen would look at her and say, 'Why didn't you do better?'

Or, if he didn't, she would look in the mirror and say the same thing.

The time had come to act, to face the shame that had crippled her so long. Slipping into the library, which was empty, she found a sheet of paper. Filling Sir Gideon's pen with ink, she wrote her Hill Street address at the top of the page and put the date, 8 September 1940, then:

To the matron of The Royal London.

Dear Miss Littlejohn, my name is Grace Philomena Whelan and I do not suppose you remember, but I was a trainee nurse at your hospital. I was unable to sit my exam and left before I completed my training, but now, with so much suffering in the East End, I would like to come back.

Would Miss Littlejohn remember their last interview?

Grace lifted the pen and a glob of ink fell on the middle part of her name which, she felt, was appropriate. She had blotted her copybook relentlessly as a probationer and had left in what was generally known as 'a bad odour'. They wouldn't want her back.

She screwed the letter up and threw it into the library fireplace.

39

BETONY

An entire weekend without a date, telephone call or a letter was a novelty and not one Betony appreciated.

Not even a meal out, all her women-friends having either left London or busy nestling up to fiancés or new husbands. She could not believe she had spent a Sunday helping her landlady and drab little Jess varnish a chicken coop.

She'd got varnish on her hands too, which Ambrose had found hilarious. She had also discovered that chicken feathers made her sneeze violently.

If that weren't enough, Mrs Kesgrave had patiently explained that Jess must keep the bed she was sleeping in – Betony's bed – as she'd suffered badly and needed as much solitude as could be managed. She had cut off Betony's counterargument by reminding her that it was her turn to cook.

'Or had you forgotten our rota, dear one?'

Betony hadn't forgotten as she'd not yet looked at it. The certainty that Winter had washed his hands of her made everything feel utterly bleak. He'd handled their parting without a flicker of jealousy. Well, she hadn't expected him to challenge

Owen to a duel, but a dash of hot-blooded fury would have made her feel a little better about herself.

Not once since that toe-curling episode in the cellar at *Practical Modes* had Owen left her head. She was almost grinding her teeth, wondering when he'd call. Or had she wrecked things there, too? She'd made sure he knew where she lived. And she knew he'd returned to Hornchurch because she'd called his uncle's home and the butler had told her so. There was nothing to stop Owen phoning *Practical Modes* and leaving a message with Sybil if necessary. Or calling his uncle's and passing on a message for Grace to bring back with her.

Nothing but silence. Desperation to know if his feelings had changed had driven her into the office, even though it was Sunday. There, she found Sybil working away and begged to be allowed to use the phone. If the man would not call her, she must call the man.

Sybil sighed, 'All right, but no more than a minute.'

'Two, please? Take the cost out of my pay.'

'At this rate, you'll be paying me to work here.'

In the telephone niche, Betony asked to be put through to RAF Hornchurch. The number rang.

A switchboard operator – another saintly WAAF, no doubt – answered. 'Who is calling?'

'This is Miss Styles.' Betony projected her words through a smile as she'd read that it made the person on the other end warm to you. 'Any chance I could speak with Flight Lieutenant Henderson?'

The answering silence made her wonder if there was more than one Henderson on the base.

'That's Flight Lieutenant Owen Henderson, 54 Squadron.'

'I know what squadron he's in, Miss.'

Officious replies like that brought out the worst in Betony. 'So, can I speak to him?'

'I rather doubt it. He's on medical leave and not to be disturbed. His squadron has been deployed up north, and he'll join them when he's cleared by the medics. Until then, his orders are rest and quiet.'

'I see.'

'What message would you like me to pass on. *If* it's important enough to interrupt his convalescence?'

Betony found every excuse possible to stay in Sybil's office, even offering to proofread copy and tidy the files. Just so she'd be on hand should Owen receive her message and phone back. By early evening, she was close to tears. He'd seemed on the road to recovery last time they met. She simply didn't believe his idea of rest and recuperation would be to curl up in bed. What was the name of the pub he frequented, next to his airbase? He'd told her the first time they met. The Good Gracious? The Good Lord? *Think, Betony.*

Seizing a moment when Sybil was downstairs, Betony picked up the phone and asked the operator to put her through to the Good Intent at Hornchurch.

She was answered after about twenty rings, by a man who, from his breezy tone, had begun drinking the moment the doors opened. She asked if Owen was there. 'Owen Henderson, Flight—'

'Hang on, love, I'll go see.'

She got the impression the phone was left hanging as she heard bumps and clicks, snatches of conversation and laughter.

After a minute or so, the breezy chap was back. 'Who is it calling?'

'It's Betony, Betony Styles.'

'Betty?'

'No – Betony.' She enunciated it in three syllables.

'All right, I'll go ask.'

Why did he come back to check her name? she wondered in growing panic. How many women called, asking for Owen?

A short while later, the same man returned.

'No, sorry, darling, not in tonight.'

'Is he all right?'

'Owen? He's fine. Bye.'

The phone went dead and Betony's heart swelled with outrage and dismay. Hard not to suppose Owen had been there all along, and the chap had shouted, 'There's a Betony on the line. Want to talk to her?' and got a headshake or a mouthed, 'God, no' in response.

Sybil came back upstairs and caught her dabbing her eyes. 'Go home. Didn't you say you were cooking tonight?'

Humiliation did not improve her kitchen skills, Betony discovered, and she had the added mortification of seeing her housemates pick miserably at the fish in parsley sauce she dished up. The fish was chewy, and the sauce, which she'd burned, was full of black bits. It was a measure of how awful her meal was that she saw relief on everyone's face when the sirens went, giving them a reason to leave the table.

That night's attack went on until three a.m.

The morning post brought nothing with a Hornchurch postmark. *I can't let it rest*, she repeated to herself. *I can't let Owen think I don't care, or that I'm seeing another man. I have to explain about Winter. But how, if he won't speak to me?*

Her eye fell on some knitting Jess had taken up. The pattern was for a cardigan, and when she'd first seen it, Betony had thought, *That's too dowdy even for someone's dear old mum.* It was the inspiration Betony needed. Not bothering to tidy her hair, she sprinted to Upper Brook Street, catching up with

Grace on the doorstep. Uniformed, bag in hand, Grace was about to take over from the night nurse.

'You have to help me,' Betony gasped. 'You have to help me get through to Owen's mother.'

40
___

Betony hadn't taken to Grace on first meeting. Or, frankly, on the second or third. Not only was Grace palpably not her type, that copper-gold hair, peach complexion and blue-blue eyes were just unfair. One person should not possess the whole colour palette, while she, Betony, applied make-up twice a day so as not to appear insipid. Another unsettling ingredient to Grace was the way she stood her ground, making you feel ever so slightly as if you'd been ushered into a boxing ring.

The greatest obstacle to liking her, however – and Betony knew this was unworthy and contemptible – was her profession.

People loved nurses. Nurses brought babies into the world, sewed up wounds and mended limbs. Simply by getting up in the morning and putting on a starched wimple and a blameless white apron, they earned their place in the world. Nobody called a nurse 'frivolous' or a 'pointless clothes horse' or described her wages as 'pin money'.

So, as she stood in Sir Gideon and Lady Ventnor's front hall, looking at Grace as Grace looked back at her, Betony experienced a fresh wave of antagonism.

To her surprise, Grace said, 'Why don't I fetch Buckland. He'll help.'

Betony followed Grace to the library and watched her pull a bell rope, then eyed the telephone on a side table as though it were a succulent cake.

'It wasn't working the other day,' Grace said, seeing the direction of her gaze. 'It should be mended by now, as Sir Gideon does war work. You said you needed to speak with Owen... I mean, Flight Lieutenant Henderson's mother?'

'My last resort. I can't get him; I've been trying.'

Betony saw shock cross Grace's face, and when Grace asked, 'You haven't heard anything bad, have you?' realised her words had been misconstrued.

Betony replied that she hadn't heard anything at all. 'That's the thing. We're an item, you see.' She put a finger to her lips, and whispered, 'In love.'

Fresh emotion darted across Grace's features. Puzzling, because, surely, she cared nothing about Betony's love life. Though, come to think of it, Grace read *Peg's Paper*, so perhaps romance was all she did think about. 'I just need a way of getting through to him. I thought his mother—'

The butler came in, looking put out when he realised Grace had summoned him. Though he straightened up when he saw Betony. 'Miss.'

It was Grace who explained that Betony needed a telephone number.

The butler clearly felt the need to repeat the information in different words. 'You wish to call Mrs Henderson at home? It is rather early.'

'If you don't mind.' Betony found her smile again. 'It's important.'

Buckland located a telephone address book and turned to the letter H. 'Mrs John Henderson. You'll find the number under her address. Sir Gideon has left for the morning, but would you like me to take a message up to Her Ladyship?'

'No thank you.'

'Very well, Miss.'

Having given Buckland the smile that dismissed him, she offered the same one to Grace, who ignored it, saying, 'Jess is cooking tonight. You didn't clean your saucepan yesterday, Betony.'

'Didn't I?' Who cared. Life and death, and Grace was wittering on about pans.

'You know perfectly well you didn't and it's burned black. I daresay Jess will do it, but you'll owe her a favour.'

'Received and understood. May I make my call, please?'

Grace still didn't leave, and Betony spread her hands, implying, *Well?*

'You and Owen are together, is that right?'

'That's what I said.'

'And you're serious about him... you won't drop him for someone else? That American, for instance.'

'American? Oh, you mean Winter. He's Canadian. And he's out of the running. We were only ever, you know...'

When Grace still didn't go, just stood looking anguished, Betony described the moment she had realised Owen was the one for her.

'We were in the Café de Paris, and the lights failed. You could feel electricity run across the dance floor. He kissed me as though he never wanted it to stop, as though he couldn't bear to let me go. A man only does that when he's in love. A moment like that doesn't lie.'

'I suppose not.' With a curt nod, Grace went.

Finally alone, Betony lifted the receiver and requested an Ealing, West London, number.

The call was answered after a few rings by a woman who sounded like a nanny Betony had once had. A Welsh woman, one of the nicer staff members employed to manage her. 'Could I please speak with Mrs Henderson. Is she in?'

'Who is this?'

Betony gave her name.

'I'm sorry, did you say Bethany?'

'No. Betony. Betony Styles. I need to speak with Owen's mother, if that's no trouble.'

'What is it about, please?'

For heaven's sake. All right, humour her. 'It's about Owen.'

Betony heard a little intake of breath from the other end.

'What about Owen?'

'I'm worried about him as I haven't heard from him. I know he's been hurt and was grounded, and is desperately tired, but he's back at his base and I need to talk to him.'

Silence followed.

'Hello, are you still there?'

'I know exactly how tired he is. Do you wish to speak to him, or his mother?'

'Him, but he's being rather elusive. His mother might know a bit more.'

'I wouldn't bank on it.'

Honestly, whoever this was, maid or housekeeper, she was either stupid or being deliberately obtuse.

'What do you want me to do, Miss Styles?'

This was going nowhere. 'Say Betony called and, well, that I called. Will you remember?'

'I think I can remember that, dear, yes.'

'May I know who I'm speaking with?' When next they met, she'd tell Owen that his mother's Mrs Mop needed to brush up her telephone manner.

'This is Primrose Henderson, Owen's mother.'

'Oh God! I'm so sorry. I don't know why, but I didn't imagine you were...'

'What, my dear?'

'Welsh.' She'd pictured Mrs Henderson entirely differently. Smiley, motherly, pearl necklace, one hundred per cent English. 'I feel terrible—' Betony's apology was wasted as the other party disconnected. Replacing the receiver, she became aware of Buckland in the doorway.

'Fourpence in the box for swearing, Miss Styles.'

'I didn't swear.'

'You did inside. May I check you've disconnected and placed the receiver down properly?'

'Go ahead. I don't care about anything anymore,' Betony said slowly, 'I've just mortally offended the woman I intend to be my future mother-in-law.'

'Oh dear. Nurse Wheeler is still downstairs. You can tell her all about it.'

41

GRACE

Grace saw Betony come out and took a couple of steps towards her, trying to get out the words she'd been rehearsing during the last few minutes. All that came out was, 'You need to listen. There's something I have to tell you.'

She could see Betony was in a state. The conversation with Owen's mother could not have gone as she hoped. The two of them met in the middle of the hall, and for a moment, they stared at each other, each in the grip of emotions neither could explain.

Grace thought, *I can't go home tonight and share a room with this woman. Can't lie in a bed next to her, eaten with jealousy, imagining that kiss that changed her life, and not say anything.* Only one of them could have Owen, and if Betony was his choice, Grace wanted to know. Now. If you were being shot down, better be killed outright than endure a drawn-out, smoking plummet to the ground.

'You need to know what happened yesterday,' she said. 'It was in East London – where I come from. I come from East London.'

'So what?' Betony was looking nervous, weighing up her escape route. 'What did happen yesterday?'

'Outside my house, I—' Grace heard a key in the front door. It opened and Sir Gideon came in with an air of urgency. Seeing Grace, he stopped.

'Ah, Nurse Wheeler, you're here. Thank goodness.' He came up to her. 'There's no easy way of saying this; I'm afraid I have to communicate something rather dreadful.'

There was no time to ask what, only a second in which to feel the floor bend under her feet and the shadowy dread that had stalked her for days harden into absolute fear.

Somebody was hammering violently at the door, and between bursts of knocking was shouting, 'Mary, Mother of Jesus, will you let me in to find my sister?'

Buckland strode by to open up, and Immie bludgeoned past him, a toddler in her arms and two small boys clinging to her skirt. Her cardigan was filthy and her hair hung in coils. Not spun gold this morning, but grey, as was her face. Tear trails had burned through the dirt, leaving streaks of clean skin on her cheeks.

Grace ran to her. 'Immie, what's happened?'

'The Peabody. In the early hours... A bomb, dozens dead.' Immie's voice echoed off the cream-white walls of the Ventnors' hall.

'Which flats?' Grace could hardly breathe.

'K Block.'

Where Granny Driscoll lived. 'Tell me she's safe!'

Immie hitched Liam higher into her arms. 'No. Buried. And Mam is under there too.'

It was a hatchet blow, but Grace could still think rationally. 'Why was Mam in Granny Driscoll's flat?'

'And Ricky,' Immie said.

'No. No.' Grace took hold of her sister, needing to hear

Immie say it was all a mistake. 'Immie, why were they inside the flat and not in the shelter?'

'They were in the shelter.' Immie's face tightened, her lips parting in an inhuman snarl. 'It's your fault, all your fault, Grace.'

Her cry echoed up the stairs and they could hear Nurse Gill coming out, on her way off-shift, wanting to know what was going on.

Through sobs, Immie piled on more. 'You told Mam not to stay in the flat. You told her to go to the Peabody shelter.'

'It was the safest place. I thought it was.'

Immie gripped Liam so hard, he whimpered. 'Me and the kids, we're alive because we didn't go. We got in the Morrison shelter in the kitchen. If Mam had stayed in her bed, and Ricky too, they'd be all right. They wouldn't be under a thousand tons of burning rubble! You left them. Got yourself out nice and safe, so now you can live with it. I'll never forgive you, Grace, never.'

Sir Gideon cleared his throat. 'I heard about it from one of my chaps, and, er, Buckland had said something about you having family in that area, Grace. I'm so sorry. And you, my dear' – he took Liam into his arms, because the little boy was squirming in his mother's grip – 'you have my deepest condolences, but it isn't your sister's fault and you will see that in time. Buckland,' he said, 'would you and Mrs Shotley please take care of this lady and her children. Grace?'

'I have to go,' Grace said. 'I have to go.' She repeated it like a machine at the fair you put a penny in. 'I have to go.'

'You can't—' Sir Gideon began, but she interrupted.

'You can't stop me. I'm going even if I have to pull my family out with my bare hands.'

He put a hand on her shoulder. 'I was about to say, you can't go on your own. Let me put on my greatcoat and you fetch your things. Gas mask and ID card, let's do this properly.'

'What about Lady Ventnor?'

'Nurse Gill can stay on a while. She owes you a few hours.'

Grace went to put on her cape, aware of Betony following her. She heard the girl say something, fumbling at compassion. 'So awfully sorry.'

Grace turned on her. 'Just go away and leave me! What d'you care? You've got everything you want, tied up with ribbon. I don't need your pity.'

42

John Fisher Street, where K Block had stood, was completely shut off by lorries which had probably got caught in an earlier raid and abandoned.

Grace led Sir Gideon down Dock Street, giving Victory Buildings a cursory glance because it was too painful to think of empty rooms, empty beds. On Flank Street, an ARP volunteer stopped them. Grace could hear men shouting above a rhythmic pumping sound.

Taking in Sir Gideon's uniform, the volunteer changed his blocking gesture to a smart salute. 'I can't let you through, Sir, Miss. We're restricting access.' He pointed to a sandbag wall.

'Good man.' Sir Gideon nodded approvingly. 'However, I am escorting Nurse Wheeler, who has been called in to help. I can lend a hand shifting rubble, if necessary.'

'There are heavy rescue lads on the scene, Sir. Leave the rubble-shifting to them.' The home guard took in Grace's tunic, white apron and cap. 'Which hospital, Nurse?'

'Royal London,' she said, because anything else would get her sent away. 'How many wounded have been brought out?'

Hard to say. 'Fifty dead, probably more. Burns, blast and crush injuries, so the numbers will go up.'

'And...' She could hardly swallow around the hard lump in her throat. 'Are people still trapped?'

'Bound to be. It's a mess.'

In the courtyard behind K Block, flatbed trucks were parked haphazardly next to ambulances. Last time she'd been here, there had been lawns each side of the sandbagged mouth of the shelter. All she could see now was a huge crater, with wooden props shoved in at odd angles like a giant game of pick-up-sticks. Men in tin helmets inched over the rubble, using poles to lift the corrugated sheets that had been the shelter's skin. Every time they lifted a segment away, they shone their torches into the hole they created. Other men with shovels stood in a loose ring, waiting. There were firemen, regulars and auxiliaries, the double rows of buttons on their tunics dust-hazed and dull. ARP volunteers stood ready with black steel stretchers. The pump she'd heard from two streets away was attached to a fire tender, its hose snaking through a window of K Block, in the only corner of the building still standing.

Sir Gideon muttered, 'Burst water main, or are they drowning out a fire?'

K Block's rear elevation had entirely fallen away. Smoking rubble and broken glass spewed over what remained of the lawn, reaching to the edge of the bomb crater. The debris was dotted with chairs, upended Morrison shelters, bedframes and sinks. The block's interior was laid bare. It felt almost indecent to Grace, to be staring at papered walls, trailing fabrics, children's toys, pots and pans.

Grace went up to one of the ambulances, aware of the residents of other blocks staring down from their lattice-taped windows. They must be thanking providence for their near miss. Or, more probably, weeping for friends and relatives. She approached a female ambulance driver who was talking with two Red Cross nurses. 'Excuse me.'

Noting Grace's uniform, the women broke off. 'Have they sent us reinforcements?' one of them asked, a mite superciliously.

'I don't know. My family was in that shelter.'

'Oh, dear, I'm so sorry. Look, most have been taken to the Royal London, some to Mile End and Wanstead. You should probably go there.'

Grace shook her head. 'They're under that lot.' She knew, just knew. The choking feeling of being trapped was getting worse.

For an hour, she watched the rescue effort. Sir Gideon moved about, taking advantage of his uniform and authoritative air to glean information. An unearthly calm reigned, except when the heavy rescue teams shouted instructions to each other. The pump maintained its dirge. Bodies were brought out, many of them children. Grace, who had offered to help with identification, glanced at each when the grey blankets covering them were briefly lifted. Some she could name. Others not. All the faces were encrusted with soil and dust.

At around two that afternoon, she identified Granny Driscoll. The collar of Granny's blue dressing gown and the liver-spotted fingers curled around the rosary beads told their story.

After a few minutes, a hundred heartbeats, Mam was brought out. Eyes shut, all life gone.

'Mary Imelda Whelan,' Grace said, her voice crashing into a sob, composure regained because nobody else was crying. They were all doing their jobs. 'From... from Dock Street.' Unlike Granny, Mam looked as if she had fallen asleep and couldn't be woken. 'Her son Ricky – my brother – is there, somewhere.'

She was waiting, hands clasped, when someone came to

stand beside her. A shoulder nudged hers and the scent of hair oil stole into her nose. She glanced to the side. 'Cormac!'

He looked terrible, and exhausted, as if he'd run miles in his suit.

'How did you know?' she asked.

'I was back at my digs, where you came that day? Immie called. Brought the kids. God, Gracie, what the hell happened?'

'A bomb. Immie says it's my fault and it is. I read them the riot act about staying home during a raid, so Mam and Ricky came here—'

A shout interrupted her. 'Got one alive!'

They went as close as they were allowed to the crater's edge. A rescue team was painstakingly easing up a sheet of steel, freeing it from the weight of split sandbags and subsoil. Stretcher bearers walked along planks, porting a black pallet between them. The heavy rescuers carefully lifted out a man wearing maroon and grey striped pyjamas, a tweed jacket on over the top, and placed him on the stretcher.

'That's our Ricky.' Cormac's voice scraped.

'I know.' She'd bought those pyjamas for him from Columbia Street market. *He did what I told him, got Mam into the shelter, God bless him for a hero. Now look at him...* Alive, though. Hope battled against the fear that this was only a temporary reprieve. The delaying of a complete, terrible, loss.

The stretcher was lifted clear and brought forward. Grace intercepted it.

She reached for one of Ricky's hands. His knuckles were raw and she knew without being told that his nightmare had come true.

In the dark, can't move.

He'd said that to her, at Gunter's when they'd eaten choco-late cake. At the time, he'd feared it was Immie and her boys who were trapped. But no, he'd seen his own fate.

'Ricky, darling, it's good to see you.'

His eyes flickered. 'Hurts, Grace.'

'I know. But they'll patch you up in hospital, and I'll sit by you.' The blood spots in his eyes and the scarlet flecks in the spittle that shot out on each out-breath mocked her optimism. 'I won't leave you until you're back on your legs.'

'Legs hurt. Belly hurts.'

She gripped his hand tighter. The bearers wanted to take him. 'Can I come too?' she asked.

'And me,' insisted Cormac.

The crew were reluctant, but Sir Gideon came up at that moment, and after learning who Cormac was, made the point that if Grace travelled with the patient, one of the ambulance staff might stay behind and help other casualties.

'Best use of resources, don't you think? Besides, you can't separate twin brothers at a moment like this.'

Mentioning his name and military rank – 'Colonel, Blues and Royals, retired' – did the trick. Grace and Cormac were allowed to ride along, Grace never letting go of Ricky's hand. His eyes had closed, the lids blue veined. It looked like the kind of sleep a person struggles to climb up from.

'Hey, you, wakey-wakey,' she said. How would they tell Ricky that Mam was gone? What would he do without her? 'I'll always be with you now. I'll never leave you. That's a promise.' A hot tear fell from her eye and Ricky half-opened his.

'Would I have gone to be a soldier, Grace?'

'Oh, yes. Course you would. You will. You'll be grand. The handsomest soldier on parade and won't the girls be swooning when you march past.'

Ricky grimaced, trying to smile. His beard was black as a shawl.

Grace nudged Cormac. 'Say something to him.'

Cormac had his hand in Ricky's jacket pocket.

'What are you doing?'

'Making sure he's got his identity card.'

'We can identify him right enough.'

Cormac withdrew his hand. 'Course, but you know what Ricky's like – has to have the little book in his pocket. He'd hate to think he'd lost it.'

Ricky was trying to speak.

'Grace...' He breathed her name as if remembering it after a long absence, then his hand slipped from hers. She laid her ear against his heart, picked up his wrist to feel for a pulse. Training took over. 'Pulse has ceased at...' She checked her watch. 'At sixteen hundred hours and fifteen minutes.' Four-fifteen, teatime, for folk who were lucky enough to be enjoying a quiet war. 'He's gone, Cormac. Our brother's gone.'

She knew then what it felt like for a heart to break.

When they reached the Royal London, and the back doors of the ambulance were opened, they were asked, 'Name of patient?'

Grace couldn't find her voice and Cormac said, 'You get out, sweetheart. I'll do the necessary.'

Relieved to be able to let tears flow, Grace watched from a distance as Ricky was brought out on his stretcher, a blanket drawn up over his face.

Grace followed the stretcher with her eyes, grief blurring the front of the hospital where she'd trained for nearly two years before walking out.

Couldn't take the discipline, she mocked herself. *Now you're on the outside, looking in.*

Cormac came back, asking what she planned to do.

'Go back to work. You?'

'The same.'

'What – relieving bombed warehouses of their surviving stock?'

'Not now, Grace.'

Looking at his jacket, cut to show off his physique, she saw a rectangular outline in the breast pocket. 'Are you finally carrying your identity card too?' she asked.

'Could be.'

'Does that mean you've gone straight? What's changed?'

'Everything, from now on,' Cormac answered with what Grace took to be deliberate ambivalence. He always played things close.

He asked her if she'd write to the family in Ireland, where Mam had four sisters still living. She said she would. 'And you need to stick around Immie for a while. She won't want me, so you need to play the good brother and uncle, till she's on her feet.'

'I know.'

'And there'll have to be death certificates and funerals to think about. For Granny too, because she has no one. I won't see Mam's dearest friend go into a pauper's plot.' Her voice broke into splinters.

'There's no point thinking about all that now,' Cormac said awkwardly. 'Nothing happens quickly and the hospitals have better things to do than bother with bodies.'

'But we'll do the decent thing, Cormac. Yes?'

'Course. This is our family.'

At last, the sobs came. She'd lost her mother and the brother she loved most. Almost, it seemed, between hellos and goodbyes. No last hug, no chance to say all those things that never, somehow, got said.

Cormac chewed his lip a moment, then asked, 'Who was that swanker who flashed his rank at the ambulance crew? Looked like he had a poker sewn into his uniform?'

'You heard. Sir Gideon Ventnor. I look after his wife.' She wiped her eyes.

'Watch his type, Grace.'

'He isn't "a type". He's kind.'

'They're all kind.' Cormac's lip curled, reminding Grace that her brother had an irrational hatred for the moneyed class. 'Is he loaded?'

'Not really. I suppose they're comfortable.'

'They should pay you properly, then.'

She had no stomach for this conversation. 'Will you drop by Victory Buildings? The water went off some time yesterday, and I wouldn't put it past Mam or Ricky to have left a tap turned on. If the supply comes back on, the place could flood.'

'Sure.'

She was surprised, Cormac being so obliging, then she remembered that the Hearts of Oak was next door and Cormac had a soft spot for the landlady. He'd pop in for a pint when the doors opened.

He was handing her a scrap of paper and pencil.

'Write your addresses down, both of them, in case I need you.'

'Immie knows where I work.' Grace had no desire to share either her work address or that of her lodgings. Not with Cormac. Even now, when they should be united in grief, mistrust of her brother ran hot.

'Write them down.'

Something in his voice warned her he would get the information from Immie anyway. She jotted '34 Hill Street' and 'Ventnor House, Upper Brook Street'. 'Just don't turn up throwing your weight around.'

She touched his arm briefly before walking away. Not in the direction of the nearest bus stop, but towards the hospital.

At the reception desk, she asked the nurse on duty if she could possibly, just possibly, be granted a moment to speak with Matron.

43

———

Saturday 14 September

Lady Ventnor had a new pressure sore, and Grace asked Sir Gideon to call the doctor. She knew why it had happened. Leaving Nurse Gill to cover for her when she went to watch the rescue efforts at K Block had given the dratted creature a free hand with the traditional treatment. An area of skin behind Lady Ventnor's shoulder was raspberry pink, and the patches on her buttock and heel had ulcers the size of drawing-pin heads. Leave them untreated, they'd be on their way to incurable.

Grace stood silently as the doctor made his examination. So much on her mind. Not only the raw grief of losing loved ones, but the BBC news had reported that St Thomas' and Guy's Hospitals had been hit by high explosives, several members of staff killed. Grace felt torn between 'It could have been me' and 'I should have been there.'

Lady Ventnor let out whimpering sounds as the doctor examined her. For once, Grace had some sympathy. These weren't known as 'bedsores' for nothing.

'Hm.' The doctor allowed his patient to lie more comfortably. 'Somebody's been a little heavy-handed with the methylated spirits.'

'Fresh air and movement work best,' Grace muttered. 'I'll go to my death saying it.'

'I trust you won't have to, Nurse. I shall leave you with iodine tincture. Go cautiously. If it causes irritation to the skin, desist.'

'Yes, Doctor. Meanwhile, I shall carry on persuading Lady Ventnor to allow some fresh air on her skin.'

'Do you always argue with the medical profession?'

Grace flinched. 'It's my downfall.'

'Continue your fresh air therapy, so long as my patient doesn't catch a cold. Tincture of iodine.' He handed a small, brown bottle to her. 'Change the dressings regularly.'

Grace followed him out of the room. 'The best thing for Lady Ventnor would be to get up and move.'

'In an ideal world,' the doctor agreed.

'Her gout is painful when it flares up, but other than that, she's as well as anybody her age. It's lying in bed all day that's killing her.'

Grace didn't care if she ruffled the doctor's vanity. She didn't care about anything at all. The memory of Owen's kiss was tainted now she knew how things stood with Betony. She couldn't stop the visions of Mam and Ricky in the seconds before the bomb fell on their shelter. For once, Grace hoped Mam had been insulated with gin. And dear Granny Driscoll too. If only she could persuade herself that Ricky hadn't suffered, but she knew in her heart that his premonitions were his gift and his curse. She blinked to stop her tears.

The doctor was asking, was she suggesting that Her Ladyship was malingering?

'Not like the homeless folk we had at the Royal, who would invent anything just to get an extra night in a warm bed. She *believes* she's ill. She could just as easily believe the opposite, if the right person told her.'

'Who might that be, you?' The doctor's eyebrow rose: amused, verging on disdainful.

'God, no, but you'd be a good start.'

The telephone was shrilling downstairs.

Buckland came up to tell Grace there was a call for her.

What now? 'My sister?'

'Not on this occasion. It is Flight Lieutenant Henderson and he is using a public call box.'

Grace all but flew, not caring what either man thought. Rather than take the call in the library, she darted down the side passage to snatch up the house telephone. 'You're still there?' she gasped.

He was. 'Have to be quick – are you all right?'

'As I can be.'

'I know, stupid question. Uncle Gideon phoned and told me about your family. I am so sorry, Grace.'

'Is that why you've called?'

'Partly, but look, I think I can get away Tuesday if you fancy leaving your sorrows at home for a night... Course, you might not want to—'

'No, I do. I do!' There was a chair by the phone table and she sank down. 'Owen, I do. But what about Betony? She's saying—'

The pips were going but he must have shoved in another coin. He started speaking quickly. 'Shall we say eight o'clock? Late, but I can never predict how the roads will be.'

'Yes, all right. Where, though?'

He had time to yell, 'Ealing, Mother's house. She wants to —' The call cut out.

Grace was shaking as she put the receiver on its cradle. A shadow touched her, Buckland's.

'All well, Nurse?'

She asked, did he know Flight Lieutenant Henderson's home address?

'It's in the address diary in the library. Didn't you see me show it to Miss Styles?'

'Yes, I did. And I know what you're saying in your unsubtle way.'

'What is that, Nurse Wheeler?'

'Oh, call me Whelan. I don't give a flying fig anymore. Call me whatever takes your fancy. If Owen doesn't mind, neither should you.'

He followed her to the stairs. 'Lady V will blow her top. You and her nephew.'

'Only if she finds out. Only if some canary bird sings.'

'You're leaving us, aren't you?'

Was she? Grace waited with one foot on the stairs.

'I found your screwed-up letter in the library fireplace. You want to go back to hospital nursing. *Somebody* should inform Her Ladyship that you have itchy feet.'

Instead of going upstairs, Grace went to the cloakroom where she always hung her cape and bag. She took out a letter that had come the previous day from the Royal London and passed it to the butler. 'Read it. It'll answer your question.'

Buckland cleared his throat: '"Dear Miss Whelan, I am given to understand that you requested a meeting with me a few days ago, with the view to being reinstated as a probationer nurse at the Royal London. I see no purpose in holding out false hope. Your misconduct and the abrupt manner of your leaving in February of this year demonstrated that you are unsuited to hold any position within this hospital. G. M. Littlejohn, Matron."'

'And you know what?' Grace said, before Buckland could add his opinion. 'I'm glad. I'd have gone back to being shut up in the nurses' house by ten, no life to call my own. If I'm dating

Flight Lieutenant Henderson...' She paused to give the butler time to get out his best sneer. He didn't, he just waited. 'If we're dating, I want us to have time together. Because you never know, do you?'

'Indeed no. As your sister Imelda said the other day, with philosophical acuity, "If a bomb's got your sodding name on it, you're done for, so you are."'

Never had Grace wanted more to boot a man up the backside, but she made do with saying, 'Well, Mr Buckland, don't you give a fine impression of an overwrought Irishwoman.'

The doctor had given Lady Ventnor some kind of sedative, which in turn gave Grace time to think. It afforded her no pleasure to be stealing Betony's man. Was that what she was doing? Not deliberately. Not with malice.

Had Owen really kissed Betony passionately in the dark, in that café place? Or had Betony been indulging a fantasy?

Meanwhile, talk about an overwrought Irishwoman... from thinking of nothing but Mam and Ricky, Grace was now feverishly worried about her date. *Please, please, don't let it be spoiled by a raid.*

Would Mrs Henderson like her? Or hate the very redheaded sight of her? She'd rather have gone out just with Owen, to a dance hall. She imagined herself in his arms, swaying to some band. She'd just got to the part when the music stopped and he bent to kiss her, when Betony's face got between her and her eyelids.

'Oi, Grace, you've nicked my boyfriend!'

She doubted Miss Styles would say 'oi', but she'd be enraged all right. Only this morning she'd heard Betony telling Mrs Kesgrave that she was planning to 'liberate a gorgeous dress' from work to wear on her next date. Sharing a room with a vengeful Betony Styles would be worse even than being punched by Cormac.

She hoped Owen would let Betony down gently. 'It's not my news to break,' she told herself and, putting the matter aside, considered another burning question. What 'gorgeous dress' could she possibly 'liberate' to meet Owen's mother?

44

In reality, the answer to 'what shall I wear?' was simple. Grace had only two dresses anyway and the green cotton one would be most suitable. Maybe a silk scarf at the neck?

'What d'you think?' she asked Jess, who, like her, had finished a long day at work and was sitting elf-like on her bed with a book open on her lap. Betony hadn't yet come in.

Jess regarded the dress from under her lashes, as if she feared to meet anything head-on. Grace wondered for the fiftieth time, how on earth this girl had got tangled up with Cormac. There'd still been no show of recognition, so Grace continued to keep the knowledge to herself.

'Is it too plain, are you thinking? Should I dress up a bit?'

'Have you seen Betony's evening gowns?' was Jess's reply, after more consideration.

'From the side. I wouldn't dare take them off their hangers,' Grace replied. 'That midnight blue... I've never owned a long dress in my life. An hour in the confessional on Sunday won't purge me of the sin of envy.'

Jess bit her lip. 'I always thought confession meant you could do something bad, then get off, like a free pardon. I always envied Catholics that.'

'You do bad stuff?' Grace shook her head. 'I doubt it.'

Jess looked away. 'I lied to my father.'

'Show me a girl who hasn't. Come on, tell me what you think... will a green day dress do for meeting a lady at home?'

Jess came to the bed. 'I think so. Green will suit your colouring. Who is this lady?'

'The mother of a friend.'

'A man friend?'

'I suppose so.' Grace gave Jess a thoughtful look. The girl seemed reliable, not the gossipy type, for sure. And as she worked for the government, apparently in the Censorship Office, she could probably be trusted. On the other hand, if she'd been one of Cormac's bits on the side, trusting her was a no-no. 'He's in the services and we haven't started going out properly,' she said, keeping it vague.

'But he's invited you to meet his mother? He must think a lot of you.'

'I hope so.'

'Then why do you look so sad, Grace?'

'Because I'll never be able to take him home to meet mine.' Fearful she'd start crying again, Grace put a question she'd sworn not to ask. 'How about you, any romance in your life?'

The headshake was telling. Nobody. 'Anyway, that's not why I came to London.'

Grace wondered now if she'd been mistaken, and that Jess just happened to look like the girl she'd encountered briefly in a darkened room. 'You came to London to work, to do your bit?'

Jess gave that due thought. 'To do my bit, but, really, to find someone.'

'Who?'

'Never mind. I love my father,' Jess said hurriedly, 'but his rules... I couldn't go on with it, the same thing every day. Church on Sunday. Jumble sales. Mothers' Union teas. And Miss Hillingdon, who is only his parish secretary but who orders me around as if she's Mother – I was at screaming pitch. Just like—' She broke off and began biting her lip.

That lip was ragged, Grace noticed. Jess's features were emerging from the bruising and soft tissue swelling acquired in her fall, revealing a face that would be attractive if it wasn't permanently cast in an attitude of worry. Had she really been drunk that time on the escalator? The more she got to know Jess, the less Grace could believe it. It must have been an accident, or a dizzy spell.

Jess was speaking. 'I'm so sorry what happened to your family. I wasn't sure whether to say so. Not everyone likes sympathy.'

'I don't like too much of it,' Grace acknowledged. 'A little is all right. I'm afraid I bit Betony's head off.'

'She told me. Will you miss your brother?'

'Dreadfully. He was such a dear character and I always looked out for him. I have another brother called Cormac who doesn't need anyone looking out for him.' Ah, at last a flicker from Jess. 'He and Ricky are... *were*... twins.'

'Identical?'

'Mm. Alike in looks, but not character. I often think Cormac has the brains and Ricky all the heart.' Grace felt her face quiver and changed the subject. 'It's Betony's turn to cook again tonight, isn't it?'

Jess nodded. 'I'm helping. It's cauliflower cheese. I don't think she's ever had to do much kitchen-work, but I kept house for Father since I was fourteen. Until Miss Hillingdon took over.'

. . .

It was a good meal, and they got to enjoy it and to wash up at leisure because, that night, the German bombers delayed until around two in the morning, by which time all the residents of No. 34 Hill Street, and the chickens, were tucked up in the Anderson shelter behind the house. Grace had still not decided what to wear to meet Owen's mother.

45

TUESDAY 17 SEPTEMBER

Grace took the Central line to Ealing Broadway. She had written down Mrs Henderson's address: Ravenscroft, Regent's Grove off Pitshanger Lane.

Houses with names, particularly single-word names, made her nervous. They implied a confidence beyond her scope. The closer Grace got to Regent's Grove, the larger and more imposing the residences seemed.

Ravenscroft's name was carved on its gate pillars. The sun was going down, but it was light enough for Grace to appreciate the large, detached house set behind hedges and a low wall. Square bay windows added an imposing touch. They were taped up, of course, as were the sidelights of a gabled porch.

Grace walked slowly up the path. Before she left, Jess and Mrs Kesgrave had said how nice she looked. Betony had been there too. She wasn't really speaking to Grace yet, her attempts at condolence having been rebuffed, but she'd said in a backhanded way, 'Green suits redheads because it's the opposite colour on the spectrum.' And then she'd asked where Grace was going.

'Just out, to a friend's,' Grace had muttered but must have looked self-conscious because Betony had narrowed her eyes as if she suspected something. She'd also been preparing to go out and was wearing a black evening dress: 'an old thing'. Not a date, apparently, but a trip to the theatre with the people she worked with. Betony had made it sound as though she was doing her colleagues a favour, and Grace's guilt over deceiving her had vanished, and she'd wanted to smack her instead. A night out at a play for Grace, and probably for Jess too, was the rarest of treats. Betony was so spoiled.

The roar of a motorbike stopped Grace ringing the doorbell. A moment later, Owen was parking against the kerb.

'I'm so glad you've pre-empted me,' she said, striding back to meet him as he took off his helmet. 'I was getting the colly-wobbles.'

'Frightened, you?'

'It's terrifying meeting someone's mother for the first time. I don't know if she'll like me.'

'If she doesn't, she won't show it.'

'How is that meant to be a comfort?'

'It isn't. It's information.' Owen tucked his helmet under his arm and took flowers off the rack behind his seat. 'A chap at base had these going spare. His girl dumped him.'

'Are they for me?'

'No, for Mother. When I buy you flowers, I'll buy white roses.'

'Not red ones?'

'Red is a cliché, and you are definitely a white rose kind of girl.'

'Could be worse,' she said. 'Just never pink, all right?'

Someone was calling from the porch. It must be Mrs Henderson.

'Don't hang about, darling, we're all desperate to meet Grace.'

We? Grace had assumed Owen's mother lived alone. Large gatherings unsettled her. They'd take one look at her and think, *Wrong side of the tracks.* However, it was too late for second thoughts. Owen had taken her hand and was pulling her to meet his mother.

Mrs Henderson let them into the darkened hall, and once the door was shut, blackout drapes pulled, she turned on the light. She wore a dress of dark peach with a brown trim. Her grey-blonde hair was cut square around a delicately pretty face. She smiled at Grace.

'Are those flowers for me?' She took the ragged chrysanthemums from Owen and Grace saw her close her eyes as she leaned towards her son and kissed his cheek. It was a brief moment of vulnerability, after which she became businesslike. 'I hope you're both hungry. Rabbit pie and Dr Marek's famous potato salad.'

Primrose Henderson met none of the preconceptions implanted in Grace's mind by Lady Ventnor. She wasn't the fussy, nervous drab of Lady Ventnor's complaints, nor did she appear over-anxious towards Owen, though Grace noticed her eyes following him as he shook hands with the small crowd in the sitting room. It had taken Grace only a minute to realise she was Welsh. She was familiar with the accent from girls she'd trained with at the Royal London.

Five other people, it turned out, called Ravenscroft home. There was the Polish doctor, known as 'Marek' because, according to Mrs Henderson, his surname was spelled z, w, y and c, repeated, with no vowels in between. Grace gathered that he was a refugee from Nazism. She was next introduced to two young women who taught at the local secondary school, and to a pair of elderly sisters who had been bombed out of their home, whom Mrs Henderson was sheltering. Everyone talked at once, and while they welcomed Grace, they were more interested in Owen.

She didn't mind, content to sip sherry and observe. The sitting room became busy with people moving about, fetching things, passing little dishes. It was nothing like her own home, no discord, nobody shouting for attention, no Cormac thumping his fist into his hand to get his way. The aged sisters were very deaf, and Dr Marek was learning English, so the schoolteachers translated while Mrs Henderson fetched more cheese biscuits and nuts from the kitchen.

Dinner was a huge rabbit pie served with the famous potato salad. That, to Grace's eye, was a mound of boiled spuds with finely chopped onion, dressing and greyish seeds which she'd never tasted before.

'Poppy,' Mrs Henderson said, seeing her uncertainty.

'As in "opium"?'

'Not opium poppy seed. Well, I don't think so. Dr Marek is introducing me to a whole new culinary world. Owen tells me you're a nurse.'

'I am. You must know by now, I'm Lady Ventnor's private nurse.'

'I wasn't going to mention that.' Mrs Henderson had a lopsided smile, almost identical to her son's. 'That mark on your face...'

Grace touched the scab left by a ruby ring. 'It's all right now. I don't think it'll scar.'

'That's not the point. If she ever does it again, call on me. I'll be straight round.'

Grace didn't want to spoil the evening by thinking of her job. 'Do you enjoy having all these people in your house?'

'I do. For some years, after Owen's father died, it was just me and a couple of maids. I like company, though I'm also working again.'

'Oh?' Grace tried to predict this woman's job. Secretary. Teacher. Librarian.

She wasn't prepared to hear, 'I'm a draftswoman. I worked in an architect's office before I married. I've gone back.'

'You design houses?' Grace's astonishment leaked out.

'Nothing so glamorous. Bridges and tunnels mostly. Civil engineering, the dull stuff, but I enjoy it. Do you like nursing?'

'Sometimes. No – that's not true. I always enjoy actual nursing, but I hate the system around it. It's soul-destroying sometimes.'

'That's sad to hear. I always thought of nursing as a sisterhood. Passionate women, running their own show.'

'Maybe when they start. Nurses get pressed into shape and the fire goes out. As for running the show... ward sisters have power, but they always give way to doctors, even the young ones who don't know much. They didn't like me.'

'Why not?'

'Because I'm Irish and working class.' *Get it out, get it said.* 'My dad was a docker and I don't take criticism well. Oh, and I had a habit of dropping specimen bottles.'

'Quite a charge sheet.'

Grace knew she'd overdone the downside, but it mattered, desperately, that this woman should like her. Or if she wasn't inclined to, then to know it. 'I am also Roman Catholic, if that happens to be important.'

'Important to you, I should think.' Mrs Henderson filled her glass and Grace's with water from a jug.

'To me it's normal.' Her hostess seemed to be taking all these revelations in her stride. 'You'd be surprised how big a problem it is in London, around certain people.'

'Dr Marek is Roman Catholic. So are the Misses Wilberforce.'

Mrs Henderson nodded towards the sisters in their lace collars and violet buttonholes. 'To me, it doesn't matter a jot what church you belong to. I was brought up in the chapel tradition, and I believe faith of some sort is important.' Her gaze found Owen. 'One has to feel there's something to aim for, so one never gives up hope.'

Owen was talking with the doctor, saying that he was still grounded: another medical next week. His voice seethed with frustration. Tonight was the first time Grace had seen him in civilian clothes, an ordinary tie, collar and knitted waistcoat. He had one elbow on the table and his fingers moved restlessly.

'Do you love him?'

The question springing from a mother's lips made Grace go momentarily still, and mute. 'I think so,' she said after a while.

'Think?'

'We haven't known each other a month. If you said to me, "Have you got flu?" and I said, "I think so," you'd suggest I take a tonic and see how it develops.'

'Indeed I would. Good answer.'

Looking into Mrs Henderson's eyes, chestnut brown like her son's, Grace felt she understood Owen's reluctance to come home more. Not because his mother fussed or invented illnesses, as Lady Ventnor had accused. It was because she fired out those blunt, unavoidable questions.

Grace imagined Mrs Henderson leaning towards Owen and asking, 'Are you all right? Are you scared?' and Owen unable to hold that steady gaze and trot out the usual half-truths.

'What are you deciding about me?' Mrs Henderson asked, proving Grace's private opinion: nothing passed this woman by.

'I'm imagining you and Lady Ventnor face-to-face and you saying, "What on earth keeps you in bed, Maude, when there's a war on?" She must be terrified of you.'

Grace thought she'd overstepped when her hostess widened

her eyes in a long, questioning look – before bursting into laughter.

'I never thought of it like that before. She's frightened of me!'

Grace's observation had come off the cuff, but now she thought, *I wonder if I've hit the truth, and Her Ladyship is actually more frightened than any of us?*

After dinner, the Misses Wilberforce performed gentle duets on a baby grand piano, until one of the teachers took over and bashed out 'Keep the Home Fires Burning'. Grace, nerves diminished by sherry and a sneaking belief that Mrs Henderson quite liked her, sang along and heard herself described by the doctor as, 'Most beautiful!'

You should see me at six in the morning, with a day of Lady Ventnor ahead of me, Grace thought. She hadn't spoken much to Owen, but the glances he kept sending her meant she hadn't felt neglected. *I've passed muster,* she told herself. Not once had she affected a Mayfair accent.

All too soon, it was time to think of going. Owen asked his mother if he could use the phone to call his uncle. 'I'll leave my bike here and take Grace home on the train. Only, I'll need to sleep over at Uncle Gideon's as the trains will have stopped for the night by the time I've got Grace to Hill Street.' He promised to be back for breakfast. 'But not for long. I'll be on my way by eight.'

'Your other friend told me you were being elusive,' his mother said. 'Am I right to suppose you're taking more time off to recover?'

'Yes, though not by choice—' Owen stopped and frowned. 'What other friend?'

'An odd girl. Miss Styles.'

'Betony phoned here, when?'

His mother couldn't remember. 'A few days ago. I didn't tell you, my darling, because she's right. You are very hard to get hold of. I think I was rather rude to her, but I'm convinced she mistook me for the charlady.'

'Someone told me she called my local pub.'

The spectre of Betony had risen up. Owen must have noticed how uncomfortable this made Grace as he said no more.

Mrs Henderson walked them to the gate and Grace continued on to give mother and son a moment's privacy. She heard him say, 'See you tomorrow, Mum. Crack of dawn.'

'I will have the kettle on. Good night, Grace,' his mother called.

'Good night, Mrs Henderson, and thank you for a lovely evening.'

'A pleasure, and I would like you to call me Primrose.'

46

Grace and Owen got off the last train calling at Marble Arch after a delayed journey. Holding hands, they pushed through the crush of people settling down for a night on the platform. As they reached the exit, they saw the metal grilles were seconds from being pulled down. They ducked under, laughing. *Just made it.* It was twenty minutes to midnight.

A few yards from the tube entrance, they stopped to gulp in the night air.

'You are amazing,' Owen said, cupping her face with her hands. 'I have never seen my mother talk to any of my other girlfriends the way she did with you tonight.'

'Your girlfriend, then, am I?' They had mentioned Betony's name as they sat side-by-side on the train. Or, rather, she had. Unable to stop herself.

Owen had assured Grace that there was nothing serious there, never had been. Not on his part. 'First time I asked her out, she sent me to a hoax address. Second time, I lost sight of her in a power cut.'

'At the Café de Paris?'

He'd looked taken aback. 'How did you know?'

'I share a room with her, remember.'

'You assured me you don't gossip.'

'It wasn't gossip, Owen. She *told* me. For a reason.'

As they walked down Park Lane, that snatch of conversation must have come back because he said suddenly, 'It wasn't much of a kiss. With Betony, in the Café de Paris. Couldn't have been, because I don't remember doing it.' He added that the third time he'd seen Betony, another man had turned up to whisk her to the Connaught. 'I don't want to be a tennis ball in her very full bucket. Whereas you' – he put an arm round her shoulder – 'I'd like us to know each other better. Will that do, for now?'

'Yes, it'll do.'

'Good. Let's walk in Hyde Park.'

Grace pointed out that it would take them in the wrong direction, but Owen said, 'That's my thinking.'

In the smothering darkness and with the skies quiet, even if it was wrong, it felt right.

It was another milk-soft night but with the first scent of autumn in the air. For a while, they walked without purpose but Grace could feel an intention, like wires tightening. It slowed them until they sank down between the roots of a majestic tree, staring up between branches at the moonlight. 'Full moon. It's put on a show for us.'

'It's actually a day past full,' Owen said. 'We call it a bomber's moon.'

'I wasn't going to say that.' Grace rolled onto her side and put her arms around him, and for a while they kissed and breathed in each other's breath. She wanted so much to make love, and his hardness and urgency was all too obvious, but they held back because this was about getting to know each other and there was so much more to discover first.

They lay, side by side, fingers linked until the siren began to wail. Owen sat up, saying, 'There's a public shelter in the park, somewhere. Ready to run?'

Only, it was too late. As they got to their feet, tracer fire was already dropping. Almost pretty, like shooting stars, coming in from the south-east.

'They're after the docks again,' Grace said, adding, 'the bastards.'

'Maybe. Maybe not.' Owen was drowned out by a succession of deafening booms as the Hyde Park guns began to speak, puffs bright as phosphor shooting up, giving away their location. Volleys came from further off, projecting bursts of light all over London. After that, it was a continuous, overlapping cacophony. Searchlights crossed swords across the sky, searching prey to skewer. An incoming bomber was hit.

A wave of enemy planes appeared, silhouetted in the dappled moonlight. 'Mary Mother of God.' Grace clutched Owen's hand. 'They're coming this way.'

They hunkered under their tree, as explosion after explosion erupted in the West End. Maybe a mile away, then half a mile. The air boiled, as though the sky was one throat, roaring destruction. A violent explosion threw them onto their sides and littered them with leaves and twigs. They stood up, supporting each other, shaking with shock, and stared towards Cumberland Gate. Balls of orange flame punched from the roof of Marble Arch tube station.

They ran towards it until stopped by the heat. Flames leaped from the ticket hall. They heard the peals of fire tenders and ambulances as the bombs continued to fall and the great guns discharged.

The Germans got here in the end, Grace told herself. There would be casualties. *Better roll up my sleeves.*

47

———————

BETONY

Betony was trying to get a taxi to stop when the sirens went. She froze, thinking, *Where do I go?* An evening watching a not very good play in a theatre off Trafalgar Square had done nothing for her confidence. She'd told everyone at Mrs Kesgrave's she was going out with Sybil and Ambrose, so they wouldn't realise the truth and pity her: she had sat through the play all alone.

Nobody wanted her. Not in the way she craved. Coming out of the theatre, she'd bumped into a married couple she knew. You wouldn't call them friends, more hangers-on of hangers-on, but they'd invited her to a drinking club on Cockspur Street, and she'd thought, *Why not?*

Plenty of reasons, as it turned out. She'd always thought the Ridley-Suttons were on the louche side, generally sozzled and vulgar. What she hadn't realised was that they liked to mentally undress you the drunker they got. Grace had used the chimes of midnight as her excuse to leave.

Now the sirens were screaming, pushing her close to panic. She should have headed home, or to a public shelter. A warden hurrying past pointed to one of the Trafalgar Square statues, bellowing, 'Get under cover! That way, sweetcakes.'

Sweetcakes? Is that what you got called when you loitered on your own, after the theatres closed?

She began to breathe fast. The shelter would be vile, hot, crowded, smelly and a thousand times safer than staying in the open. She could feel the ground shaking now the guns were firing. The drone of incoming planes was deafening. Inescapable. Staring up, she saw their outlines etched in the moonlight.

The bombs began to fall. East of here to start with but getting closer. She was vaguely aware of someone shouting to her, but she continued staring at the moon until it blurred. She'd done nothing with her life except make a mess of it. The reality was, if she was blown to pieces tonight, not many people would care. Father and Mother would a bit, or even a lot, but they'd carry on. Friends would say, 'Oh, not darling Betts, that's frightful.' Sybil would shed a tear, but Ambrose wouldn't. Her fellow lodgers at Hill Street would probably be relieved to have the whole wardrobe. Grace hated her, with reason.

Can't stop myself looking down my snout at her.

And Owen? He had his own troubles; he didn't need hers. She'd thought he'd been head over heels for her, but since their kiss at the Café de Paris, he'd cooled. After their night together in Sybil's basement – admittedly a crowded one – he'd hardly spoken to her at all. He had someone else. It felt that simple.

An odd thing had occurred earlier in the evening. She'd noticed Grace poring over a London street map before putting it back in Mrs Kesgrave's bookcase. Curious to know where those friends of hers lived, Betony had taken it out again and it had fallen open at London W5. Ealing.

Coincidence, or could Owen Henderson really have ditched Betony Styles for an East End nurse?

It was almost funny.

'Betty, what the hell?'

Winter? Betony swung round, and round again, trying see where he was. *If* he was there at all. She might be conjuring him up.

But no. He was coming towards her, dressed for work, his tie loose. He was running.

'Jesus, Betty, you're standing around waiting to be killed?'

'I'm contemplating my wretched existence.'

'You're drunk. And it may be wretched, but it's the only one you've got.'

'Where did you come from?'

He jerked a thumb behind him, indicating the Canadian High Commission. 'I've been working late, finishing off. I was walking home and saw you.'

'Risking death too.'

'Practising,' he said enigmatically. 'Let's shelter.'

'I don't want to. You go.'

'Not without you.'

But she pulled back, only to clutch at him as bombs fell so close, the flagstones of Trafalgar Square reflected red, and the sky was briefly as bright as day.

Winter picked her up and carried her bodily to the foot of Nelson's Column, which was walled in with sandbags. He pulled her down into the shadows, hugging her close so their heartbeats merged. All hell raged as they waited for the bomb that would fall too close, the one with Admiral Nelson's name on it.

48

———

GRACE

Staying as close to Marble Arch as they could get, Grace and Owen gave first aid to people caught by flying glass and masonry, pulling out splinters, binding cuts. Owen's tie made a tourniquet for a man whose leg was laid open. Grace gave her coat to a tramp who was wandering around, shivering and dazed. Her cardigan looked as though it had been used to mop a butcher's floor, and she'd torn up her petticoat for bandages.

Owen had removed his shirt for the same purpose. All he had on his top half was the knitted waistcoat.

'We look like we went to a jumble sale and got stripped at gunpoint,' Grace said, attempting a joke in a momentary lull. Just as she felt like a shirker for not being among the emergency teams, Owen was angry at himself for having flipped his plane, as if his absence from his squadron had let in these waves of bombers.

In the early hours, ambulances took the last of the injured away. A policeman shook his head at them and said, 'Get yourselves home.' The all-clear came as dawn edged through the smoke.

They reached the front door of Ventnor House, both of

them weary to the bone. The short walk had been hard going. Though the bombers had been turned away from London, the streets were littered with splintered mortar casings. Shattered roof tiles lay everywhere, fresh ones falling as they passed by. Most of the way, they'd walked in the middle of the road, too cautious to turn on their torches and using the moonlight to go by.

Owen took out a key and wiggled it in the lock before realising the door was open anyway. 'Buckland's losing his grip,' he muttered.

Grace, glancing up, saw a gap in Lady Ventnor's bedroom curtains through which a pencil thickness of light shone. That was a five-pound fine and a severe telling-off. Nurse Gill must have forgotten to check as darkness fell.

Owen led the way to the kitchen, saying he'd knock them up an early breakfast.

'Won't your uncle mind?' Grace really meant 'your aunt'. At some point, Her Ladyship would have to swallow the idea that her beloved nephew was stepping out with a girl named Whelan, from Dock Street. Grace wasn't ready for that moment.

'They'll still be down in the cellar,' Owen said. 'Auntie sleeps right through these days, and Uncle Gideon won't be in a hurry to wake her.'

'What about Nurse Gill, and Buckland, or the cook?'

'If any or all of them catch me frying two rashers of bacon, I'll deal with the uproar.' He lit the gas jets on the stove. 'I'll point at this.' He opened one of the hinged doors of an old-fashioned range next to the modern cooker. Inside was a collection of tinned foods. There were more in the range's other ovens.

Grace shook her head. 'I don't like ration cheating.'

'Uncle Gideon won't know a thing about it,' Owen said, 'it'll be Buckland and Mrs Shotley, and I doubt much of this stuff gets served in the dining room. Tea or coffee?'

'Tea. Will you excuse me a minute?' Grace was impatient to wash out her cardigan before the bloodstains set. The sink upstairs would do. And somebody needed to shut those blackouts.

She hurried upstairs quietly, so as not to rouse the occupants of the cellar. Her face was sooty, she smelled of smoke and there was blood on her forearms. In Lady Ventnor's bedroom, she pulled the curtains closed then stared at the bed. Lady Ventnor's jewellery box was upturned on the coverlet, its contents spread out but not in a heap. Laid out as if in a shop window.

A noise took Grace's attention to the annexe off the bedroom. She was about to call, 'Nurse Gill?' when the memory of that open front door stopped her. Years of being her father's daughter, Cormac's sister, pulled a lever marked 'Caution'.

Slowly, quietly, she went to the annexe whose door was partially ajar and yanked it open. A man stood in front of the open drawers where Lady Ventnor's cosmetics, perfumes and trinkets were kept. Though his back was to her, the line of his shoulders and the way his black, greased hair tapered to a point against his neck was as good as a nameplate. She said, 'You.'

Her brother Cormac turned on the spot and hurled the same word back. 'You.'

49

Had she been more mistress of herself, Grace would not have stated the blindingly obvious. But she was scared and sick with a shame that was only a fraction of what it would become if anyone walked in on them. 'You broke in. God, Cormac, is there any pit you won't wallow in?'

He threw down a Chinese fan he'd found in a drawer and came to the doorway, gripping her jaw with hard fingers. He was smiling. 'God helps those who help themselves. Didn't Mam always say so?'

'I don't think she meant it like that. Is this why you asked for my work address?' She got free, but he gripped her wrist, twisting it so she couldn't break away.

'Course. If you're going to snivel over that collection on the bed, it's worthless. Paste and soft gold. I thought you said they were rich.'

'I said nothing of the sort.' The calamity that was building, that would once again ruin her life, weakened her self-control. 'Please, just go, Cormac. I'm begging you.'

'Begging are you? That's a change.'

His face was close, and she smelled gin on his breath.

Cormac was not a heavy drinker. He despised the vice, but she imagined him in the Dock Street flat, checking the taps and the gas, and finding Mam's gin. Necking it to drown whatever sorrows he felt. Dealing with an enraged Cormac was tough, but this one, drunk, grieving, resentful, she hadn't the tools for.

'Yes, I'm begging. Because if I lose my job, I may not get another.'

'Good!'

'What use is it to you or anyone if I can't support myself.'

'I'll find you a job, something you're good for.' He gave her wrist a further twist. 'My landlady can use you, upstairs or down.'

She gasped. 'You'd have your sister work in a brothel?'

He slapped her with his free hand. 'Mind your manners, Grace.'

'Cormac, please, for Mam's sake, just go. I won't say anything.' She could feel him edging towards a tipping point where anger flirted with madness. She'd experienced him in that state a few times and it terrified her.

'Oh, Gracie won't rat on me.' It was said in a mocking, wheedling voice. 'Even though she dobbed me in to the police not a month ago.'

'I did not. The police came because the government keeps records of who doesn't answer the call-up. It's not hard to find someone who's lived in one part of London most of his life.'

'You think that, do you? Grace knows everything.'

He was in the mood where he'd twist everything, as he was her wrist, making her bite her lip with the pain.

'I've a mind to drag you away with me, trailing worthless jewels, so they'll think it's you.'

'Why Cormac? Why have you always done your best to wreck my life?'

'You don't know?'

She shook her head, dislodging scalding tears because her wrist was excruciating, and any moment, he'd dislocate it.

'There's blood on your face,' he told her.

Breathing hard between every word, she sketched out what had happened that night. 'Idiots like me who don't take shelter, and they got caught in the tail of the blast.' She didn't mention that she'd not been alone. Please, God, let Owen stay downstairs and not come searching for her.

'What a heroine, Nurse Gracie, always where the need is greatest. Why were you seen kissing a policeman, mm? In Dock Street, outside Mam's house a week ago?'

She thought he was rambling, until she realised he meant Owen. They must have been seen. 'I have a young man. He's not a policeman.'

'He's a military policeman. That's what Brenda at the Hearts of Oak told me. She can recognise one a mile off.'

'He's in the RAF. He was wearing a leather coat because...' She was going to faint from the pain in her wrist.

Cormac was mocking again, saying something about 'flash RAF types' who were only after one thing. 'You'll get up the duff and you won't see him for dust.'

'Not true.'

'True, Grace.' He let go of her and she stumbled against the door frame, cradling her wrist.

'Please, please just go.'

'If you beg me. On your knees.'

She tried to work out if he was having fun tormenting her, or if he'd broken the bounds of self-control. His face was flushed, his eyes bloodshot. She went down on her knees. 'I'm begging you.'

He pushed past her to the bed and scooped up the rings, bracelets and necklaces. He was wearing his brown, pinstripe suit, which she realised, for the first time, had been provided with extra-deep pockets.

It was a housebreaker's suit. Her brother was a professional thief.

As if she'd spoken out loud, he turned and grinned.

'You wrote this address out for me. "Ventnor House, Upper Brook Street". That makes you an accessory.'

Grace got up, anger pushing away fear. 'You're scum, Cormac. Ricky was worth fifty of you. I take it as a compliment that you hate me.'

She knew he was coming for her before he moved and she tried to get into the annexe, but she was slower than usual and he caught her. He raised his right fist and she braced herself for a knock-out punch. It didn't come, because a voice from the doorway said, 'Leave her. Step back. Look at me.'

Owen stood on the other side of the room, and he was pointing a handgun at Cormac.

50

Cormac slowly raised his hands, but he didn't look nervous. 'That's not loaded.'

'It is. It's my uncle's and it's always loaded, in case German parachutists land in the streets. Before you ask, I can shoot. I'm military trained and you'll note that my hand is not shaking.'

Nor was it, Grace saw. Nothing in Owen's stance or tone suggested any scruples, should it come to pulling the trigger. 'Shut up and listen,' she told Cormac.

Cormac raised his hands a little higher. 'Is this the RAF boyfriend?'

'He's a friend.' It was like seeing the boulder that was going to kill you slide from the top of a hill and begin its descent. All chance of this situation being covered up was past. Owen would learn that Grace's brother had broken into his uncle's house, because she had furnished the address.

'I hope I'm more than a friend,' said Owen, without taking his eyes off Cormac. 'The bigger question is, who the hell is this?'

Cormac, hands up and an animal glint in his eye, smiled at Grace.

'He's my brother,' she said. 'Cormac Whelan.'

For a moment, Owen looked from one to the other. 'You had twin brothers.'

Grace said their names. 'Cormac and Ricky.'

Owen swore. 'He came here, knowing the family would be sheltering in the cellar?'

'More or less' Cormac said, still grinning at Grace. 'I had a tip-off. The door was a doddle. You need better locks.'

'Who tipped you off?'

'That would be telling, wouldn't it, Gracie?'

Owen again looked from one to the other, a coldness settling over his features. He barked at Cormac, 'Turn out your pockets.'

Knowing how Cormac loathed being ordered around, Grace was taken aback to hear him say in a man-to-man kind of voice, 'You look like a decent fellow, so I'll warn you about my sister. She's not what you think.'

'You don't know what I think.'

'I know you're thinking she's a nice girl, a bit of a mouth on her, but a lovely, caring nurse with her heart in the right place. What if I tell you she stole everything I had?'

Owen gave it a moment's consideration. 'I'd point out that it's a bit rich, from someone whose pockets are bulging with somebody else's jewels.'

'I'm not talking about property. I'm talking about a father's love.'

'Cormac, don't,' Grace pleaded. 'Just empty your pockets and go.' Then she could set about mending whatever remained of Owen's trust and goodwill. Or if that had disappeared, then do what she could to keep her job. 'Dad's been in his grave nine years. We've just lost Mam. This isn't the moment.'

'When is the moment?' Cormac sounded very reasonable, but Grace knew he could turn on a pinhead. 'I say it's now, Grace, when you're busy conning a good man and getting the life you've always hankered after. A nice house.' He gazed around, nodded. 'Money in the bank.'

'I don't have any of those,' she protested. 'It's Immie that has the tidy life and you never resent her. I don't understand.'

'Then let me make you understand.' It came across as a warning. Something boiling up in her brother for years was about to break free.

'Fine.' There was no fighting this.

Cormac turned his eyes to Owen. 'When I was ten, there was a teacher, Mr Bryant, who thought I had ability and he coached me. I got a scholarship to the Foundation school. It's good, boys go on to do all sorts of things from there. Only, I couldn't go.'

This was new to Grace, yet hadn't that girl in bed with Cormac said something of the sort? *'Aren't you the one who stopped him going to school?'*

Grace knew that all this was for her. She was the audience, not Owen.

Cormac continued. 'I couldn't go because Dad was out of work *again*, and they couldn't afford the uniform or the bus fare. And Mam said, if I went to a better school, there'd be no one to look after Ricky. I had to make do with a school down the road where the boys are churned out as cheap dock labour. I was clever, but they made me nursemaid to my slow wit of a brother, so Mam didn't have to and Dad needn't do a proper day's work.'

'It wasn't like that,' Grace protested.

'What would you know?'

'You're saying your education was sacrificed for Ricky? That's why you went off the rails?'

'What d'you think? And then it was your turn. Clever Gracie, top of the class in everything.'

Grace knew what was coming. Like a stage curtain hauled back, a domestic scene was being revealed, painted from her brother's angle.

'When you got your scholarship to the Foundation school, Grace, didn't they wring every penny from every corner to get you there. Uniform, bus fare, books, pencils. The Golden Girl had to have it all.' Cormac addressed the next bit to Owen. 'When our dad came home and saw her at her homework, he'd ruffle her hair and say how proud he was.' His voice shook. 'He'd go to Ricky and say, "Have you looked after your mam today, lad?" Then he'd come over and fetch me a swipe round the head. "What trouble has Cormac brought to our door today?" It's why I hated him, and her too.'

Owen didn't speak.

Grace said, 'Now I know why you've done everything in your power to ruin my chances. You can't bear me succeeding because you didn't.'

'Couldn't. Not "didn't". I could have been in a good job, holding my head up. Speaking of which' – Cormac's grin returned – 'can I put my hands down now?'

'So long as it's only to empty your pockets,' said Owen.

'Sure.' Cormac pulled out jewellery in snatches, hurling it onto the bed.

'And your top pocket.' Owen had listened so far without expression. Nor had he looked at Grace in several minutes. She wished she knew what he was thinking. Planning. Would he frogmarch Cormac downstairs, and alert Sir Gideon to call the police? Was there a tiny chance this could be kept between themselves?

Owen repeated his demand for Cormac to empty his top pockets.

'Nothing in there, except my identity card. I have to carry that, it's the law.'

'Throw it on the bed.'

'Why would you want to see it?'

Owen re-aimed his gun, this time at Cormac's forehead.

Cormac took a beige-coloured card from his left breast

pocket and flipped it so it landed in the middle of Lady Ventnor's bed. Owen reached for it.

'Why aren't you in uniform, Cormac?' he asked.

'I'm exempt.'

That brought Owen's eyes up. 'On what grounds?'

'Health.'

'There's nothing wrong with his health,' Grace burst out.

'I've been declared unfit for any kind of military service.' Cormac held out his hand for the card. 'Give it back.'

Owen ignored him. He read the card, frowning. 'This isn't yours. It belongs to a Carrick Whelan. Oh, wait. Ricky is short for Carrick, yes?' Finally, Owen looked at Grace, seeking confirmation. Rather than say out loud what those words revealed, she launched herself at her brother and hit him, over and over, with her bare fists.

'You stinking, loathsome, utter filth. Owen, tear that card up!'

Cormac shoved Grace away. As Owen came at him with the gun, he ran forward, head low like a bull and butted past. The gun went off, and plaster rained down from the ceiling onto Lady Ventnor's bed.

They heard Cormac's feet thundering down the stairs, followed by the slam of the front door. As the dust thinned, Grace coughed. Owen was coughing too.

They could hear Sir Gideon calling, 'Who's up there?'

In the seconds she had left before her humiliation was complete, she explained, 'I saw Cormac trying to take something from our brother's pocket in the ambulance, as Ricky was dying. Ricky was declared unfit for military service, through mental incapacity.'

'And Cormac is now Ricky. Very neat. While others live on a knife-edge, he's free to enrich himself off the backs of everyone else.'

Miserably, Grace nodded.

Sir Gideon walked into the room, saw the gun in his nephew's hand and the hole in the ceiling. 'Looters?'

Grace waited for the boulder to roll over her.

'Nurse here surprised a burglar, caught him red-handed,' Owen told his uncle. 'There was a tussle, and your gun fired.'

'Rather careless, m'boy.' Sir Gideon regarded his nephew, who had taken off his waistcoat to shake off the plaster dust, leaving him naked from the shoulders to his waistband. Sir Gideon also took in Grace, whose bodice was bloodied and had two buttons missing. 'What is going on with you two?'

'We got caught in the raid,' she mumbled. 'People needed help. Marble Arch got a direct hit.'

'How dreadful. We heard the explosions. Wait a sec... You two bumped into each other, in the street, during an air raid?'

Grace glanced nervously at Owen, desperate to read his expression. This was his moment to make an announcement, to say, 'She's my girl, Uncle. I took her to meet Mother.'

But he didn't say anything. All he did was empty the gun cartridges onto the bed and hand the weapon to his uncle. 'This trigger is jumpy, Uncle Gideon. You should get it looked at.'

51

The day after, Grace was having her morning tea break when Buckland informed her there was a telephone call for her. 'This is getting to be a habit, Nurse.'

She went to take it, expecting it to be the police. After Cormac's attempted robbery and escape, she had quietly left Ventnor House, unseen, and gone home. After sitting at Mrs Kesgrave's kitchen table for a couple of hours, thinking, she'd walked to Hyde Park Police Station, where she'd done something no member of her family had ever contemplated doing.

'Miss Whelan speaking,' she said in a voice ironed flat.

'Grace? You sound strange.'

'Owen?'

'I've got two minutes, tops. How are you?'

'I'm...' She tried to say she missed him, that they had to talk. Broach the festering issue of Cormac, and the kind of family she came from. Her voice wouldn't work.

'Are you all right?'

'No,' she whispered. 'You?'

'I've got a time and date for my medical, and it's with a doctor who likes to get us back flying soon as humanly possible.'

Her heart plunged. 'You'll be glad.'

There was a silence, a costly one considering they now had under a minute left to speak, so they both started up at once.

'If it's about Cormac,' she said, 'I've reported him for using Ricky's identity. I've given the police the address of his hideout.'

'Listen, Grace,' he shot the words past hers, 'I need to see you. Are you free this Friday?'

'Course I am. You don't suppose I've got someone else, do you?'

'No. No I don't. I'm the one with the complications and we need to talk.'

'About my family?'

'About us. Sorry, I'm showing some new trainees round the base in five minutes. Where would you like to go on Friday? Name anywhere, so long as you can meet me there.'

Where did she know? Several pie and mash shops or Lyons Corner House, Piccadilly? Neither felt right for a last rendezvous where she got the elbow, or whatever well-bred men called it when they no longer wanted to be associated with you. Then she thought of Betony, swanning out the first night they'd lived together at Mrs Kesgrave's.

She said, 'The Savoy? Apparently, it has a bombproof ballroom.'

'Savoy it is. Nine-ish, and Grace?'

'Yes?'

'I'm sorry.'

FRIDAY 20 SEPTEMBER

Grace was wearing the amethyst dress for her date with Owen, the one Immie had handed on. In a blind panic, because she knew, *just knew*, that Owen was going to break things off, she'd ripped the pink peony off the front. She'd done it in a moment of self-hate, and now there was a hole to show for it. She was almost in tears, wondering how to get a message to the Savoy to say she was ill, when Jess came into their room.

She surveyed Grace in her rabbit-eyed way. 'That colour is gorgeous on you.'

Grace pointed out the tags of thread at the base of the neck. 'I'm not good at sewing. Anyway, I haven't got the right colour thread.'

'Mrs Kesgrave will have something.' Jess ran out and came back with a jade brooch. 'She says, you're welcome, but please don't lose it. It was a gift from a gentleman with dishonourable intentions. Did you know she's off to Brighton tonight? A work engagement.' A dimple appeared at the side of Jess's mouth. 'Some man is getting divorced and will spend a night doing a crossword. Stay still.' She pinned the brooch over the tear and asked what Grace was going to do with her hair.

'I don't know,' Grace wailed. 'I don't get on with curlers. They get tangled up and I have to cut them out.'

'Then brush your hair out and pin it up at the sides. It's your crown, Grace. You don't need to primp it. Are those the shoes you're wearing?' Jess picked up a pair of flesh-coloured sandals with an ankle strap, gazing at them admiringly.

'I might be.' Hearing footsteps on the stairs, Grace pushed the shoes under her bedcovers.

Betony came in, wearing just her slip and stockings and eyed them both. 'Night out?'

'Not me,' Jess said. 'I'm curling up with a book. Grace has a date.'

'Anyone I know?' Betony asked in an off-key voice.

Grace hid her blush by looking for her coat in the wardrobe, then remembered she'd given it away. 'Oh, God, I'll freeze if it turns cold.'

Betony came to stand beside her. She'd been in the bathroom for at least an hour and smelled deliciously of gardenias. 'Can you wear black?'

'You mean, do I look all right in it? I suppose.' Grace watched her take a narrow-cut coat with a deep velvet collar off a hanger, not knowing if she was being granted a favour, or taunted. 'Are you... lending?'

'You can't go out without a coat. It's supposed to rain later.' Betony removed a crimson evening dress and her quilted velvet jacket. She had already done her hair and applied her make-up. Putting the dress on the bed, she sat down next to it. 'I got a letter today.'

Jess reacted with polite interest. Grace felt uneasy.

'You should know what it says,' Betony continued in her indifferent tone. 'It'll be an education for you, Jess. And for you, Grace, a lesson in never overestimating the meaning of a kiss.'

Taking a sheet of letter paper from her evening bag, Betony cleared her throat theatrically. '"Wednesday, eighteenth of September, RAF Hornchurch."'

She looked straight at Grace, who couldn't conceal a start of shock.

'"Dear Betony, I've been meaning to write, and please forgive the delay. This is not easy—"' She looked up and, to Grace's relief and frustration in equal measure, folded the letter away. 'Long story short, he's given me the heave-ho. Very courteously, being Owen. Did I mention it was Owen? And I have to say I'm grateful he didn't blather on about "these difficult times" or insult me by saying "You are far too good for me". No. He came straight out and told me that he's met someone else. What d'you think of that?' She looked from Grace to Jess and back to Grace.

'I think he's a fool,' Jess said. 'He won't find anyone half as beautiful as you.'

'Thank you. You are very sweet. Grace?'

Grace shook her head, and began putting her stockings on,

an excuse to keep her eyes down, though her hands shook. It was a relief to know Owen had finally broken with Betony, but did Betony know that she, Grace, was the 'someone else'?

Relief was short lived, as Betony said with a brittle smile, 'Owen collects hearts like souvenirs. I'm just the latest casualty. The next victim will work it out soon enough.' Her eyes took on a filmy quality. Anger or pain, Grace couldn't say.

'Who are you going out with tonight, Betony?' Jess's question broke the tension.

'My Canadian friend. We've discovered a mutual affection for Admiral Horatio Nelson.' Betony picked up her dress. 'Better get ready to go to the ball. Jess, will you be all right here alone?'

'I'm used to it.' Jess had watched their preparations without apparent resentment. She now took up her book, finding her chapter.

When Betony went downstairs, Grace gave an anguished sigh. 'How does she do it... Burst every bubble?'

Jess always gave questions proper thought and put her book down. 'It's her job to be fascinating and worldly wise. Yours is nursing and mine is reading other people's letters in case they've accidentally given away state secrets. I wouldn't be any good at being Betony, but I don't think she'd be very good at being me.'

Grace smoothed the wrinkles from her stockings and retrieved the evening sandals. She'd found them under Betony's bed when she went down on her knees to pick up an earring she'd dropped. Betony had probably forgotten she had them.

It had felt too good to be true when Owen had called to ask her out. If she was simply the next victim in a long line, as Betony suggested, and this was going to be the first and last time she danced with Owen, she would do it in a pair of beautiful shoes.

52

———

In the Savoy's lobby, a crowd of uniformed men and their dates split into groups and Grace suddenly felt like a woman left on the platform after the last train has gone. She was expecting the worst, but it hadn't occurred to her that Owen might stand her up.

It was gone nine, and he wasn't here. Be honest, why would he want her, a girl from the dingy backstreets of Whitechapel, sister to a criminal? Best thing would be to go home and escape humiliation.

'Grace?'

She turned. Owen was there, in uniform and, to her sleepless eyes, looked heart-stoppingly handsome.

Not bothering to disguise her relief, she hurried towards him. He took her hands and, for a moment, they said nothing. The marks on his jaw were fading, but there was a vivid nick below his ear. It hadn't been there the last time she saw him. She bet he'd shaved in a hurry before leaping onto his motorbike.

'Deep black.' He was referring to her coat. 'Would you have preferred not to come out?'

'It isn't black for mourning,' she assured him. 'I borrowed it because I don't have a coat anymore. Other than my nurse's cape, and I'd like to not be a nurse tonight.'

'What would you like to be?'

She could answer that: *to be more than just another souvenir heart. The woman you introduce to your aunt and uncle as 'yours'.* She couldn't say it out loud. 'Just me. Just Grace.'

'I've booked us a table. Is that all right?'

'Course.' He'd had his hair cut in the last day or two, and with a light greasing through it, it looked a shade darker. It unnerved her, even so slight a change. 'Why did you say "sorry" on the phone when you rang?'

'Shall we go to our table?' Obviously, he wasn't ready to explain and fear rushed back. It was going to be one of those horrible endings, where you have to sit tight and not cry.

He asked if she'd been to the Savoy before.

'Never. And to be honest, this sort of place isn't my...' She couldn't think of the word. 'My usual...'

'Thing?' Owen supplied. He glanced around at the potted palms, the columns and voluptuous flower arrangements. 'It's not mine either. I've just had a whisky in the American Bar, but I'd rather have a beer, to be honest.'

'Why don't we go somewhere else? You don't need to lavish money on me, Owen. I'm a plain soul.'

'Why shouldn't I lavish money on you, such as I have? You said yourself, they have reinforced shelters here, so we needn't bolt if there's a raid.'

Grace felt a flutter of dangerous hope. He was planning a whole night, then. 'If there's going to be a raid, it'll come between eleven and twelve,' she said nervously. 'If they're sticking to schedule.'

Owen looked at his wristwatch. 'Gives us two hours. Come on, let's go down the stairs.' He took her hand. 'There's another good reason to stay put.'

'Because the Savoy is romantic, as well as reinforced?'

He laughed. 'Because they'll feed us well.'

'Good,' she said, while doubting she'd be able to eat a thing, her stomach tying itself in knots.

53

BETONY

Betony's taxi drew up in front of the Savoy.

It had been Winter's choice of venue. Suggesting it, he'd said, 'I'd like one last visit,' which told her quite enough. He was taking her out as a friend, to call it quits. The romance, if it had ever been that, was over.

She felt the same regret as before, but that looming obstacle between her and Winter was still there. The uniform, or lack of.

Paying the driver, she got out, ensuring her crimson silk-jersey hem was clear of the door sill. As the cab made its anti-clockwise turn around the Savoy's court, she paused.

Would Winter guess she'd accepted his invitation in part so she didn't have to spend Friday night sitting with shy little Jess, who, sweet as she was, reminded Betony of the last evacuee child in the queue to be picked?

'He'll only know if you tell him,' she reminded herself. Winter had lived up to his name, going cool on her because she'd had someone else on her mind. In Trafalgar Square when she'd frozen like a deer in a searchlight, he had taken over, carrying her to relative safety and he'd held her. She'd never forget it as long as she lived. Their relationship deserved to go out on a high note. She would dazzle and flirt, and he would be charming and amused.

There'd been a brusque shower of rain earlier, as she'd predicted, and her gold evening shoes pattered as she ran inside. Just as the uniformed porter opened the doors to her, a tirade of ack-ack fire cut through the night, followed by the dull resonance of high explosive. An air raid? Where were the sirens?

As if they'd been waiting for her to arrive, they began blaring. In the Savoy's lobby, a bellboy beckoned urgently. 'This way, Miss, quick as you can.'

'Do you happen to know if my date has arrived?'

He looked blank. Stupid question, really.

She was hitching up her skirt so as not to put a gold toe through its hem, when she heard, 'Betty?'

She turned, intending to say something witty, and her mouth fell open. 'Winter?'

He wore RAF uniform, though a different shade of blue to the one she was familiar with through Owen and others. The peak of a cap shaded his eyes.

'Winter, what have you done?'

Instead of answering, he held his hand out. 'Come on, before they seal the doors to the lower floor.'

Her gaze travelled from his gold cap badge to the shoulder flash stating 'Canada'. 'Tell me.'

'I've gone back. Come on, move.' He all but dragged her down into a vast, lamplit area where people milled around or perched on bar-room seats. Last time she'd sat out an air raid at the Savoy, she and Winter had been in the ballroom and the band had played on. Winter had written his telephone number on her arm, when the lights had failed, only she'd thought it was Owen.

It was Owen who had kissed her, though, and she had spent the time in between aching for a reprise. It was going to be hard, accepting that he had moved to pastures new.

'Drink, Betty?'

'Champagne, of course.'

The hotel provided luxury even in its underground shelter. Walls and ceiling were painted in boudoir shades. Unlike a boudoir, steel struts buttressed the ceiling. Staff wove through the crowd with tin helmets on their heads. She heard the clank of the door behind and a man saying, 'All sealed in, sir.'

Hopefully not in perpetuity. As they made their way through the smartly dressed throng, she said to Winter, 'You might have warned me you'd re-joined.'

'I never left. I was co-opted into the diplomatic corps. I always was going back. Does it make a difference, Betty?'

'Course it does. Now I'll have to worry about you, too.'

He stopped and made her look at him. Regardless of who was watching, he bent his head and kissed her. The two things Winter Macpherson had lacked, in her estimation, was passion and a uniform. She was taken by surprise by the intensity of the kiss. The lights in the room faltered and went out. Their lips met again, and realisation made a whirring sound, a couple of clicks and dropped. *Betony, you idiot.*

A kiss in the dark had sent her full cry after Owen Henderson, only she'd been chasing the wrong fox. Wrong stag. Wrong man.

She whispered against his jaw, 'It was you, wasn't it?'

'Me, what, when?'

'Kissing me... at the Café de Paris, last time the lights went out.'

'I hope so. Who did you think it was?'

'Never mind.' She tilted her chin, inviting the kiss to go on because, suddenly, everything felt too deliciously simple. Until the lights went back on... and over Winter's blue serge shoulder, she saw Owen sitting with a girl in a violet dress. They were holding hands, speaking earnestly. The girl's hair could belong to nobody else.

Just as she'd suspected. Just as she'd feared.

How dare they come here, gate-crash her world and flaunt their stolen, second-rate romance under her nose?

Someone was going to explain. Someone was going to apologise till they were purple in the face.

54

Owen jumped to his feet at her approach. Grace stayed where she was, but guilt was painted all over her and she blushed as only a redhead could. Not enough to go behind her back, thought Betony, they had made a public fool of her.

She took a long look at Grace's dress, pricing up the fabric and the green brooch on the breast. Department store, and not even Regent Street.

The truth? *She still looks knock-out.*

It ramped up her fury. 'How exciting to bump into you both,' she said icily. 'Owen, of course you've met Winter Macpherson.'

Winter was standing at her shoulder. She was too angry to see how he was taking this.

The two men shook hands after which Betony said, 'Oh, and this is Grace.' She could almost taste Owen's discomfort. 'Thank you for your lovely letter, Owen,' she said with a glassy smile. 'I do like to be kept up to date.' Leaning towards Grace under the guise of smoothing her skirt, she whispered, 'Were you ever going to tell me?'

'I... Yes. Course.' Grace glanced uncomfortably at Owen. 'I'm sorry. We—'

'Couldn't help yourselves. I know. Passion is a sly dog, creeping up to bite you.' She wondered why Grace had tucked her feet under her chair, the way young, terrified schoolteachers did when they knew they'd lost the class's attention.

Owen was still on his feet, and Winter was looking around for extra chairs. Grace simply looked miserable. Betony refused to feel sorry for her. A waiter was passing, champagne on a tray. She gave her perfectly pitched smile and took two glasses, passing one to Winter.

'Shall we find a quiet corner?'

'Sure.'

Betony glanced down at Grace, noticing one silk stocking had a delicate darn above the strap of her shoe. A suede strap in a shade called gypsum. Only a few sample pairs had ever been made. 'Those are mine.'

Grace nodded. 'Yes. I borrowed them.'

'Borrowed?'

'It's unforgiveable, I know. I'll clean them really well.'

If the girl blushed any harder, she'd catch light.

'Keep them,' Betony said. 'New dress?' She couldn't stop herself adding, 'It's always evening wear at the Savoy. Of course, you couldn't know.'

She walked away, searching for a spare table, moving her hips as she'd learned in her very first job, as a house model at Lucile.

Someone called her name. There was always somebody one knew at the Savoy. Oh, God, no. It was the Ridley-Suttons, who'd dragged her to that evil drinking den a few nights ago. It looked like they weren't going to be snubbed.

'Betony, you luscious creature. How tasty you look. Yum, yum. All alone? Do join us.'

She turned, expecting Winter would have followed. He had

the diplomatic gift to extract her from people like this without offending them. He wasn't behind her. 'Sorry,' she said to Frances Ridley-Sutton, 'I need to find someone.' She retraced her steps and saw Winter in conversation with an older woman in gold lamé. She stalked up, saying a sharp, 'Hello?'

The golden interloper raised an eyebrow and left. Betony attempted to link her hand through Winter's arm. He shook her off, saying, 'I didn't like that. It was bitchy.'

'She shouldn't chat up my man, then, should she? And who wears gold when there's a war on?'

'I didn't mean her. I meant Grace.'

'Really, Winter, nobody comes here for the evening in a short party dress.'

'"You couldn't know". That was so...' He had to think about it.

'Bitchy, I think you said.'

'Demeaning. To you, not her.' Winter turned to look where Owen and Grace were. The way they sat, foreheads close, suggested two people trying to regain shattered intimacy. 'This might be their last time together. You want that to be their final memory?' For the first time in their acquaintance of almost a year, Winter's eyes on her were the coldest shade of grey.

'What I said wasn't that bad.'

'Did you see her face?'

Betony fought against remorse. Yes, she'd seen the wretched girl's face, but why should she back down? She was the wronged party. 'She's even taken my shoes. Not enough to pinch my boyfriend, apparently.'

'Your boyfriend.' Winter's eyes flashed colder. 'Then why are you out with me?'

Panic seized her. Just as she realised it was Winter she wanted, he was starting to loathe her again. The tears that rushed in were not the sparkling dewdrops that usually got her out of trouble. They were real, and frightened. If Winter threw her off, she'd again have nobody. It was joyless purgatory, being alone. Even Mrs Kesgrave had her chickens. The taste in her mouth was new, but recognisable. Self-disgust. She so wanted to break the deadlock, but the words wouldn't come. She considered walking out, then remembered that the doors were sealed. She was stuck for the duration.

'Betony?'

It was Grace. Owen had stayed at their table, his posture tense.

'Have you come to tell me I'm an absolute cow?' Betony said stiffly. 'Because I know.'

'Yes, you are,' Grace agreed. 'But we should have told you earlier. I'm truly sorry for that. As for what you said about my dress, don't you realise that not everybody works for a fashion magazine and has a wardrobe of clothes they can just help themselves to? D'you think I could wear what you've got on tonight on a nurse's wages? I don't have a lord for a dad. I don't have a dad. I shouldn't have taken your shoes. No excuse, except that they're lovely and you'd chucked them under your bed. But I'll take them off if you like and walk home barefoot.'

'Oh, don't be ridiculous.'

Grace was reaching down, undoing the ankle straps.

'I mean it,' Betony hissed. 'Not here. This is the Savoy. Keep them on. Please.'

Owen came over and said, 'Betony, Winter, will you come and sit with us? There's no point staring daggers at each other all evening.'

Betony looked to Winter. His return look gave nothing away, but she knew what he wanted her to say. 'All right,' she conceded. 'If we're not interrupting.'

'Owen's asked a for a deck of cards,' Grace said. 'I'm going to teach him Racing Demon. Know it?'

· · ·

It was stiff-going at first. Everyone on edge. But after a while, as they got to grips with the game, the tension lessened. Grace was so fast with the cards, she cleared the board. They drank champagne and gorged on finger food. At just after three, the doors were unsealed and they all filed out. Grace said, 'I need the facilities.'

Owen went to help her find them. Betony stood awkwardly, Winter remaining by her side but not really looking at her.

'Are you going to fly?' she asked, her eyes referencing his uniform. 'Or sit at a desk?'

'I'd hardly swap one desk for another. I report at RAF Digby on Monday.'

So soon. 'Then we might not see each other again. I suppose you'll be busy packing.'

'Oh, sure, trunks of stuff to take to the airbase.' He was teasing but not in the lazy, attractive way of old. When he said, 'Maybe we'd better say our goodbyes now,' her eyes clouded with tears.

'Betony?'

'Goodbye, Winter.' She put her arms around his neck. 'I'll miss you.'

His hands tightened on her waist and he was kissing her as if they hadn't quarrelled. It was a farewell kiss, engraving a message. 'You'd better damn well miss me,' he said.

'I will.' She meant it.

55

GRACE

Grace found Owen waiting when she came out of the ladies'. He was flicking the leaves of a potted plant. They both said 'sorry' at the same moment.

'Why?' A smile lifted his face.

'For taking so long. There was a queue. Why did you finish our telephone call with "sorry" the last time? I thought you were planning to break things off. That maybe I was just another souvenir.'

'Another what?'

'You know. A notch on the wing of your Spitfire.'

He shook his head. 'That would be insane. Making notches. Ground crew would give us hell.'

'It was a manner of speaking.'

'I know. But is that what you think, that I want to break things off when we've only just started?' He looked genuinely puzzled. 'I meant sorry for not finishing things with Betony straight away, when I knew it was you I wanted. And for not telling my uncle that I took you home to meet Mum. I've always confided in him in the past.'

'That was a strange night,' she acknowledged. 'You're

allowed to be shocked rigid, finding my brother is a thief. As for telling Betony, it's hard, isn't it, hurting people?'

'It's the worst.'

'Promise me one thing – when it's my turn, you'll write or phone immediately.'

He pulled her into his arms. 'Thing is, Grace, it won't be your turn. I don't want anyone else.'

She wriggled herself free, not sure if she'd heard properly, and overwhelmed. 'None of us know how we'll feel in a few months, or even weeks.'

'I mean it. Grace...' He thrust his hand into his trousers pocket and brought out a small box, the same blue as his uniform. He lifted the lid to reveal a slender gold ring.

Her heart tripped a beat.

'Grace, I want us to get engaged.'

She stared at the ring, then at him. 'To be married?' He looked serious. Deadly so. 'We hardly know each other,' she stammered.

'You're right. Thing is, times like these—'

'Don't.'

He was going to speak, whatever. 'If I know someone I love, who loves me, is waiting for me – my girl – it makes it easier. I can concentrate when I'm in the air because I've got someone on the ground to come back for. Does that sound mad?'

'No. What will your mother say?'

'She likes you.'

'I hope so. Not everybody does. Your aunt, for one.'

'Her loss.' He went down on one knee and Grace glanced around, flustered, in case anyone was watching.

'You don't have to do that!'

'Then give me your answer.'

'Yes, all right.' She thrust out her finger and let him slip on the ring. They kissed, held each other, until she said, 'I'd better get Betony's coat out of hock, and you need to mount your trusty steed.'

He looked at his watch. 'Should have left an hour ago.'

'Owen?'

'Grace?'

She put her hands each side of his face and stretched up to kiss him one last time. 'I'm always here, and this ring stays on my finger, come what may.'

Outside, they found Betony and Winter waiting. The sky behind St Paul's was the colour of lobster shell, streaked with smoke. Winter offered to see Betony and Grace home, so Owen could get on his way. They heard him kickstart his bike and the cough of a damp exhaust, and then he was gone.

Winter flagged a taxi down after they'd walked some time, at the entrance to Green Park. Grace got in beside the driver to give the other two some privacy. How was it going to be, sharing with Betony after tonight? The ring on her finger was gleaming proof that she'd taken what she wanted. It would be lovely if Betony paired up with Winter, but was life ever that simple?

'Hill Street did you say, Miss?' the driver asked, interrupting her thoughts.

'That's right, halfway down.'

They couldn't get in from Berkeley Square, as that end of their street appeared to be blocked off. Smoke rose in swirling clouts from its centre.

Grace got out of the cab, forgetting she was in evening shoes until she stumbled. At the barrier, she shouted to an ARP warden, 'What's happened?'

He came to her. 'Bomb, Miss. Hit a house.'

'Which street?'

'This one. Hill Street.'

Betony joined her. 'What number Hill Street?'

'Not sure. Has a "thirty" in front of it.' The man added grimly, 'Direct hit. Wait, you can't—' He spread his arms to stop Grace and Betony climbing over the sandbags.

Behind them, Winter shouted, 'Don't, the building might collapse on you.'

Betony's long legs made easy work of the barrier. Grace was slower, but she managed to slither past the ARP warden. She heard Winter swearing, and then his feet behind as he pelted in pursuit. All three caught up where the smoke thickened and auxiliary firewomen stood in a line, preventing them getting closer. Flames roared above the chimney pots of the house two doors from theirs.

Grace and Betony glanced at each other in horror, two glamorous night-owls in evening clothes with the lipstick kissed off their mouths and voiced the same thought at the same moment.

'Jess.'

56

JESS

In the yard behind No. 34, Jess lay in a corrugated steel shell that bulged inward like a canvas tent after a rainstorm. She was pinned down and could do no more than blink and breathe. Beside her crouched three of Mrs Kesgrave's chickens. A fourth hunkered in the crook of her arm. She had left the house when the siren went and had heard the birds in their coop clucking in distress.

Not long after she'd shut the door, a terrifying whistle, followed by an unearthly detonation, had made the shelter convulse. The night itself had seemed to collapse on top of her and all she knew was that something close by had been hit. She was entombed and nobody knew. Mrs Kesgrave had left for Brighton. Betony and Grace were somewhere in the sprawl of London. She shivered violently and bade a mental goodbye to everyone she cared about. Her purpose in London had dwindled into failure. 'I never found you, Charlotte. I'm sorry.'

She slipped into the sleep that comes with deep cold.

Hours passed, or was it days? Without a speck of light, time lost meaning, but she could still hear. Was that a faint tapping, of metal on metal? From miles above, so it seemed, a man's voice called, 'Anybody down there? Knock if you can hear me.'

A LETTER FROM NATALIE

Thank you for picking up *The Irish Nurse at the Lodging House*. If you did enjoy it, and want to keep up to date with all my latest releases, just sign up at the following link. Your email address will never be shared and you can unsubscribe at any time.

www.bookouture.com/natalie-meg-evans

This is the first in a trilogy of stories set during one of London's darkest – and most defining – chapters: the Blitz summer of 1940.

In this novel, you have met Grace, a nurse with Irish roots and a London spirit. You have stepped into her world of ration books, air raids and long shifts under pressure, but also of dreams – for a better future, for love, for freedom. Grace's heart will continue to be tested because falling for an RAF Spitfire pilot, who daily risks his life in the skies above a burning city, is never going to be easy. Loving him will mean living with constant fear, but also with fierce pride.

At the lodging house in Mayfair, Grace's story is shared with two other young women whose paths will become deeply intertwined with hers. Each young woman has her own reason for seeking independence and staying in London despite the dangers. Betony's motives are perhaps the most selfish, but life has a lot still to teach her, not least that sharing everything from a wardrobe to her heart is the only way to gain true and lasting friendship. And then there's Jess, who seems shy and unassuming, but has come to London on a secret mission of her own that will put her at odds with her family and her conscience. Her story comes next.

I'm so pleased to have introduced this trio of women, whose bond will strengthen over the course of the three novels. This first book belongs to Grace, but Betony and Jess will each have their time to shine. Through heartbreak, danger, joy and friendship, they will hold each other up as they navigate a city under siege and a world in upheaval.

I'm deeply grateful to you, my readers, for welcoming these stories into your lives. Your kind messages and your support mean more than I can say. If you enjoy Grace's story, please do tell a friend – or two! Word of mouth is still the greatest gift a reader can give a writer.

With warmest wishes,

Natalie Meg Evans
Suffolk 2025

www.blythe-evans.com

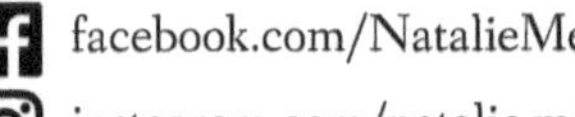
facebook.com/NatalieMegEvans
instagram.com/natalie.meg.evans

PUBLISHING TEAM

Turning a manuscript into a book requires the efforts of many people. The publishing team at Bookouture would like to acknowledge everyone who contributed to this publication.

Audio
Alba Proko
Melissa Tran
Sinead O'Connor

Commercial
Lauren Morrissette
Hannah Richmond
Imogen Allport

Cover design
Lesley Worrell

Data and analysis
Mark Alder
Mohamed Bussuri

Editorial
Natalie Edwards
Charlotte Hegley

Copyeditor
Jade Craddock

Proofreader
Becca Allen

Marketing
Alex Crow
Melanie Price
Occy Carr
Cíara Rosney
Martyna Młynarska

Operations and distribution
Marina Valles
Stephanie Straub
Joe Morris

Production
Hannah Snetsinger
Mandy Kullar
Nadia Michael
Ria Clare

Publicity
Kim Nash
Noelle Holten
Jess Readett
Sarah Hardy

Rights and contracts
Peta Nightingale
Richard King
Saidah Graham

Dear Reader,

We'd love your attention for one more page to tell you about the crisis in children's reading, and what we can all do.

Studies have shown that reading for fun is the **single biggest predictor of a child's future life chances** – more than family circumstance, parents' educational background or income. It improves academic results, mental health, wealth, communication skills, ambition and happiness.

The number of children reading for fun is in rapid decline. Young people have a lot of competition for their time, and a worryingly high number do not have a single book at home.

Hachette works extensively with schools, libraries and literacy charities, but here are some ways we can all raise more readers:

- Reading to children for just 10 minutes a day makes a difference
- Don't give up if children aren't regular readers – there will be books for them!

- Visit bookshops and libraries to get recommendations
- Encourage them to listen to audiobooks
- Support school libraries
- Give books as gifts

There's a lot more information about how to encourage children to read on our websites: **www.RaisingReaders.co.uk** and **www.JoinRaisingReaders.com**.

Thank you for reading.